## A CHRIS...

Andrew pushed ope_____on
is right. These pies sm_____

"Oh, no!" she cried

Looking across the ki_____, Andrew saw a row of pies set
on the table. In the center of each pie was a set of kitten-
sized footprints. He came around the table just in time to
see the kitten jump to the floor, knocking a pie pan off the
table. Cutie Pie landed on her feet, but the mince pie fell
upside down on the stone floor.

He glanced at Rosemary, not sure if he expected she
would be wearing tears or simply a scowl on her face at the
ruin of her long hours of work. Instead, he saw her wry
smile.

She bent to pick up the overturned pie pan. Setting it
on the table, she picked up a bucket. "Andrew, the pump
is just outside the back door. Please don't let Cutie Pie slip
past the door."

"How much water do you need?"

"Enough to clean up this mess and a tiny kitten, and to
make some tea for the children."

"You don't have an obligation to serve us anything."

"It's not an obligation." Shoving the bucket into his
hands, she smiled. "This kitchen won't clean up easily or
quickly. While you help me clean up the kitchen, the children won't want to wait on their tea."

"And what makes you think I will help you clean up the
kitchen?" He took the bucket and set it on the table. As
she started to reach for one of the pies, he caught her
elbow and brought her to face him. His breath caught in
his throat as he gazed into her eyes. It was an endless delight to find them so close to his. He saw the glow of wonder in her eyes—not only wonder, but the same craving
that carved through him like a heated blade. . . .

—from "Beneath the Kitten Bough" by Jo Ann Ferguson

# MISTLETOE KITTENS

*Jo Ann Ferguson*

*Judith A. Lansdowne*

*Regina Scott*

Zebra Books
Kensington Publishing Corp.
http://www.zebrabooks.com

ZEBRA BOOKS are published by

Kensington Publishing Corp.
850 Third Avenue
New York, NY 10022

First Printing: November, 1999
10 9 8 7 6 5 4 3 2 1

Printed in the United States of America

# Contents

# Beneath
# the
# Kitten Bough

Jo Ann Ferguson

# One

"Are you sure this is a good idea?"

Jenna glanced at her younger brothers as she put her finger to her lips. There was no worry about being overheard here by the banks of the River Wye. The last vestiges of autumn had vanished, and the wind blew cold from the mountains in the heart of Wales. No one who had an excuse to remain close to the hearth came out into the crisp afternoon.

"But, Jenna, are you sure this is a good idea?" asked Simon.

"It's the only one we've had," Donald stated with all the certainty of his five years. He reached for the pie basket on the ground.

Jenna slipped the basket from under her brother's hands. She should have left these two back at Uncle Andrew's house. They were going to make a bumble-bath of everything. Although she had explained to them how important it was to be quiet while they skulked into the village, they had pelted her with questions since they crossed the field toward the river that divided Wales and England.

Putting her finger to her lips, she led the way into the village. She kept the basket close to her coat, hoping that no one would notice that Lord Snoclyffe's wards were sneaking along the street. Glancing guiltily at the stone church, she hurried past the pub at the base of the street that curled up the hill.

The village's narrow streets were edged by shops. On the hill above them, the shell of an old castle that had burned years ago threw shadows over the cobbles. Jenna did not slow to look in the shops, and urged her brothers to hurry along after her. It must nearly be time for Miss Tranter to come to the nursery for tea. If they were not there . . .

She did not want Uncle Andrew to guess that they had left Snoclyffe Park this afternoon. Then he would ask them where they had gone, and why. She realized that she needed to have her brothers drilled in a good alibi by the time they returned. Even if they were back before their absence was noted, Donald had a habit of being honest at the very worst times.

"Stay here," she hissed.

"Jenna—"

"Stay here." She motioned for them to wait by the hitching post on the corner.

Tightening her grip on the basket, she rushed around the corner to the neat house that was set only a stone's throw from the castle ruins. She set the basket on the large stone that served as a front step.

"Hurry!" came the call from the corner.

Jenna glanced over her shoulder at Simon, then rapped hard on the door. She ran back toward the corner and hushed her brothers. Peeking around the side of the building, she watched the door.

No one came to answer it.

Was no one home? She had not considered that. Someone was always home there.

"How long will it take?" Donald asked. "I'm hungry. Cook told me she is making iced cakes for our tea this afternoon."

"Iced cakes?" Simon tugged on her sleeve. "Let's go now, Jenna."

"Not until we're sure someone will answer the door." Jenna took a deep breath. She did not want to go back and knock on the door again. If no one was home . . .

She was not sure if they could sneak away like this again. She had thought every facet of this plan out carefully, talked to the staff at Uncle Andrew's house of Snoclyffe Park, visited the village herself with Miss Tranter to be certain of the whispers that she had heard. Then she had waited for this moment when everything was set to go. Never had she considered no one would be home this afternoon.

So much depended on this.

Not so much.

*Everything* depended on this, because she did not know any other way to give Uncle Andrew the Christmas present everyone belowstairs said he needed.

A wife for him, and a mother for her and her brothers.

# Two

Rosemary Burton set her book down and lifted her spectacles off her nose. *That* had been something more than the wind. She was certain of it. Looking across the room to where her cousin sat on the comfortably soft chair by the back window, she saw that Charlotte was napping.

That was good. Charlotte needed to rest after her long struggle with the illness that had confined her to her bed for most of the autumn. Still as pale as the beeswax candles on the table beside her, she must have this rest to recover back to her usual jovial self. Nothing must disturb her.

Hearing the sound that seemed to be coming from outside, Rosemary stood. The soft whisper of her dark green dress flowed along her feet as she crossed the slate foyer and opened the front door.

No one was waiting on the step. The sound must have been a branch being blown along the street. No, that was not possible, because the air was still. Up on the hills rising beyond the village, the sheep were gathered beneath the trees that were as unmoving as a sculpture.

She turned to go back inside, but paused when she saw a covered basket on the step. It was a small basket, not more than six inches deep. Was it a holiday pie?

That was not possible. It was not even Stir-up Sunday yet. That would not be until next Sunday, the last Sunday before Advent began. Why had one of her neighbors left a pie here on the step before Advent arrived? The mincemeat would not have had time to age properly for a Christmas pie.

She looked both directions along the curving street, but saw no one. A few specks of snow drifted through the air, reflecting in the lights from Mr. Nicholas's store. Glancing at the narrow walkway, she saw a maze of footprints in the thin layer of snow. Several people had come past her door since it had begun to snow.

Lifting the basket, she carried it into the house. She closed the door and set it on a table. Mayhap it did not contain a pie, for it was light, as if empty. The tasty mincemeat pies the neighbors shared over the holidays were weighty when decorated with ribbons and greenery for gift-giving.

Rosemary lifted the top. "Oh, my!" she gasped as she stared at unblinking green-yellow eyes. "A kitten!"

A tiny mew came from the creature. When she reached into the basket, she found she could hold the kitten in one hand. It nuzzled at her fingers, licking them eagerly. Stroking the fur, which was almost the same shades as her tortoiseshell hair clips, she raised the small kitten to her cheek.

It shivered, purring wildly. She knew it was not purring because it liked her attention. The poor thing was terrified. It strained to see past her, looking for anything that was familiar.

Who had abandoned this kitten, which appeared too young to be away from its mother, on her doorstep?

"A caller, Rosemary?"

She heard the hope in Charlotte's voice. Few people called on a stormy afternoon at the beginning of December when the sun had already fallen past the western hills. "No caller," she said, settling the kitten against her as she walked into the parlor, "but mayhap a guest."

A smile eased the lines left by the pain Charlotte had suffered. Holding out her hands, she cooed, "A kitten! Rosemary, you are always so kind. You thought of this kitten to entertain me during my convalescence."

Rosemary knelt beside her cousin and placed the kitten

on her lap. "I did not think of a kitten for you. It was left in a basket by the door."

"Left?" Charlotte's eyes, which were a brilliant blue in her wan face, widened. "Who could be so cruel to leave this tiny baby alone on such a chill day?"

"I do not want to guess, but I shall find out."

Rosemary listened to the other patrons in Mr. Nicholas's store. Even though the village of Baedd-upon-Wye was on the English border, Welsh phrases and words flavored the conversation. She understood more of them each day, for she had been only a child when her father took his family to live in Plymouth. Except for an occasional visit, she had not been back until her cousin took ill. Then, as she was the only unmarried daughter, it was decided that she would come to sit by Charlotte's deathbed.

Charlotte had gotten well. Rosemary had been determined she would. Some of her fondest memories of visits here had been playing with her cousin, who was only two months younger than she was. They had been inseparable on those holidays—blonde Charlotte, who was as delicate as a child's china doll, and tall, thin, and regretfully red-haired Rosemary, who never would be mistaken for anything fragile or petite. The hills around the village had offered them places to take walks, to paint, and to pretend to be fairy princesses made of flowers, like those of Welsh legend.

Soon Charlotte would be able to take over management of her home again, and Rosemary could return to Plymouth. She was not anticipating that event, because there was no place in her father's household for her since he had remarried last year. Her stepmother was a dear woman, but she wanted the house to be hers, not her husband's youngest daughter's. Although Charlotte had not said anything, Rosemary wanted to postpone making a decision about leaving Wales until after the first of the new year.

"Miss Burton," crowed the shopkeeper as she reached

the battered wooden counter where he presided over his shop like a Welsh prince of ages past, "how does Miss Griffydd fare?"

"My cousin is doing better with each passing hour." She smiled at his enthusiasm and her joyous tidings. After those long weeks of having nothing good to share with Charlotte's neighbors, it was a delight to wear a sincere smile.

"And what can I get for you today?"

"Charlotte's usual order." She set the basket she was carrying on the counter. "And, Mr. Nicholas, can you tell me if you have seen a basket like this before.?" She tilted it so that he could see the odd design on the bottom. She was unsure if the pattern woven into the basket was supposed to be a blossom, or something else.

"Of course I've seen its like." He tapped the pattern. "That's the snowflake design that's on every basket made at Snoclyffe Park."

"Snoclyffe Park?" She noted how the heads of the other patrons turned at her question.

"On the other side of the River Wye, miss. Home of the Whitfields." He set the basket back on the counter. "The old viscount liked this pattern, so he decreed that all baskets used in the household would have it." He cocked a dark eyebrow at her, wrinkling his forehead toward his bald pate. "Usually these baskets stay on the estate, but the young viscount may have changed his father's tradition."

Rosemary bit her lip to keep from announcing to Mr. Nicholas and all the blatant eavesdroppers that she was as curious as they were about how this basket had come to sit on her cousin's doorstep. However, to do that would require her to own as well that a kitten had been abandoned in the basket. She did not want to stain the viscount's name with such accusations of cruelty before she understood the whole of this.

"Thank you, Mr. Nicholas," was all she replied.

He glanced at her again and again as he gathered her order. She simply put the items in the basket and bid him

a good day. Ignoring the glances in her direction as she
went out of the store, she hurried along the street.

Charlotte called to her from the kitchen when Rosemary
entered the house. "I'm out here!"

Setting her hooded cape of green wool over the hook
by the front door, Rosemary went to the kitchen, which
was as tiny as the other rooms in the house. The kitchen
and a cozy parlor shared the first floor with a small dining
room. Upstairs, the two bedrooms battled for space beneath the slanted roof.

"Charlotte, what do you think you are doing?" she
gasped when she followed the stone floor into the kitchen.

Charlotte set down the knife she was using to cut beef
into small pieces. She held her finger to her lip and
pointed to a blanket in the corner by the hearth.

Rosemary smiled when she saw the kitten curled in the
blanket. "She seems to be making herself right at home
here."

"She ran about, up and down the hall, until she dropped
with exhaustion."

"She truly is a cutie pie."

"Then that is what you should call her."

"What?"

"Cutie Pie."

Setting the groceries on the counter beneath the room's
only window, Rosemary took the knife from her cousin
and turned the cutting board toward herself as she sat on
the bench on the other side of the table. "It is appropriate
because she arrived in a pie basket."

"That basket . . ." Charlotte's smile vanished.

"Apparently is from Snoclyffe Park."

"Oh, dear!"

"Why do you say that?"

That question contained the last words Rosemary had
a chance to speak for the next half hour. As she chopped
the meat that would be used in mincemeat for the holidays, she was regaled by her cousin with a list of the esca-
pades and misadventures carried out by the present Lord

Snoclyffe. None of them excused his inexcusable act of depositing this kitten on their doorstep on a cold afternoon.

As she watched the kitten sleep, oblivious to how close it might have come to freezing to death, she was determined that, somehow, Lord Snoclyffe would learn that, even though he might be the Pink of the *ton,* that did not give him *carte blanche* to disregard the peril to a kitten that still should be nestled next to its mother.

Somehow, he must be told, and, as she worked on the mincemeat, she was sure exactly who should tell him.

# Three

Andrew Whitfield, Fifth Viscount Snoclyffe, tapped his pipe against his hand, then set it down on the table beside his chair. To own the truth, he was a complete failure.

He stood and walked over to look down at the fire on the hearth, where the mantel was even with his shoulder. How loudly he had boasted to everyone in Town that he could succeed at this task of being guardian for his orphaned nephews and niece at the same time he maintained his bachelor's fare! Now, he was stuck here at his family's country seat while he tried to keep track of the antics of three children who seemed, regretfully, to have inherited his ability to be in the wrong place at the wrong time.

For the past trio of fortnights, he had not held the flats once. A bottle of wine was not so enjoyable without someone to share it, and no callers had come to the imposing doors of Snoclyffe Park.

Footsteps sounded behind him. He turned to see Souder, the butler, who had seemed to Andrew, during his childhood, as ancient as the walls of this huge house that was still half-castle—from the years when those on the other side of the river twisting through the valley were enemies. It was odd now not to look up at him. Andrew was accustomed to being taller than most of his fellows, but, when he was younger, he had been certain that Souder's height challenged the remaining tower on the east wall.

"Lord Snoclyffe, you have a caller," the butler said quietly.

He pushed away from the hearth, unable to judge from Souder's tone who might be calling. He doubted if Souder would lose his aplomb even if the specter of Death came knocking on the door. The butler would ask the Grim Reaper to wait in the foyer to be announced to the viscount.

Trying to keep his lips from twitching at the unseemly thoughts, Andrew nodded. "You may bring the caller here, Souder."

"As you wish, my lord."

Andrew sighed as the butler walked away. He could not miss the flicker of dismay in the butler's eyes. True, he should have asked who was calling, but, dash it, what did he care if the caller were of the gentry or a petitioner? Anyone's company was better than suffering only his own.

He reached for his pipe, but froze when he stared at the woman following Souder into the small parlor.

Souder said in the same quiet voice, "Miss Rosemary Burton, my lord, from the village."

She stepped forward and held out her hand so boldly that he doubted if she had ever endured a London Season. "Lord Snoclyffe, I assume."

He hesitated on his answer, giving himself a chance to enjoy the sight of this pretty lady in her bright green cloak which opened to reveal a pink gown that matched the ruffling within her bonnet. Her cheeks were chafed with the cold, nearly to the shade of her auburn hair. She was tall and slender, and clearly—by the timbre of her voice—about to fly up to the boughs.

For that, he knew there was but one explanation. He had become familiar with such tight faces confronting him since he had become the guardian to his sister's children.

Bowing his head slightly, he said, "Your assumption is correct, Miss Burton. Will you sit and allow me to offer you something warm to drink?"

"Thank you, no." Her fingers clenched and unclenched on the handle of the basket she carried. A Snoclyffe basket, he noted, wondering how she came to have it. The staff was very possessive of these old baskets. "What I have to say shall not take long."

"I was afraid of that." He locked his own fingers together behind him as Souder bowed his head and left. No doubt, the butler had no interest in being a witness to the *contretemps* that was sure to ensue. "I suggest you say what you feel you must, Miss Burton, before you explode with whatever wrath you believe is rightly aimed at me and my household."

She opened her mouth, then closed it. For a moment, he congratulated himself on defusing her anger. He was disabused of that assumption when her hazel eyes snapped with renewed fury.

"My lord, I have never heeded the tales spouted by others, for rumor is seldom based on truth."

"True." The wrong thing to say, for those eyes narrowed until each spark seemed aimed at piercing through him. "I must own to being pleased that you have decided not to judge me before I had a chance to defend myself."

"You feel you must *defend* yourself?"

Everything he said was wrong. Blast it! Why was he allowing this redhead, this very enticing, lovely redhead, to unnerve him so that he was prattling like a child? "A poor choice of words, I fear."

"I care nothing for the choices—whether words or other things—made by my neighbors, for each person's life should be one's own to use or waste as one wishes."

He did not doubt how she perceived his life. His only question was why she had chosen this moment to tell him of her opinions. Had *he* done something to rouse her ire? Quite unlikely, because he had not seen her before. Odd, because he thought he had met most of the residents of these backwater hills along the Welsh border.

"Yes?" he prompted when she paused.

Again that was a mistaken thing to say, for she raised her chin which was just a bit too square to be declared beautiful in London. "My lord, your life is yours to spend as you wish, but you must consider the lives of those who are dependent upon you. To do what you did, risking even a single one of those young lives, is beneath reproach. I could not rest another night without coming here to tell you that myself. Good day."

As she turned to take her leave, Andrew grasped her arm, not caring what she thought. "Risking a young life? Whose? Has something happened to one of the children?"

"Children?" She looked down at his hand, her nose wrinkling as if he had wrapped a dead fish instead of his fingers around her arm. "I don't know what you're talking about, my lord. However, I do know that a gentleman should not treat a lady like this."

He paid no mind to her gracious indignation. If something had happened to harm one of the children . . .

"Nor do I know what in the blazes you are babbling about, Miss Burton."

"My lord, there is no need for such language from you in my presence."

He resisted rolling his eyes at her prim tone. However, no temptation to laugh teased him. If something had happened to one of the children . . . He could not even think of that. "Miss Burton, there would be no need for words that unsettle you if you would be so kind as to explain what brought you here."

"Your lack of concern about—"

"About whom? Miss Burton . . ." He took a deep breath before he was the one to fly off in a pelter, sent there by the unspoken accusations in her eyes. What was it about lovely women that beguiled him, but always left him portrayed as a villain among the *ton*? In a calmer tone, he said, "I have endeavored to be a good guardian to those young lives entrusted to me. If you know of some manner in which I have failed to succor those dependent upon me for their welfare, I would have you be blunt, Miss Burton, and do not think to spare my feelings."

"As you wish, my lord." She drew away from him. Setting the basket on a chair, she lifted the lid and reached inside.

"I do not know how you could be so thoughtless as to leave this poor creature on my step, where it might have frozen to death."

Andrew stepped closer to see what she was pulling out of the basket. His heart had slowed its frantic beat because he realized she could not be speaking of one of the children. It sped up again as a faint, flowery scent drifted from her. The aroma tempted him closer, to discover if it was something she had used to wash her hair or if it came from the sweet flavor of her skin. He was intrigued with her height, which brought the top of her head only a few fingers' breadth beneath his own, for he had accustomed himself to the tiny misses of the London Season, those sweet maidens who had the wiles of a serpent as they tried to catch him in the parson's mousetrap. All he would need to do was tilt his head slightly now, and the soft flesh of her cheek would be against his lips.

"Do you deny, my lord, that one must be heartless to abandon this helpless creature?"

He back-pedaled as she turned and held up something dark and furry in his face. It spat at him. With a curse, he took another step away.

"Helpless?" he asked. "I fear you are championing something that has no need of your help."

"This poor kitten has no defenses against the beasts of the wood."

Andrew stared at her. She was quite serious. When she drew the kitten back against her bodice in the shadow of her cloak, he fought to pull his gaze from the enticing fullness beneath the pink muslin to look at her face. It was taut with her fury, but the uncompromising angles of her pretty face somehow retained their gentle curves even when she was frowning.

"A kitten?" He dropped into a chair, laughter bursting from him. "You came here, as righteous as a judge sentencing a felon to hang, because of a kitten left on your doorstep?"

"Left on my doorstep in a basket from your house, my

lord." Rosemary released the breath she was holding
through clenched teeth. This man was completely without
conscience, as well as without manners. Even when he
stood again, leaning on the chair as more laughs rippled
out, she did not speak. She tried to calm Cutie Pie, who
clung to her as the only familiar object in the whole room.

"Miss Burton," he said through his chuckles, "forgive
me, but you must own that your fervor is oddly placed."

"Is it?"

"You are accusing me of a crime where I see none. The
kitten is not injured, and it seems quite attached to you."

"That is true, but I fear I cannot forgive you, my lord."
She stroked the kitten's soft fur. "This poor kitten would
have died if I had not chanced to hear some noise from
outside my house that led me to open my door."

"You believe I played a part in abandoning the kitten
on your doorstep?"

"The basket, I am told, is one that is made here, and
that these baskets seldom leave Snoclyffe Park."

He picked it up. "Yes, it was made here. The emblem
woven into the bottom—"

"That was already explained to me, my lord." She
glanced down at the kitten as she took the basket and set
Cutie Pie in it. Closing the well-vented lid so the kitten
could not flee and be lost in the maze of rooms in this
house that had awed her as she passed through the gate,
she said, "What I would like you to explain is how this
kitten came to be on my doorstep in a basket from your
household."

"To explain, I believe I shall need some help." He
grasped a bellpull. A quick tug brought answering footsteps from beyond the room. When a footman appeared,
he ordered, "I would like the children to attend me here
at once."

"My lord, they are at their lessons."

"It appears they have learned some things quite well
already. Bring them here without delay."

The footman nodded and rushed out.

Lord Snoclyffe called after him, "And send in tea for five."

"My lord," Rosemary said, "there is no need to include me for tea. I wish only to receive your explanation. Then I shall return to Baedd-upon-Wye."

"And you shall have an explanation as soon as I have one."

"You?"

"I'm not certain which combination of three young minds devised the idea of leaving that kitten in a basket on your step, Miss Burton, but I intend to find out if my suspicions are accurate, and why they decided to do such a thing."

"Three young minds?"

He motioned toward the settee. "Please sit, Miss Burton. I fear you and I have been brought together by the mischief my three wards delight in perpetrating."

Rosemary hesitated, then sat. Dismay coursed through her. Had she wrongly accused the viscount, and committed an unforgivable *faux pas* herself?

"Do not look so distressed, Miss Burton," he said, warning her that her reaction was displayed on her face. When he sat facing her, he smiled, and she understood how all those women whose names were connected with his had been dazzled by such a smile of bright warmth beneath his dark hair. "If it eases your chagrin, you may remind yourself that, as their guardian, I am responsible for the antics of these children and any resulting trouble."

"That is kind of you, my lord, but I should not have been so quick to assume that you were involved."

He relaxed against the chair, but she doubted if it was more than a pose. Every motion he had made reminded her of a tightly coiled spring, ready to strike out in any direction at any moment. His ebony hair and his eyes, which were nearly as black, kept one from noting how fascinating his sharply molded face with its deep tan was. Dangerously fascinating, she was sure, recalling the tales

Charlotte had made sure she knew before calling at Sno-clyffe Park.

She pulled away from his mesmerizing gaze. Each one of those tales she had heard about Andrew Whitfield raced through her head in a wild cacophony. Tales of the rake who lured one unsuspecting woman after another into his arms and left all of them with empty promises and tarnished reputations. Tales of the rogue who would risk anything on the turn of a single card, but was wildly successful at the board of green cloth because Lady Luck was as taken with him as any mortal woman. Tales of the roué who delighted in every sport available during a London Season, not caring about the cost as long as the sport was fast. There were even whispers that Charlotte had warned her might be true that he had been part of a duel in which a man died. He was a man whom mothers warned their daughters to stay far from, and feared their sons would emulate.

"You looked at the facts before you, Miss Burton," he replied, a hint of humor lightening his voice, "and they pointed to my involvement in this crime. If—"

An insistent mew came from the basket.

Rosemary opened it and drew out the kitten, calming her. "Hush, little one," she whispered. "It will be fine, Cutie Pie."

"What did you call the cat?" Lord Snoclyffe asked.

"I needed to give her a name, so I decided to call her Cutie Pie."

"You are jesting!"

"No." She stroked the kitten's fur. "You see, I was expecting that the basket contained a pie. When she was so cute—"

He groaned and shook his head. "Please spare me the details. By all that's blue, Miss Burton, I would say you have developed quite a *tendre* for this kit."

She was spared from answering by the loud sound of a trio of footfalls that must be coming down the staircase that curved upward from the one she had climbed to reach this parlor.

Lord Snoclyffe set himself on his feet and again clasped his hands behind him. Then, with a smile, he held one out to her.

She glanced at it before setting the kitten back in the basket. She watched her fingers rise to settle on his palm. He drew her with polite indifference to her feet, but there was nothing indifferent about the sensation that shot up her arm to explode in her mind as his fingers cradled hers. When he released her hand as he turned to the door, she hastily laced her fingers together so no one would discover how they trembled.

"A stern facade will work best, Miss Burton," Lord Snoclyffe said in a near whisper.

"For what?"

"For getting the answer to the puzzle of that kitten with all due haste, so you may be on your way and not have to suffer my company any longer."

# Four

Rosemary was glad that, again, she had no chance to reply as three children came to a skidding stop in the doorway. The girl, the oldest of the three, looked to be no more than eleven. Her hair was a honey-blonde, not far in shade from Charlotte's. The taller boy also was light-haired, but the younger boy was as dark in coloring as Lord Snoclyffe. Each of them had a younger version of the viscount's determined jaw.

"Miss Burton," Lord Snoclyffe said with a hint of a smile hovering along his lips, "my niece Jenna Morsey. Her younger brothers are Simon and Donald, in that order."

"How do you do?" Rosemary said, not sure what else to say. None of the children would meet her eyes, so she guessed the viscount had been right in suspecting that they had played a part in bringing Cutie Pie to her cousin's door.

"How do you do, Miss Burton?" Jenna dipped in a curtsy. A poke with her elbow brought a bow from Simon.

Donald looked at both of them, clearly torn between bowing and curtsying. He tried to do both at once, and nearly toppled on his nose.

As she reached forward to steady him, her hands became entangled with the viscount's. She pulled back and bumped into a chair. When the children giggled, she knew her face must be aflame.

The viscount brushed his hands together, and her lips

tightened. She could not be angry at him for wanting to be rid of her touch simply because, at the brush of his skin on hers, her heart had leapt like the river at springtide.

"Miss Burton has come to Snoclyffe Park with a tale that distresses me," Lord Snoclyffe said. "It seems that she found on her—"

A furious mew came from the closed basket. Donald ran to it and cried, "Look, Jenna! Our kitten is back."

Simon rolled his eyes, and Jenna seemed to be very interested in the laces in her light blue dress.

"I believe that saves me the trouble of asking for you to reveal the truth." Lord Snoclyffe took Donald by the hand and motioned for the others to come into the parlor. "You should know better than to leave a tiny kitten outside like that on a chilly day."

The children appeared properly chastised for their misdeed, but Rosemary was not fooled. She took note of the glances they exchanged, and the littler boy's lips had a tendency to twitch—very much like Lord Snoclyffe's.

She became more sure of that when Jenna stepped forward and stared up at her. "You aren't the lady who usually lives in that house, are you?"

"I have been staying there with my cousin Miss Griffydd since she took ill this fall."

"Oh."

Lord Snoclyffe arched his black brows. "*Oh?* I suspect you mean more by that than you want to share with the rest of us, Jenna."

"I meant that I was surprised, Uncle Andrew. I had not heard that anyone was ill there."

Rosemary almost laughed aloud at how Jenna's chin jutted in an exact copy of her uncle's. "So the kitten was meant for my cousin Charlotte?"

"No . . . I mean . . ." She brightened. "There are three more in the kitchen. I would be glad to get you another one for your cousin, Miss Burton. I know Cook would be delighted to have another one gone. She keeps complaining that she will trip over one and spill dinner on the floor."

Glad that a maid interrupted by bringing in a tray with tea and freshly baked biscuits, Rosemary decided the best response to such an offer was nothing. A single kitten would brighten Charlotte's days, but two were sure to get into far too much trouble. She took the basket and set it on the floor, hushing Cutie Pie's protests. When the kitten curled up with a yawn, she closed the basket again and untied the laces of her cloak. She folded it over the back of the settee.

"Do sit, Miss Burton," Lord Snoclyffe said.

As she did, the children scrambled to claim the chairs on the other side of the low table. Again Lord Snoclyffe's brows rose, but he said nothing as he sat beside her on the settee. She had not realized how small the settee was until then. Unless she almost leaned over its arm, she could not keep hers from brushing his sleeve.

He faced her, and she clasped her hands in her lap, once again to hide their quivering. A pulse of heat washed over her as she met his raven gaze. She waited for him to speak, but he remained silent as he searched her face. Looking for what? She wanted to ask, but no words reached her lips.

His arm slid along the back of the settee, so it no longer brushed her. Now she seemed surrounded by him. Even though she needed only to stand and step away, she could not move. She did not want to move.

"Would you pour, Miss Burton?" he asked.

"I—"

"It would be so nice for the children to see how a lady handles the niceties of serving tea."

Rosemary tore her gaze from his. What kind of widgeon was she? Charlotte had warned her of Andrew Whitfield's less than pristine reputation in London. She must take care that he did not practice his fascinating arts on her here in the country.

Forcing a smile, she said, "Of course, my lord, I would be honored to serve."

That was the best decision she had made since she entered this house. Her fingers were kept busy as she poured the tea, for each child wanted it prepared differently, and passed the plate of biscuits. When she saw how nicely even the smaller boy balanced his saucer and biscuit, she knew someone had seen closely to their training.

When Rosemary bent forward to pour her own cup, Jenna asked, "Will you be keeping the kitten?"

"I'm sure she will," the viscount answered before she could. "After all, she has given it the absurd name of Cutie Pie."

Simon grinned. "That's a silly name."

"I think it's the perfect name," Donald returned with all his young fervor.

"So do I!" Jenna's smile was shy.

Lord Snoclyffe turned back to Rosemary, again making her heart batter her breastbone with its furious beat. "It appears the consensus on this is very divided, Miss Burton."

Looking at the children, she released the breath she had been holding. "Mayhap I might change your mind, Simon, when you realize that this basket you brought the kitten in is one very like the ones that neighbors use to deliver pies for the holidays."

"You thought there was a pie in the basket?" Donald giggled again.

"Yes, I did. Then I opened it and saw a cute kitten. The name seems to fit her."

"Cutie Pie," said Simon slowly, rolling each syllable off his tongue. "Yes, it does seem to fit her."

"Traitor!" Lord Snoclyffe reached across the table and ruffled his nephew's hair.

"It makes sense, Uncle."

"Or you are growing up, Simon, and find green eyes too intriguing to be ignored?" He flashed a smile at Rosemary.

"The kitten's eyes?" the perplexed boy asked.

Lord Snoclyffe laughed with a warmth that brought grins from the youngsters. "Mayhap you haven't grown up that much yet. One day, you shall understand that a kitten's eyes are not the most intriguing green eyes one might encounter."

Wishing she had some excuse to take her leave when she could not still her gasp at his provocative words, Rosemary reached for another biscuit. She was not hungry, but she would eat each of the remaining biscuits herself if it would bring this uncomfortable tea to a close more quickly.

Donald slid down from his chair and came around the table. He leaned toward her, his hand on her knee, as he whispered, "What kind of pie did you think the kitten was?"

"Miss Burton shall answer your question," the viscount said, lifting his nephew's hand away, "when you recall your manners."

"I asked nicely." His lip stuck out in a pout.

"But you do not put your hand on a lady's knee without her permission."

"Remember?" interjected Jenna as she plucked another biscuit from the plate. "Remember when Uncle Andrew had his face slapped by Lady Yatesville?"

A flush along the viscount's face surprised Rosemary. Embarrassment, or dismay that the children spoke so? She was amazed, as well, by her own reaction, so she hastily said, "Donald, I expected the pie to be mincemeat, for that is what neighbors usually share. That was why I was so shocked to see the basket on my step, because it is still a few days until Stir-up Sunday."

"Stir-up Sunday?" Jenna looked at her brothers and frowned. "What is that?"

"Haven't you ever celebrated Stir-up Sunday?"

Lord Snoclyffe held up his hands, and she knew her glance had been accusatory. "They have been here with me only since summer began, Miss Burton. At that time, when I decided to return here from London, I thought they might enjoy being in the country."

"Instead of at school?"

"They have a governess and a tutor. Their education is not being ignored."

Rosemary knew she had overstepped herself again. Delving too deeply into the children's personal lives was something she should not do. She could not accuse the viscount of a sad want of manners when she was proving she was no better. She hoped no one would suspect that she was finding it difficult to curb her questions about the children when all her thoughts were on their guardian.

That Lady Yatesville had given him a facer only confirmed what Charlotte had revealed about this devil-may-care viscount. She should put an end to this conversation immediately, but when she looked back at the wide-eyed children, she hesitated. Stir-up Sunday had long been one of her favorite days, for it signaled the beginning of the Christmas holidays and all the fun that would follow through the next weeks.

Each year, her mother had worked long hours in the kitchen on Stir-up Sunday. The kitchen had been fragrant with spices that were used only at this time of year. As soon as each of her children was old enough, Mother had welcomed them to join in the traditions that began by a hearth.

"Stir-up Sunday," she said, her smile becoming more sincere as she savored her memories, "is the day when puddings and mincemeat are made, so they will be ready for Christmas Day. The pots must be stirred just so, so your wish will come true."

"Uncle Andrew, can we do that?" Jenna asked, rushing to his side.

"Cook makes what we need for Advent and Christmas. If you check with her—"

"I would be glad to show the children the traditions I grew up with." Rosemary wished she had kept her mouth shut when the children cheered and Lord Snoclyffe regarded her with an expression halfway between a scowl and bafflement. How could she have made such an offer when she needed to maintain quiet in her house? Charlotte must have quiet for her healing.

"Please, Uncle Andrew!" cried Jenna.

The two boys jumped up and down, cheering. They paused when their uncle stood.

Putting a hand on each shoulder, he said, "If Miss Burton is willing, she is welcome to come here to our kitchen and share the traditions with you."

Simon grasped her hand. "Will you, Miss Burton?"

"Yes, I would be glad to, as long as your uncle and his cook agree."

"Simon," Lord Snoclyffe said, "you do not take a lady's hand without her permission." He slowly drew Rosemary's fingers out of his nephew's grip. As he lowered it to her lap, his hand grazed her leg. The motion, which she would have barely noticed with another, threatened to send her head reeling with the potent sensation.

Hastily, she came to her feet. As he stood, too, she raised her eyes to his. She had become so accustomed to being the tallest that this was also an unexpected pleasure.

Did she want for sense? Picking up the basket, she edged past the table.

He matched each of her steps. When she turned to leave, he blocked her path. She stared at him, unsure what to say or do, especially when her fingers still tingled from his touch.

"You will want this, Miss Burton." He held out her green cloak.

She put the basket on a table as she tied the laces around her neck. She was a beef-head to let her own vagrant thoughts betray her like this. In spite of his reputation—which Charlotte had mentioned with dismay and his wards spoke of matter-of-factly—he had not overstepped the boundaries of propriety this afternoon. Instead, she had been the one who made one social solecism after another.

"Thank you, my lord."

"I look forward to your return on Sunday."

"You will be joining us in the kitchen?"

His smile broadened, and she wondered what her face revealed. Her hope, or her dismay?

"I am understandably interested in what you will be teaching the children." His voice held no hint of anything but sincerity. "I suspect we all are in for a stimulating afternoon. Don't you agree?"

She replied something, but as she grabbed the basket to rush down the stairs and out of the house, not slowing along the road toward the river and the village, she was not sure what she had said. The only thing she was sure of was how his smile urged her to toss caution aside . . . just once.

# Five

Hearing the kitten mewing anxiously, Rosemary looked into the parlor. She smiled and shook her head when she realized the kitten seemed only to want to make sure it was not alone. She bent and patted its small head.

With a buzz of sound deep in its throat, it scurried under the settee, chasing some scrap of paper that Charlotte had found for her. Then it flew up the stairs and back down. When it landed hard on the stones at the base of the steps, Rosemary picked it up. It squirmed, obviously not hurt and eager to continue its play.

"She's been running about like that for nearly an hour," Charlotte said as she sat by the window and picked up her knitting. She was making mittens for the church to give out in the Christmas boxes.

"She did this yesterday, too, then collapsed and slept for more than an hour." Laughing, Rosemary rested her shoulder against the door. "After that, she ran around like a crazy creature again."

Charlotte smiled. "She exhausts me just to watch her."

"Mayhap we should return her to—"

"No, no!" Grasping Rosemary's hands, she said, "I know you fret about my health, sweet cousin, but do not deny me this bit of excitement that eases my long days." She looked down at the half-finished mitten on her lap. "I have spent too many days doing nothing. Now I can watch Cutie Pie flit across the room like a sunbeam, adding warmth and a spot of color."

"As long as you are sure that the kitten will not slow your recovery."

"I believe it shall be quite the opposite. When she has a rare moment of quiet, I adore sitting and petting her. She has such a fierce purr for such a tiny creature." Raising her eyes, she added with unusual intensity, "And I do not want to cause you to have to make another journey to Snoclyffe Park."

"I am going there this afternoon."

"To Snoclyffe Park? Why?" Her eyes grew wide. "Don't tell me that you have fallen under the spell of that rake?"

"Of course not!" She wished she was as certain of her words as she sounded. "I discovered the children aren't familiar with the traditions of Stir-up Sunday, so I offered to show them the fun of preparing some of the dishes for Christmas."

Charlotte sniffed. "One should not be amazed that *he* failed to oversee their proper education."

"Quite the contrary, Charlotte. He has hired a tutor for them, since they came to live with him only a few months ago."

"Oh!" She sighed. "You must understand that my comments were not meant to disparage the viscount unfairly. I simply assumed—"

"That a man so focused on his own pleasure would not bother to spend his time teaching his wards about the fun of the Advent season?"

Charlotte picked up her knitting, twisting the yarn with speed about the needles. "You defend him with such fervor, Rosemary. I do not like the tone of that."

"You have warned me well to distrust him, and I will not fail to heed that. But I shall not allow these children to miss out on the traditions we have long enjoyed."

"Be wary." Charlotte gripped her hand again. "Promise me, Rosemary."

"I can promise you that I shall be very wary if I see Lord

Snoclyffe." That was one vow she knew she would not falter on.

She must not.


"This way, Miss Burton." The maid walked through an arch that was one in a group of three that looked as if they belonged in a cathedral grotto.

On the other side was Snoclyffe Park's kitchen. It awed her as she slowly turned to look at the series of rooms and larders. It must be as big as her whole house. Hearths rose higher than her head. Tables, which were long enough to hold a full boar or deer, took up only a small portion of the stone floor. Hanging overhead from a metal rack, brightly shined pots and dull, cast-iron pans waited to be used.

"You must be Miss Burton." A slender, dark-haired woman, who looked no bigger than a large stew pot, came from around one of the hearths. "I'm Mrs. Jones, the cook."

"How do you do, Mrs. Jones?" Mindful of the protocol she had heard existed in these big houses, she added, "I hope you don't mind me intruding on your Stir-up Sunday."

"Not at all." She smiled. "You know that it is a day that can always use extra hands."

Shouts and giggles preceded the children into the kitchen. Donald bounced right over to Rosemary and threw his arms around her. "Can I have my story now?"

"Story?" She laughed and bent over to ruffle his hair exactly as she had Cutie Pie's fur. "This is *Stir-up* Sunday, not Story Sunday."

"Oh, I thought—"

"But I'd be glad to tell you a story if you'd like."

He brightened again and put his hand in hers.

"Mrs. Jones," she said as she included the older children in her smile, "we shall need four more aprons and four big spoons."

"I have them ready, Miss Burton." She pointed to a table in the very center of the room, far away from any of the hearths. "I thought the children might want to do their work here."

"An excellent idea."

In quick order, Rosemary tied aprons around herself and Donald. Mrs. Jones helped Simon. With a superior smile, Jenna managed hers on her own. Although Rosemary despaired at the stains that were certain to slip past the aprons and onto the children's pretty clothes, she said nothing. She could not guess what sort of play clothing a viscount's ward would wear.

Before she could begin her work, Rosemary turned as her dress was tugged on. She looked over her shoulder to see Jenna holding a box with a swarming collection of kittens inside.

"This is the rest of the litter." The little girl smiled. "You should bring Cutie Pie to play with her sisters and brothers." She sat by the box and let the kittens run over her crossed legs.

"Don't you think that seeing them would make her sad when she doesn't live with them any longer?"

"It wouldn't make me sad to see Mama and Papa again."

Rosemary pressed her hand over her heart. She was sure it had halted at the sorrow in the little girl's voice. Glancing at Mrs. Jones, she wondered if Lord Snoclyffe knew that the children's grief had not eased with the passing of the months since they had come into his care.

Even though she wanted to ask Mrs. Jones what had happened to the children's parents, she silenced her curiosity. It was not her place to gossip with the viscount's servants, even if the children had not been there to overhear.

"Don't forget my story," Donald said, climbing onto a sturdy stool so he could reach the pot on the low table.

Glad for his request that pulled her away from her dreary thoughts, Rosemary began to chop the meat for the mincemeat and drop it into Donald's pot while Simon and Jenna began to crack and shell nuts with Mrs. Jones. In rhythm with her knife, she told them about the mishaps she had enjoyed on Stir-up Sundays when she was a little girl.

They laughed when she told how she had fed pieces of the meat to the dog at the same time as she was working, and left a guest wondering how a dog hair came to be in his piece of pie. She watched their eyes get wide when she related the story of a pudding that seemed to appear and disappear until they discovered that her older brother had been playing a holiday jest on all of them. By the time she had finished telling of how she decided, one year, to help in as many kitchens as she could to enjoy the day for as long as possible and ended up sick in bed with measles, which meant all the puddings and mincemeats had to be thrown out so others would not sicken, the pot was ready to be placed on the fire.

"One at a time," Rosemary cautioned as the children followed her to the hearth. "It won't work if more than one is at the pot at a time." She glanced at Mrs. Jones and saw the cook trying to hide her laughter.

"Me first!" cried Donald.

"I think we should let Simon go first this time."

"Why?" asked Jenna.

"I'm sure you get to do many things first because you are the oldest. Donald gets privileges, too, because he is the youngest." She smiled at Simon, who had been working the hardest, although she knew better than to say that and start a quarrel among the children. "Today, we will start with the middlest."

"Is there such a word?" Jenna frowned.

"If there's not," her brother retorted, "there should be." He held out his hand for the spoon.

Making sure he stayed back from the flames, Rosemary put the pot in place. "Now, Mrs. Jones, we need a wooden spoon."

"Not a metal one?" asked Simon. "I like how metal spoons clang in pots."

"For Stir-up Sunday, when we are stirring the Christmas treats, we must use a wooden spoon." She smiled. "My mother always told me that was because the manger in Bethlehem was made of wood."

"That's what my mother told me, as well," Mrs. Jones added as she handed Simon a long-handled wooden spoon. "And she said one like this was the very best."

Rosemary chuckled as Simon took the spoon with all the gravity of a king accepting his scepter. Holding his hand, she showed him how to turn the spoon clockwise. "Always in this direction, like the movement of the sun across the sky."

"Why?"

"I don't know." She laughed. "But I do know that if you close your eyes and make a wish while you're stirring in that direction, it should come true before Christmas dawns."

"And what should one wish for?" asked a voice much deeper than the children's.

As she looked over her shoulder, the children swarmed to greet their uncle, who was coming in from outside. The cool breath of the afternoon breeze had followed him in, teasing the fire to dance to its silent melody.

He hugged each of the children, and she hastily picked up the spoon Simon had left leaning against the pot and began to stir before the mixture burned. She should not intrude on this private moment of happiness that belonged to the viscount and his family.

In spite of herself, she sighed. Once her family had been like this, loving and demonstrative and laughing with one another. Even when her older siblings married and made their own homes, the house had been filled with laughter. That had ended when her mother died, when Rosemary was no older than Jenna. She had tried to figure out when to share a jest with her father to give him some relief from his pain, but it had not worked. Only when he met her stepmother and began to court her had the twinkle come back into his eyes. She had not guessed then how lonely he had been with just a young daughter. Now, as she faced leaving Baedd-upon-Wye when Charlotte was well enough, she understood all too well. She could return to her father's house, but she was not sure where she would find home again.

"Miss Burton?" called Simon, rushing over to grasp her hand. "Come and tell Uncle Andrew about the dog."

"Yes," the viscount added, "please share this story that has the children giggling so hard they can barely speak."

Handing the spoon to Mrs. Jones, Rosemary wiped her hands on her apron and brushed her hair back from her face, which must be scarlet from the heat. "It is nothing but a silly mishap of my childhood, my lord." She edged around a pair of kittens who were playing tag among the tables. "I would be glad to share it with you some other time, but I need to return to my cousin's house to do our own cooking."

"At least honor me with an abridged version of it while we walk to the front door, where I suspect your cloak is waiting." He held out his hand toward the arch in what she recognized as an order.

Vexed that he would expect her to follow his commands with the alacrity of his servants or the obligation of his wards, she paused long enough to thank the children and Mrs. Jones for their help. She again turned down the offer of another kitten, at the same time she invited the children to visit Cutie Pie at her cousin's house. She let Donald give her a wet kiss on the cheek.

"A lucky lad," the viscount murmured as she joined him by the arch.

"That's what comes from working together on Stir-up Sunday," she replied, determined not to let him put her to the blush with his outrageous comments. Nor would she be overmastered by the breadth of his shoulders, which seemed even more awe-inspiring beneath his ebony cloak. And his gaze must not be allowed to hold hers, seeking something she was sure he should not find—even though she was not sure what it might be. "You get good luck and wishes come true."

"Mayhap I should have endeavored to return with more speed, so I could have helped."

"The children would have enjoyed that," she said as they climbed the stairs toward the front of the house. "They speak of you constantly, and with the greatest affection."

Rosemary wondered if she had overstepped the bounds of propriety again when he did not answer. She risked a glance at him and saw his gaze had turned inward. Again curiosity teased her, and again she tried to submerge it.

Only when they stood in the foyer and a footman had brought her green cloak did Lord Snoclyffe speak again, "You are kind to come to share this tradition with the children. They seem quite taken with it, and with you."

"They are lovely children, eager to have fun." She drew on her left glove. "They are rambunctious, but that is the way of children."

"I did not realize that you had children."

"I don't, but one need not be a painter to enjoy the beauty of a sunset, my lord."

He laughed. "The point is very well taken, Miss Burton. I thank you again."

"It was my pleasure." She smiled. "You have brought much pleasure into my life and my cousin's by allowing us to keep Cutie Pie."

"That name!" He shook his head with a grimace. "I am glad the *cath fach* brings you happiness."

"I did not realize you speak Welsh."

"A bit. I was raised here, as I understand you were, Miss Burton."

"Yes." She was unsettled at the thought that he had been asking about her. And why shouldn't he, before he allowed his children to come under her supervision in the kitchen? "In the hills beyond Baedd-upon-Wye."

"Odd that it took this many years for us to meet. Or mayhap, it is not so odd. By the time either of us were old enough to stray in search of adventure, I had been sent to school."

"My lord—"

His smile grew wide again. "Would it make you uncomfortable to address me as Andrew? I find I like the idea of calling you Rosemary."

"As you wish, my—as you wish, Andrew."

He took her right hand and drew her glove along her palm and up her wrist. His fingers slipping beneath her sleeve sent quivers deep within her. The motion of his fingertips, so ordinary, became extraordinary.

When she pulled her hand away reluctantly, he released it, but not her gaze. That he held, in spite of her resolve not to be spellbound by him once more. She knew she should look away, but she could not, not when his eyes revealed what she longed to believe was genuine emotion.

"I cannot thank you enough," he said softly, "for the sound of their joy. No matter what each of them wishes as the pot is stirred, that delightful laughter is my wish come true."

"Do not be deluded by it." She could not imagine being anything less than honest with him at this moment. "So much sorrow remains within each of their young hearts."

"I understand their grief, Rosemary." He sat her beside him on the carved bench by the door. "I share it. My sister and brother-in-law died so suddenly that none of us had a chance to be prepared."

"They took ill?"

"No." He clasped his hands between his knees. "They were killed when the boat they were sailing about the Mediterranean Sea capsized. All aboard were drowned."

She put her hand on his arm. "How horrible!"

"That was the thought of many in London when it was realized that the wastrel Lord Snoclyffe was to be the poor orphans' guardian."

"You are a good guardian to the children."

"I thank you for your testimonial, but few share your generous opinion." His fingers slipped over hers, pinning them to his sleeve. "One gains a certain reputation by the acts of one's youth."

"So you did do all those things?"

He laughed coldly. "You must be more specific, Rosemary. I have been accused of many things. It would be impossible for one man to commit so many crimes in a single lifetime, and I have yet to reach the end of mine. I would gladly give you an abridged version of my so-called exploits, if you wish."

"That, too, should be left to another time." She stood. "My"—she corrected herself when a frown flashed across his lips—*"Andrew,* Charlotte is expecting me back before dark. It is already darkening, so I must hurry."

"Let me call for the carriage. I can have you back in the village in ripping time."

"No, thank you. I think the children would be very happy to have you stir the pot a few times with them."

"Are you certain?"

"Most certain, thank you." She hurried out the door before he could guess that her refusal had less to do with the children than from the way her heart leapt at the thought of being alone with him in the closed confines of the carriage. She could rush away from him, but not from the fantasies that his offer had created in her imagination.

# Six

Andrew was aware of every eye focused on him as he stepped from his coach on the narrow street. He looked up at the box.

"Take the carriage up toward the old castle, so people may pass on their business," he said.

The coachee touched his cap and nodded.

Jumping back so the wheels did not roll over his toes, Andrew pulled in his cloak. It was dusty enough from the ride over the bridge to the village. He did not need more dirt sprayed upon it.

"Good afternoon," he said, touching his own brim when a pair of women paused in the street to regard him with unabashed curiosity.

They rushed away, whispering together. He understood only a single phrase—*Arglwydd tir.* He had heard it spoken to his father on several occasions, but, even though the words meant *lord of the manor,* they had been addressed to his father with little respect. Mayhap that was why his father had seldom come to the village on the other side of the river from Snoclyffe Park, even though Baedd-upon-Wye was within the feudal boundaries of the estate.

For the first time, these thoughts disturbed him—mayhap, because for the first time he was looking at an extended stay here. It had amazed him when he decided to come to Snoclyffe that he could not recall any time when he had spent more than a pair of fortnights in his family's ancestral home. His parents had been there even less frequently. He could return to London and face the coterie of lies there, but not with the children. They had suffered enough already, and for now they needed him more than he needed the excitement provided by the *ton*.

He shoved those thoughts aside as he paused in front of the door that had been pointed out to him. It was painted a bright red. Somehow, that did not surprise him, for, in spite of Rosemary's attempts to remain quietly in the background, she could not. Not solely her glorious red hair, but her fiery emotions, too, refused to be concealed.

At his knock, he heard, "Let yourself in, please!"

Andrew opened the door, not sure why there had been such exasperation in the muted voice. He understood as he quickly closed the door and pressed back against it, as Rosemary came running toward him in pursuit of the kitten, which seemed to have made itself quite at home here in the past fortnight. With candid admiration he viewed her slender ankles, letting his gaze rise along her delightful curves to her eyes, which snapped with irritation.

"That kitten is utterly impossible." She jumped aside as a blur of black and light brown came down the stairs and tried to turn the corner into the foyer. With a bang, it slid on the tile floor and spun into a stack of cut greens, its back quarters hitting the wall smartly.

Andrew winced. "She'll learn to be more cautious after she does that a few more times."

"She already has managed to strike a wall or a table or the settee at least a dozen times since this morning. She seems to consider it a small price to pay to chase a mote of dust or a scrap of paper."

"She apparently considers it fun." He took a step toward her. "You know, Rosemary, fun is not sin."

"Of course, it isn't."

"Then why do you take everything everyone says to you so dreadfully seriously?"

"I don't take everyone's words so seriously."

"Just mine?"

She bent and captured the kitten. Holding Cutie Pie close to the alluring curve of her bodice, she said, "I believe you are misunderstanding me."

"Then, mayhap, you might clarify all this for me."

He watched as she hesitated, and he could guess her thoughts as clearly as if they were his own. She regretted not asking who was at the door instead of shouting for him to let himself in. He was glad she had. With her hair falling from its bun to curl along her neck and her dress littered with apple peel and mint, she was a charming sight.

"Forgive me for leaving you standing in the foyer," she said, "but I must check my pie."

"It smells delightful."

"If you will wait for me in the parlor—"

"Of course, Rosemary." As she turned toward the back of the house, he asked, "What sort of pie is it?"

"Beef, potato, and apple."

"An interesting combination. Your invention?"

She regarded him as if he had taken a knock in the cradle. "It's a traditional receipt from the hills around the village."

When he did not reply she paused, then handed him the kitten. He smiled down at the big eyes in the kitten's narrow face before looking up to admire the sway of Rosemary's skirts as she rushed back into the kitchen.

He yelped as the kitten decided it must follow Rosemary into the kitchen. Trying to keep it from scurrying away, he was rewarded with a trio of bloody scratches along his hand.

"I will take the kitten from you, my lord."

Andrew glanced at the staircase, realizing he had been too lost in his thoughts of his hostess to hear footsteps coming toward him. He stepped aside to allow the frightfully thin woman down the last few steps. Although he considered offering his hand to assist her, the scowl she wore warned that she was not interested in his help.

Her blond hair was neatly contained in her lacy cap, and she moved with slow grace—not at all like Rosemary, who seemed to rush here and there every time he saw her. This must be her cousin Charlotte Griffydd, who had been rescued from death by Rosemary's tender care.

When she held out her hands, he placed the kitten in them. She did not look at him as she said, "The parlor is this way, my lord."

He shivered and drew out his handkerchief to wrap around the scratches. Her voice was as cold as the wind-swept day beyond these walls.

For a moment he thought she might not sit, but she did, and he chose a chair facing her. The fire crackled on the hearth. That and the sounds of Rosemary in the kitchen were loud amid the silent disapproval displayed on Miss Griffydd's face. She did resemble Rosemary, even though her face was lean with her recent illness and her mouth pinched from her opinions of him.

"The kitten is not too troublesome, I collect," Andrew said when he could endure the quiet no longer.

Her voice did not soften, even on the kitten's absurd name. "Cutie Pie will mature to know the mistakes of her youth, my lord."

Baedd-upon-Wye might be many miles from London, but Miss Griffydd had all the skills of offering an unvoiced insult that many of the *élite* honed amid the treacherous conversations of the *ton*. She believed the kitten would come to learn from its mistakes, but that Andrew never would.

"I trust that you are right." He leaned back in his chair, hoping his nonchalant pose covered the annoyance bubbling within him.

"May I be blunt, my lord?"

"Always."

She blinked at his reply, which said more than its single word. The dart had found its target, for she had been frank from her first words. Petting the kitten that was stretched out on the cushion beside her, she asked, "Why do you want to make my cousin a part of the morass that seems to surround you?"

This woman did not mince words. He could be as forthright.

"Miss Griffydd, I have no intention of doing anything to damage your cousin in any manner whatsoever. I called today simply to express that the children would enjoy seeing her again."

"You cannot expect me to swallow that clanker on a single gulp."

"I can only expect that you will accept it as the truth, for that is what it is."

She continued to stroke the kitten, which curled up against her, purring with enthusiasm. "I find it unconscionable that you would use those orphans as a route to entangle my cousin's life with yours."

Mayhap she would do poorly in London, for half of the Polite World would swoon at such outspoken comments. The other half would have nothing to do with Miss Griffydd from that point.

"I do not use those children to obtain myself anything," he said quietly. "It would be a mistaken thing to use someone else in that manner."

"Then one would question where the children obtained the idea to use a small kitten to make a match for you."

He set himself on his feet. "I do not have the foggiest idea what you are speaking of."

"I'm speaking of a kitten left on *my* doorstep by *your* wards. As I have it on excellent authority that the children were amazed to see Rosemary with the kitten, I can only assume they expected that I would appear at Snoclyffe Park to accept the invitation offered by this gift."

"Miss Griffydd, every word you speak baffles me further." He wondered who among his staff had witnessed the children's meeting with Rosemary and then hastened to spread poker-talk on both sides of the river. That must be corrected with haste, for he needed no additional gossip about him that would bring pain to the children.

Slowly she stood. "Lord Snoclyffe, a gentleman would

understand that leaving a gift on a young woman's step is a profession of affection."

"May I remind you that I played no part in putting that kitten in a basket and depositing it here?"

"Yes, you may. At the very same time I remind you that I do not wish to see my cousin ruined because you find her charming and a way to ease your boredom with country life." She held up her hand as he opened his mouth to protest. "Grant me enough respect, my lord, to know that I am able to understand what I see with my own two eyes. You find Rosemary captivating."

"That is true, but—"

"I believe I have repeated my opinions enough. I bid you good day, my lord." She glanced toward the front door.

He considered reminding her that he had called to speak with her cousin, but this was Miss Griffydd's house. The blasted constraints of polite society gave her the license to toss him into the street.

With a tip of his hat, he said, "Good day, Miss Griffydd. I do hope you will pass my message on to your cousin."

"You may be sure of that."

He wished he could be. As he walked out of the house and stomped along the street, he refused to acknowledge that Miss Griffydd had, mayhap, been a bit more accurate in her assessment of his call this afternoon than he wished to own. The children *had* been asking when Miss Burton would be calling again. That was true. But it was also true that he had been looking for an excuse to invite her back to Snoclyffe Park, where she brought laughter and a thrill that began somewhere in his center and curled up around his heart.

Andrew dropped into his chair and glowered at the fire on the hearth in his book-room. It flickered as merrily as the one in Miss Griffydd's parlor.

Blast that woman!

And blast her vexing comments that still rang through his head!

Even if she had been right about his motives, she had not considered that Miss Burton made no secret of the fact that she had consented to come to the Park on Stir-up Sunday solely to brighten the children's holiday season. And the idea that he would leave a kitten on a doorstep in a feeble attempt to gain a lady's attention—it never had occurred to him.

Blast his own honesty!

He had had enough of the silliness of women and their demands in London. For once, coming to Snoclyffe Park had not seemed like exile when he brought the children here. Yes, it was often too quiet, especially when the children were at their lessons, but he was learning ways to fill the long hours to avoid *ennui*. Spending time with the children or riding about the estate offered endless entertainment when he saw the hills as if through their young eyes. Every tree, every fence, every brooklet, might be the perfect place for an adventure.

Adventure. There was one adventure he would enjoy greatly, but he doubted if Rosemary would consent. A single sample of her lips might ease the longing within him.

Blast it! He needed no woman ruining his life again. But then, why could he think of little else but her sparkling eyes?

A throat was cleared.

Andrew looked up to see Souder in the doorway. "Yes?"

"You have a caller, my lord," the butler replied.

At the moment, he wanted to see no one. He almost laughed. On previous visits, he had been sure he had been left to molder in the country, and he had been desperate for visitors. Now, when someone was calling, he had no interest in conversation.

That, he knew, was a falsehood of the first degree. He would be glad to share a conversation—and more—with Miss Rosemary Burton. That seemed less and less likely to happen. She had not been able to hide her eagerness to be done with his company this afternoon, and her cousin had been even less circumspect. Defending himself would have been a waste of time, for Miss Griffydd had her opinion of him firmly formed and just as vigorously voiced.

"Who is it?" he asked. "If—"

"Why are you making me wait in the foyer like a stranger?" came a laughing voice he had not expected to hear this far from London.

Standing, Andrew watched a man who was nearly as round as Miss Griffydd was spare bounce into the room with all the ebullience of the children. Terence Connors's dark hair was the only part of him that had thinned since Andrew last saw him, for he was plump from his cheeks to his knees, which seemed ready to pop out of his stylish breeches.

"Terence, what are you doing so far from Town?" he asked.

Tossing his riding gloves into his hat, he handed them to Souder. "It has been too quiet since you took your leave, Andrew. I miss our rollicking good times."

"The Season and the Little Season are both long past. What else did you expect to discover in Town but quiet?"

"True, but now I hear that you plan to remain here in grassville even when the Season begins with the new year. I considered it my obligation to come and acquaint you with the folly of that idea."

"Advent is only half done. We have weeks before the Season will be underway."

"True," he repeated with a gusty laugh, "but, in spite of your comments, I can assure you that there are entertainments awaiting us in London even now. Not everyone retires to their dirty acres for the Christmas celebration."

He chuckled. If he had thought to ask for someone to drag him out of his dismals, it would have been . . . Rosemary. He ignored that thought. Terence Connors always had known just the jest to cheer a dull day.

"But enough of the *ton* has gone down from London," he replied, "so we would be hard-pressed to gather enough hands for a decent game of whist. Sit, Terence, and let me get you something to wash the dirt of the road out of your mouth. Souder, let the staff know we have a guest."

"Of course, my lord." Souder glanced at Terence and away.

Andrew did not let his butler's hardly hidden impressions of his guest slow his feet as he went to the cabinet by the largest bookcase. He took a tray containing a bottle of brandy and set two glasses on it.

Walking back to where Terence sat on the chair closest to the fire, he set the tray on a table next to his friend and poured two generous servings of brandy. He wondered why he had not considered sampling this ball of fire before, so it could burn away these thoughts of Rosemary that he did not want plaguing him.

He sat and listened with a smile as Terence outlined every indignity of every mile between London and the Welsh border. That Terence laughed loudly about his mishaps was one of the reasons Andrew had always enjoyed his company.

"So who is she?" Terence asked in mid-story of the vermin in a country inn.

Andrew scowled. "She?"

Terence crossed one leg over the other. "Come on, old chap, you know you never have been able to hide anything from me. Didn't I know even before the countess herself that you intended to put an end to that absurd *affaire*? Didn't I warn you that Larkin would bring you nothing but trouble? Of course, you did not heed me, and went with him to that tragic duel."

"I don't wish to speak of that." His fingers tightened around his glass until he had to force them to ease their grip before it shattered. He had owned to no one, not even to himself, that he had come to Snoclyffe Park in the hopes of putting that horrible dawn behind him. His attempts to escape it had been useless, because it had trailed him here.

"Then speak instead of this woman who so clearly has

your mind all a-jumble. You are not reminding me that I am at fault for my own mistakes, as you do so often." He leaned forward and pointed at Andrew's hands. "She clearly has claws to make her feelings known when you don't do as she wishes."

" 'Tis not as you think."

"No?" He laughed and took an appreciative sip. "You have said that before, and it has always been exactly as I think."

"This time is different."

"How?"

Andrew opened his mouth to reply, then found that he did not want to reveal, even to his best tie-mate, the nascent emotions revolving around his reveries of Rosemary. Glancing down at the scratched hand holding his glass, he smiled. "The wounds are caused by a female, but not a woman. They were put there by a most recalcitrant kitten that the children gave to one of the villagers on the other side of the river."

"A villager you clearly have called upon recently, for I can tell by the way you're avoiding looking me straight in the eye that my guess is close to its target." He chuckled. "Is she blonde or brunette?"

"Both, actually."

"Both?" He sat straighter.

"Dark and blonde, and a bit of orange tossed in for good measure."

Terence's mouth twisted. "I did not mean the cat. I spoke of the woman."

"One is blonde, and the other auburn."

"Two? You have two women you are calling upon? Do you think that wise when you are now guardian for your sister's children?"

Andrew chuckled. "Actually the children are the ones usually pestering me to call upon them." When his friend scowled, he relented. "The children left the cat on the doorstep of Miss Charlotte Griffydd, who has been in the care of her cousin, Miss Rosemary Burton."

"Aha!"

"Aha what?"

"I can see that you are quite taken with this Miss Rosemary."

Blast it! He should be more careful. Terence knew him far too well. Some variation in his voice must have pointed Terence to the right name.

"The children, I assure you, are quite taken with her. She's introduced them to Advent traditions that my sister did not have the time to teach them."

"So she'd be a good mother to your wards?"

"Egad, Terence, leave off with your probing about my relationship with Rosemary Burton. You sound like an old tough."

"So you own to a relationship?"

"I believe she might count me as one among her many friends."

He drained his glass and reached for the bottle to refill it. "A beginning, although a most peculiar one for you. I do recall you once stating that friendship and women went together no better than a racehorse and a rainy day."

"How is that you remember what I said years ago, and you are unable to heed what I am saying now?"

"Because," Terrence said, holding up his glass in a salute, "I believe that I chose exactly the right moment to give you a look-in here in the country. This shall be a most interesting visit."

# Seven

"Good afternoon, Miss Burton!"

Rosemary turned to see three heavily bundled forms rushing toward her. With a smile, she asked, "Where have you been this afternoon?"

"Uncle Andrew took us sledding on the hill beyond Mr. Roberts's sheepfold." Jenna bounced from one foot to the other.

"What fun!"

"It was." Donald grabbed her hand. "I wish you could have come with us."

"Mayhap next time," said Andrew as he walked toward them, dragging a long sled behind him. "Miss Burton may not be interested in flying down the hill to land in a heap in a drift of snow."

"It sounds like so much fun," she replied.

"If I had known you liked sledding, I would have stopped by for you."

As the children hurried along the street to press their hands and noses to the shop windows, she walked more slowly with Andrew. The soft fall continued, warning that their footprints would be swept beneath new snow.

"It is just as well that you didn't tempt me with sledding today." She patted the basket on her arm. "I have spent the past two days baking, and I would have been glad of any excuse to escape the kitchen."

"And what good things have you baked?" He reached for the cloth covering the basket.

"It's empty!" She slapped his fingers away, then drew back, shocked at her own action.

When he laughed, she relaxed—or tried to. She could not forget Charlotte's dismay that she had welcomed Lord Snoclyffe into the house.

"You never answered the notes the children sent you," he said quietly, again warning her that he was too privy to her thoughts. "Was it because you wanted to avoid having us call?"

"I have been busy with preparations for Christmas."

"Too busy even to send the children a note that said you were too busy?" He slowed, putting his hand on her elbow to bring her to face him. "They were quite hurt, Rosemary."

"That was never my intention."

"I know that, but they have been hurt so much already. I want to keep them from any other hurts."

She looked from his oddly solemn expression to where the children had stopped to wait for them to catch up. She wanted to take them all in her arms and plead their forgiveness. But then she would have to explain to them and herself and to Andrew that she was so unsure of her own feelings that she needed time to think. Avoiding Andrew and the children had not cleared her mind in any way, even though seeing them today had sent a pule of delight through her.

"Then," she said, "it is time for me to atone for not considering the consequences of my actions."

"You?" He gave a laugh, but it was as chilled as the winter afternoon. "You consider every aspect of everything until you find that time has passed you by with nothing accomplished except your baking."

"Then mayhap I should do something now."

His eyes widened. "I did not mean to—"

With a smile, she called, "Children, would you like to come into my house for some hot chocolate?"

Their cheers rang along the street.

"You need not entertain us this afternoon if you are busy, Rosemary."

"The children are chilled. Having a cup of chocolate here will give them a chance to warm up before you return over the Wye and back to Snoclyffe Park." She let her smile copy his most self-satisfied expression. "See? I have considered all the facts, with time to spare to prepare some chocolate for the children."

"I suspect I shall come to regret that appraisal of you."

"I suspect you shall."

He drew her hand within his arm as they continued along the slippery street. "The children are delighted to accept your invitation." His voice lowered to be as velvety as the early twilight. "And so am I."

"*You* should have been aware of how long a walk it is to Mr. Roberts's farm for those short legs. Poor Donald. He must be exhausted."

"He must."

"You could have taken them there in your carriage."

He put his hand over hers on his arm. "True, but then it would have been nigh onto impossible to have this chance meeting with you, Rosemary."

"You are diabolical."

"So I have been told."

The children swarmed over them as they got closer. Listening to their happy chatter, Rosemary knew she had been wrong to set the notes from Snoclyffe Park aside, unanswered.

When she opened the door to her house, the children surged inside, eager for warmth after their chilly adventures on the hillside. She set her basket on the stairs and turned as Jenna spoke her name.

"Yes?"

"Where is the kitten?"

"Cutie Pie is—"

"Terence!" Andrew said from where he stood closer to the parlor door. "What are you doing here?"

A dark-haired, very round man stood and bowed to Rosemary. "Good afternoon, Miss Burton. Allow me to introduce myself. I am Terence Connors."

"Good afternoon, Mr. Connors. Are you visiting Baedd-upon-Wye?" She glanced at Andrew, who clearly was well-acquainted with this stranger. That did not explain why Mr. Connors was here in Charlotte's parlor.

"Today I am." Looking past her, he smiled. "Andrew, as I did not wish to intrude on your outing with the children, I thought I might enjoy a bit of the fresh air myself with a walk through the village. When I passed the door of this house, I paused, guessing that you might be calling here yourself. Imagine my surprise when I discovered Miss Griffydd sitting here with only a kitten to keep her company while Miss Burton was busy with her errands and you, my friend, with your fun."

"Mr. Connors has been entertaining me," Charlotte said, her eyes brighter than Rosemary had seen them since her illness, "with stories of his visits to London. Oh, Rosemary, someday we must think of traveling up there."

Rosemary drew off her cloak and hung it on the peg. As the children scrambled around her, she could not pull her eyes from her cousin's face. It was emblazoned with healthy color, which deepened to an appealing pink when Charlotte turned to speak to Mr. Connors.

But who was he?

As if she had spoken those words aloud, Andrew said as he helped Donald untie his scarf, "Terence is a tie-mate from London."

"One who clearly feels he can run tame through the village, putting aside all the canons of society."

Andrew stood and draped Donald's scarf over his coat. Wagging a finger at her, he smiled. "You are judging him without facts, Rosemary. He is respected throughout the *ton* and beyond as a gentleman without peer. He would no sooner break one of society's rules than trod about town in his smallclothes."

She knew she was blushing when he chuckled. "You could have chosen another analogy."

"Very well. He would no sooner break a rule than your kitten would sit quietly while someone teased her with a ribbon."

Rosemary could not keep from smiling when she saw how Jenna was entertaining the kitten with the ribbon that had been holding back her hair. Cutie Pie stalked it, leaping as if she thought she was after dangerous prey.

"He is a very good friend," Andrew continued. "He would do anything for someone he cares about."

Before she could answer, Simon intruded to say, "The house smells so good. I love mincemeat pie."

"Would you like a piece of pie to go with your chocolate?" Rosemary asked.

Charlotte's eyes widened. "Rosemary, if we cut one of the pies—"

"There is time to make another." She held her hand out to Simon. "Would you like to help me slice it? I want to make certain all the pieces are the same size."

He started to nod, then shook his head. He rushed back to play with the kitten, who skittered away, clearly overmastered by all the attention.

"Cutie Pie usually hides in the kitchen or upstairs," Rosemary said.

"Can I go look for her?" Simon asked.

"Are you sure you wouldn't rather help me with the pie?"

He was shaking his head as he rushed out with Donald on his heels. Jenna picked up the ribbon and tied it into her hair again.

"Allow me to help you, Rosemary." Andrew smiled. He glanced over his shoulder as a door opened and closed. "I guess the kitten is not in the kitchen." Without a pause, he added, "Terence, I trust you and Miss Griffydd will excuse us."

For a moment, Rosemary thought her cousin would protest. Then Mr. Connors asked Charlotte a question about

the mittens she made for the church, and she began to
smile again as she said, "You may need to cut into two
pies. Rosemary makes the tastiest mincemeat."

"I cannot wait to sample it." Mr. Connors included all
of them in his warm smile.

"Don't look so suspicious," Andrew said quietly as Rosemary turned toward the kitchen. "Terence is, as I assured
you, every iota a gentleman." He cocked a brow at her.
"Shall I say before you that our friendship proves the old
saying that opposites attract?"

"It might be better that you do."

He chuckled. "You share your cousin's skill of firing off
an insult without saying anything impolite." He pushed
open the door to the kitchen. "Simon is right. These pies
smell wonderful."

"Oh, no!" she cried.

Looking across the kitchen, he saw a row of pies set on
the table. In the center of each pie was a set of kitten-size
footprints. He came around the table just in time to see
the kitten jump to the floor, knocking a pie pan off the
table. Cutie Pie landed on her feet, but the mince pie fell
upside down on the stone floor. Mincemeat and crust splat-
tered everywhere.

He glanced at Rosemary, not sure if he expected she
would be wearing tears or simply a scowl on her face at
the ruin of her long hours of work. Instead he saw her
wry smile.

She bent to pick up the overturned pie pan. Setting it
on the table, she picked up a bucket. "Andrew, the pump
is just outside the back door. Please don't let Cutie Pie slip
past the door. The last thing I need to do now is chase
her across the garden."

"How much water do you need?"

"Enough to clean up this mess and a tiny kitten, and to
make some tea for the children." She shook her head. "I
think chocolate is out of the question now."

"You don't have to be obligated to serve us anything."

"It's not an obligation." Shoving the bucket into his

hands, she smiled. "This kitchen won't clean up easily or quickly. Neither will the kitten. While you help me clean up the kitchen, the children won't want to wait on their tea."

"And what makes you think I will help you clean up the kitchen?" He took the bucket and set it on the table. As she started to reach for one of the pies, he caught her elbow and brought her to face him.

His breath caught in his throat as he gazed into her eyes. It was an endless delight to find them so close to his. He saw the glow of wonder in them—not only wonder, but the same craving that carved through him like a heated blade.

"This is your fault." Her voice was no louder than a whisper, but it rang in his head with the power of a heavenly choir.

"How so?"

"Cutie Pie came from your house."

"True."

"And your nephews must have allowed Cutie Pie into the kitchen when they came in here looking for her."

"That is true, as well." He grinned and watched her lips quirk in an answering smile. "But, it's true as well, that I am your guest."

"As I was when I worked in *your* kitchen."

He gave an emoted groan. " 'Tis good that you are not a man and wish to win a seat in Parliament. You would pulverize someone in a debate."

Rosemary laughed and picked up the bucket. Pushing it into Andrew's hands, she said, "Please get the water before the mincemeat turns to stone on the floor."

When he went out, careful that Cutie Pie did not edge past him, she clenched the side of the table. Letting him draw her so close had been skimble-skamble, but she had not been able to resist. She tried to steady her breathing. Her frantic heartbeat refused to be stilled. She *had* been right to resist the temptation of going to Snoclyffe Park.

She pushed away from the table, gathering tea cups and

putting them on a tray decorated with small purple flowers. Cutie Pie jumped back up onto the table and gave a furious mew. Shaking first one foot, then another, the kitten glared at her.

"It is clearly your fault that her explorations left her covered with mincemeat," Andrew said, chuckling, as he came back into the kitchen and set the bucket on the table.

"She will be even more vexed when I try to clean her off."

"You could let her clean herself."

She pointed to the pattern of pawprints across the floor. "I would rather endure the task of washing a cat's feet than having her leave those prints throughout the house."

Taking the bucket, she poured some water into a pot and pushed it over the fire. A smaller amount she put into another pot, and set it next to the fire. She set the bucket back on the table and reached for a brush.

"You can start with the pawprints, Andrew," she said as she tied on her apron, "while I clean up the spilled pie. As soon as the water warms, I'll wash off Cutie Pie and put her out of the kitchen."

When he agreed, she was astonished. He shed his coat and worked with fervor as he followed the trails left by the kitten around the kitchen. His lighthearted whistle made her smile. He was such a mercurial man, his moods changing as rapidly as the clouds rising out of the sea and over the Welsh mountains. Learning more about him could be an invitation to disaster. Only Mr. Connors's charming company had lured Charlotte into welcoming Andrew.

If the two men had arranged this . . . No, Andrew had been genuinely surprised to see his friend here.

Rosemary checked the water in the smaller pot and found the chill was gone. Cutie Pie nosed around her, curious as to what she was doing. When the kitten rubbed mincemeat against Rosemary's dress, she knew she must not delay any longer.

Picking up the kitten, she brought the water over near the table. She gave Cutie Pie no chance to react before she dunked the kitten's feet into the water. The kitten wiggled wildly, trying to escape, but she held Cutie Pie still in the water.

"Here," Andrew said, handing her the brush. "I got the last of the pawprints cleaned up, so you might find this helps."

"Will you let the others know why there's a delay?"

"Are you sure you don't need help?"

"Don't delay to chat with the children." She grimaced as Cutie Pie tried another escape.

Bending to her task, she lifted one of the kitten's feet and tried to get the mincemeat out from between Cutie Pie's toes. It took longer than she expected, because she was still working on the first foot when the door opened and Andrew came in.

"I needed to persuade the children that their assistance was *not* necessary." He sat beside her on the floor again. "Do you need help?"

"Can you get a towel?"

"From where?"

She smiled without humor as she struggled to hold the kitten and clean its feet without getting more mincemeat all over her dress. "There is a towel under the pies on the table."

Andrew drew the towel carefully out from under a pie whose crust had been broken with two sets of pawprints. Rosemary glanced back at the kitten, trying not to think how many hours she had worked to have those pies ready for her neighbors. After all her work, the pies now were fit only for the pig sty.

"It would be easier if her paws weren't so close in color to the mincemeat," she said.

"Mayhap you should just scrub until you find some other color."

She looked up at him in shock. His face was serious. A grin uncurled along her lips, then she was laughing.

"That would work," she said, "except she's pretty much the color of mincemeat everywhere."

"You are very gentle with her."

"She's just a baby."

He watched her in silence until she was working on Cutie Pie's last foot, then asked, "Are you always so forgiving of misdeeds?"

"How can I blame a kitten for doing what a kitten does? She is young, and has much to learn."

"Do you forgive humans as easily?"

She hesitated as she finished Cutie Pie's last foot. Taking the towel, she began to dry the kitten. "If you are concerned about your nephews, you need not be."

"That I assumed."

"Then—"

"You never have asked me about the stories I'm sure your cousin wasted no time telling you about me."

"No."

He put his finger under her chin and tilted it toward him. Ignoring the kitten, which wiggled free from the towel and scurried across the kitchen to lick its fur by the hearth, he said, "Much of it is true."

"Oh."

"It is true that I enjoy playing with the flats, wagering that the next turn of the card will make me the victor. And I have enjoyed the company of many lovely women, who have enjoyed my company, as well."

"You don't have to tell me this."

"I think, for once, you are very, very wrong." He gave a short laugh as she stood and wiped her hands on her apron. "Or mayhap it is simply that I want you to know that the rumors of one of the most reproachful antics linked to my name is wrong. I am sure you have heard that I brought a man back dead from a duel."

"Yes, I have." She picked up a bucket and scraped more of the pie into it, but he took it and set it on the floor. When he took her sticky fingers in his, she could not keep her eyes from rising to meet his. Again his face was as grave as it had been outside on the walkway.

His fingers caressed hers with a strange sensation of the

mincemeat, trying to keep them motionless. "Would you believe me if I were to share the truth?"

"You have never lied to me." She bit her lip. "Have you?"

"I have found it most satisfying to be honest with you. Most satisfying." He continued to stroke her fingers. "Rosemary, I did go to that duel. I did bring a man dead back to his house, but I was neither the wronged nor the challenged party in that duel. I went there in hopes of persuading Carl Larkin to withdraw his challenge. He refused, and he died before I could get him back to his home on Soho Square."

"I'm so sorry that you lost your friend."

His hand curved along her cheek. She gazed into his dark eyes. Every alarm rang through her head, but she paid them no mind. She wanted to lose herself in those eyes, even though she knew the peril of letting them beguile her.

He pressed his lips to her palm. Her gasp echoed through the suddenly silent kitchen as rapture raced up her arm to explode through her. Raising his head, he lifted her hand so that it remained only a breath away from his mouth.

"I know you are," he murmured, his breath cool against her palm.

A crash from the other side of the kitchen sent pieces of porcelain rolling across the floor to stop at her feet. A flash of black and orange headed for the door, which opened as Jenna peeked in.

"What was that?" the little girl asked. She did not wait for an answer as she rushed after Cutie Pie.

Rosemary looked down at the shards of the cups she had set out for tea. With a sigh, she reached for the broom. She paused when Andrew put his hand on her arm.

"I need to clean up this mess," she said quietly.

Another crash came from beyond the door.

Andrew grimaced. "Mayhap it would be for the best if I took the children home now."

"Mayhap it would be."

"Will you give us a look-in at Snoclyffe Park?"

"I'll try. I need to bake more pies. Also I have to—"

"I understand." Something flashed through his eyes. She was not sure what it was, but he said nothing else as he went out of the kitchen.

She followed, wanting a chance to ask why he was reacting as he had. She had no opportunity, as he gathered the children and Mr. Connors and bid her and Charlotte good afternoon.

When the door closed, Charlotte prattled about the call. She did agree to rest while Rosemary finished cleaning the kitchen.

Rosemary did not leave the foyer. The house was silent now that the children's happy voices were gone, but it was not the lack of their voices that disturbed her. It was not hearing Andrew's voice. When he had spoken to her on the walkway, somehow, his voice had found its way into the very center of her heart.

A mew came from by her feet. She bent and picked up the still damp kitten. Holding Cutie Pie close, she sighed. The kitten stretched up its nose to touch hers. She buried her face in its fur, wondering if she had ever been so alone.

# Eight

Rosemary was not surprised when a case of teacups was delivered to the house, along with a dozen mincemeat pies. What amazed her was that Mr. Connors brought them.

Without Andrew.

As she sat in the parlor and listened politely as Charlotte and Mr. Connors chatted over endless cups of tea, she glanced again and again toward the front window. Several people passed by, but not Andrew.

Mr. Connors took his leave with a promise to call again, and Rosemary did not linger to listen to her cousin delight again over every facet of the conversation. Tossing her cloak over her shoulders, she hurried through the village to the hills.

She knew she was addled to look for Andrew and the children while she gathered greens to decorate the house. No matter what she told herself, she could not keep her ears from straining to catch the sound of childish glee and the deep, rich tones of his voice. By the time her basket was filled with cuttings of greens, she was annoyed at herself. This task, which she looked forward to from the beginning of the holiday season, had been ruined by her own silliness. She had no notion of why Andrew had left in a huff, and she was wasting time and this wondrous season by fretting about it.

She hurried back to the house, determined to enjoy the rest of the day, no matter how hard she had to work at it.

* * *

Andrew's scowl must have been ferocious as he strode through Baedd-upon-Wye, because no one stopped him while he hurried along the streets that were becoming dim tunnels as twilight swept out from beneath the storm clouds. Bending his head into the rising wind, he stopped before the bright red door.

His knock went unanswered. With a curse, he turned from the door. He paused when he heard a childish laugh. Hoping no one saw him, for he must look like a sneaksman getting ready to rob the house, he peered through the window. His frown became a smile when he saw Jenna dancing about with a long string of greens wrapped around her shoulders.

This time, his knock was answered almost immediately by Jenna. "Uncle Andrew!" she gasped, her eyes wide.

He brushed snow off the shoulders of his cloak and stepped into the house. Motioning for her to lead the way to the others, he walked behind her into the kitchen. Donald was chasing the kitten about, trying to get back a piece of greens. At the table, Simon worked, lacing greens around an iron hoop, with Rosemary's help.

Andrew would have enjoyed a moment to admire Rosemary's slender profile. As always, her hair was escaping from her demure bun, accenting the lightly brushed color of her cheeks.

Before he could do more than notice that, Donald cried, "Uncle Andrew, what are you doing here?"

"I might ask the same of you," he replied as Rosemary straightened and faced him. "You have worried Miss Tranter almost to apoplexy with your disappearance."

Rosemary frowned at the children, who looked chagrined only then. "You told me that you had left word at Snoclyffe Park where you were bound."

"Simon was supposed to write a note," Jenna said.

"I did!" He raised his round chin in defiance. "And you were supposed to put it on Miss Tranter's bed."

"I was not," she fired back.

Donald stood and jabbed at his chest. "No, I was supposed to do that. I put it on her pillow, but the breeze from that window she leaves open kept blowing it off, so I put it—"

With a groan, Andrew said, "No need to explain that you put it beneath her pillow. Mayhap when she goes up to take a rest to ease her aching head, she will hear its crackle. No matter. I knew I would find you here." He tweaked Jenna's nose. "If you spend much more time with Miss Burton, I vow I shall have your clothing and beds moved over here."

"And our toys?" piped up Simon.

"He is teasing you, children," Rosemary said with a forced laugh. Andrew might be hoaxing the children, but his stance announced how uncomfortable he was to be here. Noting how his gaze went to the shelf where the new teacups sat, she looked back at Simon. "Be careful there. You will jab yourself with that pin." She put her hands over his and helped him loop the sprigs of holly more tightly around the metal bar.

Jenna glanced up from where she was sitting on the edge of the hearth with Cutie Pie on her lap. "Can we really stay here, Uncle Andrew?"

"I'm afraid not. We must return to Snoclyffe Park without delay." Over the protests, he continued, "A storm is brewing, and I don't want you children out in it."

"You didn't bring the carriage?" Rosemary asked.

"I didn't want to wait for it to be brought about," he said.

Seeing his shock at his own words, she bent to help Simon again. She froze when Andrew's enticing fingers curved around her elbow again. She let him draw her toward the kitchen door. When he closed it behind her, he did not move away, leaving her with her back against it and only a hand's breadth from him.

She waited for him to speak, but he simply gazed at her. A warmth that had vanished along with him swept over her with the enthusiasm of the children. There was nothing childish about this wanting to be even closer to him, to be swallowed by his arms, to risk everything to sample even a single bit of the powerful emotions glowing in his eyes.

"I believe I owe you an apology," he said.

She wished he had not said anything, for then she could have continued to lose herself in his eyes. She sought for words to answer, but each one had vanished.

"You have every right to be vexed with me," he continued, and she realized he had taken her silence as anger. "My manners were ragged when I stamped out of your house."

"I don't understand why you left like that." Finally she could speak the words that had plagued her. "If I said anything—"

"You said nothing but the truth. I heard nothing but the truth."

"I don't understand."

He framed her face with his hands. "Rosemary, I know what I was. I have tried to put that behind me to be a good guardian to these children, but my past haunts me. When you hesitated, I thought you were seeking an excuse to put an end to our visits."

"No, I was being honest. I had to replace all those pies that the kitten ruined."

"I know, and so was I being honest, because I could perceive your dismay at the recital of my past exploits. I simply assumed that . . ." He smiled suddenly as he drew his hands away. "Where is Miss Griffydd this afternoon?"

The question about her cousin startled her, for she had thought—*hoped*—he would speak of other things when they stood so close. "Charlotte often must rest in the afternoon to aid in her recovery."

"The children—"

"Have been very good about being quiet."

"I did not intend for you to have to keep them occupied every time they took a notion to pay you a call."

" 'Tis been no trouble." She faltered, then said, "I do have one request for you. I was speaking of St. Thomas's Day coming soon, and Jenna is excited about the tradition of women going door-to-door to ask for goodenings for their families and kitchens. She would like to be part of it."

He smiled. "Jenna is a child."

"She is old enough to share in the fun."

"Begging?" His nose wrinkled. " 'Tis not my idea of what a viscount's niece should be a part of."

"Surely you have had women coming to your house asking for goodenings on St. Thomas's Day."

"Of course, but 'tis the place of the poor to ask, not of the gentry."

She laughed. "Andrew, how can you be so worldly and so naive at the same time? The true poor are given food and alms by the parish at this time of year. Any who come to your door are enjoying a tradition that is older than anyone can recall, and this offers a chance for the women to take a break from the tasks of preparing their household and kitchens for the holidays. Can you imagine anything better than a walk on a crisp December afternoon?"

"To own the truth, I can." His finger coursed along her cheek, reviving the hunger in her that his gaze had invoked. "I can think of a much more delightful way to spend a crisp, wintry afternoon." As he slanted toward her, his voice became a husky whisper that resonated within her like the last note of a song. "And it would not be cold if you were within my arms, Rosemary."

Exerting her flagging willpower, she drew away. "You have not answered my question."

"Nor you mine."

"I didn't hear you ask a question."

"I didn't speak it with words." He gave her that smile that threatened to dissolve her into sweet desire. "But you know what it is."

"I know you have not told me if Jenna may go with me about the village, and to the farms on your side of the river for St. Thomas's Day."

His finger traced her cheek before slipping behind her ear to caress its curve. As she closed her eyes, unable to escape the indescribable pleasure, he murmured, "I suspect my permission or lack of it matters little. My niece will run off to join you."

"Oh, no!" She looked up at him. "The children will not be so unthinking again. I know how fearful you and Miss Tranter must have been when you discovered them missing. If you wish, I will speak to them of that."

"I will speak with the boys, and, if you would speak to Jenna of this while she is begging about the countryside with you, I would greatly appreciate it. She is at an age where she questions everything I say. I believe she would listen to you, a woman she admires."

"Thank you for giving her permission to go. Being with the other women and girls may help her find her way. I fear I spoil them."

He smiled. "Odd that you should be the one doing that, when upon our first meeting you accused me of being far too lenient in their upbringing."

"You are their guardian. It is your place to set certain limits. I am—"

"You are what?" He put his crooked finger under her chin and tilted it up so she could not avoid his ebony gaze. "You are their friend, Rosemary?"

"I would like to think so."

"Are you mine, too?"

"Your friend?"

He smiled. "I did not intend to put you to the blush with that question."

"I think you did intend exactly that."

"All right, I probably did." He chuckled. "However, I did mean the question to be taken with all the gravity it deserves."

"And how much is that?"

His smile faded as the radiance in his eyes became a flame. "I really wish to know. Are we friends? Can we hope to be friends, or can we hope to be more?"

"More?" She pushed past him and began to pick up the scattered leaves on the foyer floor. "I think friendship is enough of a goal for two strong-willed people like us."

His hands caught her shoulders, and he whirled her back toward him. With a smile, he tugged her to him. "I disagree."

Before she could retort, his lips covered hers. His hands slid from her shoulders and down her back, drawing her even closer. She could not keep her fingers from inching along his sleeves to curve around his nape. As she touched the hair falling over his collar, his mouth became more insistent, demanding a share of the pleasure he was offering her.

Mayhap she was being taken in by his easy seduction, but at that moment she did not care. Even when the children spilled out of the kitchen, asking for her help with the kissing-bough they had been making, she smiled at the memory of his lips on hers.

If this was madness, she wanted a full serving.

# Nine

Jenna grasped Rosemary's hand as they walked up the driveway. "This is such fun, Miss Burton."

"It is, isn't it?" Looking down at the girl, she was thrilled to see Jenna's unabashed smile. She knew how little joy this child had had in the past year, despite Andrew's attempts to ease their grief. Who would have guessed that a simple tradition would bring Jenna such happiness?

As they had walked ahead of the others from Baedd-upon-Wye, Jenna had confided that her parents had seldom been in the children's lives, for they suffered from a *wanderlust* that had led them across two oceans and into almost every cranny of the civilized world. Jenna's mother had been home for only one Christmastide with the children, and that had been several years ago. The customs that Rosemary was sharing with them were delightfully new, and the children grasped them as eagerly as Cutie Pie did a proffered string.

Their parents' prolonged absences might have smoothed the harshest edges of their grief, but that emptiness was still there. The loss of their home and all that had been was something she understood.

Rosemary did not allow those thoughts to show on her face as Jenna smiled up at her. The little girl pulled away and ran up the drive, past the somnolent flower beds, to the front door of Snoclyffe Park. Behind her, the women of the village were gaping with candid curiosity at the house that was hidden from the road behind a wall and tall trees.

The air was crisp despite the bright sunshine. She was glad that Charlotte had decided to remain in the village. Although the freshness of the day would have lightened her spirits, her cousin must not risk getting chilled and becoming ill again.

"You should not knock on your own door," Rosemary said as she reached where Jenna was bouncing from one foot to the other. "Let someone else do that."

One of the women stepped forward, with a tentative smile, and lifted the iron knocker that was in the shape of a heavily knuckled fist. The days when the lords of this manor needed to guard the rest of England from the chieftains of Wales were long past.

A rumble of amazement rushed through the score of women as the door opened to reveal Andrew. He smiled and winked at Jenna, who giggled.

"I trust you are out and about on this fine day to celebrate St. Thomas's Day, ladies." Reaching behind him, he lifted a basket. He pulled out a packet of finely ground flour and another containing a small cake and handed it to the closest woman.

*"Diolch, arglwydd tir,"* she said, curtsying and handing him a cutting of holly.

"You are welcome. *Nadolig llawen.*"

The woman smiled more broadly at his wish of Christmas joy. He offered two packets to each woman. When Jenna stepped forward, he held out her packets. She took them and curtsied as the others had.

"Thank you, m'lord," she said with a grin.

"And do you seek a goodening, as well?" he asked, turning to Rosemary.

She heard whispers behind her, but she was lost in the sweet fire in his eyes. Her fingers craved the chance to touch the resolute lines of his face. He was a man who did not change his mind easily, and was most certain of his own opinions. Yet, he loved these three frequently naughty children as if he were their father. He was determined that they would be raised with a sense of learning, duty, and love. He was quick to reprimand them, and just as quick to show them that they were in a home where they were loved.

"We all come seeking goodenings, my lord," she said, glad that her voice held nothing but amusement.

He handed her two packets, and she held out some holly. His fingers engulfed hers as he reached to take it. In a near whisper, he said, "Some of the others brought me mistletoe, Rosemary. You bring me holly."

"Yes."

"Does that mean you think only of the greening of the kissing-bough, and not the mistletoe within it that lures two beneath it to share a kiss?"

Aware of the ears straining to eavesdrop on every word she and Andrew spoke, she said, "Some thoughts a lady wishes to keep to herself."

"Not for long, I hope." His fingers caressed her gloved ones as he lifted the holly from them.

"I hope so, too."

Jenna tugged impatiently on her other hand. "Rosemary, we have to go."

"Why in such a hurry?" asked Andrew.

"If Simon and Donald find out how much fun I'm having, they're going to want to come along, too. We need to leave before they realize we're here."

"An excellent reason." Raising his gaze to Rosemary's, he said, "I shall send the carriage for her before tea."

"Send the carriage?" She clamped her lips closed, but it was too late. Every ear had caught her dismayed reaction.

Andrew nodded, his face still wearing a cheerful smile. This close, she could see what the others could not. Disappointment as vivid as hers smoldered in them. "I have promised the boys an outing of their own this afternoon. I doubt we will have returned in time."

"All right," she said, although it was not. She had anticipated sitting over tea with Andrew and Jenna and Charlotte and laughing about the collection of goodenings on both sides of the River Wye. With a smile that she feared looked strained, she said, "Then you shall miss out on all our tales."

"You and Jenna will have to share them with me and the boys someday soon." Again his voice lowered to a husky warmth. "Or mayhap you can share them with only me, when you are in my arms once more very soon."

Taking Jenna by the hand, she turned to follow the others back toward the gates of Snoclyffe Park. Her smile, as she thought of Andrew calling, could not be hidden.

Rosemary shook snow off her shoes as she came back into the house. Waving to Jenna, who was leaning out the carriage window to wave widely at her, she closed the door. It had been a wonderful day, with the promise of more wonderful things to come. She had not been so happy in longer than she could recall.

Her hands were grasped by her cousin. "Oh, Rosemary, you will never guess what has happened."

"It must be wondrous, because you are aglow like a kissing-bough with all its candles lit."

"It is truly wondrous." Charlotte led her to the settee in the parlor and urged her to sit.

"Tell me please, or I fear I shall burst with curiosity before you burst with your tidings."

"While you were out with the children, Mr. Connors called."

Rosemary's eyes widened. "And you received him when you were here alone? Charlotte, you should not make a habit of sitting alone with him and enjoying a conversation. It will create a scandal that will tarnish your reputation."

Charlotte giggled, sounding as young as Donald. "You may rest assured that the next time I enjoy Mr. Connors's company, I will not be alone."

"Good. Now these tidings—"

*"Those* are the tidings, Rosemary." She jumped to her feet, clearly unable to sit still. "Mr. Connors has asked me to join him at the Christmas Eve ball at Snoclyffe Park. To join him as his guest." She whirled around and nearly collapsed.

Rosemary stood and caught her by the arm before she could fall. "Charlotte, do not over-exert yourself with celebrating. You should not—"

"Do not tell me that I should not go! Simply because Lord Snoclyffe has not—I mean—"

Rosemary did not attempt a feigned smile for her cousin. From their childhood, they had been honest with one another. That could not change at this late date. "Charlotte, if you would let me finish, you would hear that I do not want you to strain yourself *now.* You must be able to dance every set at the ball with Mr. Connors, if you wish."

"Oh, Rosemary!" Tears stole the happiness from her eyes. "You are thinking only of me, and I said those dreadful things to you. Can you forgive me?"

"You have always forgiven me. I can do no less."

She hesitated, then asked, "Has Lord Snoclyffe said anything to you about the ball?"

"No."

"Then Mr. Connors was right. Oh, dear—"

"Oh dear what?"

Charlotte sat again and folded Rosemary's hands between hers. "Mr. Connors is very fond of Lord Snoclyffe, Rosemary. He assured me of that fact over and over again, but he warned me as well that Lord Snoclyffe is so intrigued with the pursuit of ladies that he is determined not to give it up even when one catches his fancy. As soon as he inveigles his way into a woman's heart or"—she flushed—"or into her bed, he grows bored and seeks the chase of another. Dear Rosemary, has he held your hands like this?"

"Yes."

"And kissed them?"

"Yes."

"And kissed you?"

Rosemary gathered up Cutie Pie when the kitten jumped into her lap. Holding her close to her heart, she whispered, "Yes."

"Has he—?"

"Nothing more."

Charlotte breathed a deep sigh of relief. "Thank goodness for that. When did he kiss you?"

Standing, she continued to hold the kitten. "Charlotte, do you have a reason for prying like this?"

"I want to protect you. Lord Snoclyffe has found a way to intrude on you too often."

"A way?"

"His wards."

She laughed. "Charlotte, the last time he called here was when he was frantic with fear because they were missing from Snoclyffe Park."

"That's what he told you."

"Yes, and the children explained how they had mistakenly hidden the note to their governess where she could not find it."

"A governess would know her charges' tricks." She sighed and set herself on her feet. Putting her hands on Rosemary's shoulders, she said, "I believe, and so does his friend, that he has seen the children as a way to touch your heart."

"If so, he has succeeded."

"You don't love him, do you?"

"I—I'm not sure." That was also the truth. Did she love Andrew, or simply the idea of being with him and the children so that she did not have to be alone?

Andrew paced from the ballroom on the upper floor of Snoclyffe Park to the top of the staircase at the entry foyer. It had been only three days since St. Thomas's Day. In that time, the house had been transformed with greenery. The

Yule log was aflame in the ballroom that had been the original Great Hall of the castle that was the heart of what was now the house. Even from the stairs, he could hear, beneath the music from the orchestra, the crackle of the large fire that lit even the farthest corners of the room.

He walked into the ballroom for what he was sure was the hundredth time. Easily he saw, beyond the other dancers following a pattern around the open hearth in the middle of the floor, the children twirling about in time to the music. The delight on their faces matched the joy on the faces of Terence and his partner Miss Griffydd. They had been dancing each time he had entered the ballroom this evening.

The room was decorated with all the glory of the season. Greenery connected the rafters high above the floor, and a kissing-bough was draped with more greens that followed the arch of the main entrance to the ballroom dared lovers to steal a kiss beneath it.

Snagging a glass from a passing maid, he downed the wine without tasting it. His guests were having a wonderful time. He was miserable.

Andrew heard footsteps behind him. Running footsteps. He was shocked when Rosemary rushed forward and grasped his hands. "Why are you so late?"

"Late?" She shook her head. "Andrew, is she here?"

"She? Miss Griffydd?"

"No, Cutie Pie!"

Frowning, he asked, "Why would the kitten be here?"

"Andrew, I must find her. She—"

When Rosemary's voice rose on each word, he drew her from the ballroom and along the hallway to a smaller chamber. Sitting her on the settee by the window that was edged with holly, he went back to the door and closed it. The sounds of the celebration vanished.

His heart pulsed with pain when he saw the despair on her face. Kneeling beside her, he folded her hands in his. "What has happened to the kitten?"

"I don't know."

"You don't know?"

"She's vanished, Andrew." She gnawed on her lower lip which was quivering. "At first, I thought Charlotte might have let her out of the house when Mr. Connors came to get her for the ball here. I searched the garden and the street. She was nowhere."

"If she wandered away . . ."

"I would have seen her pawprints in the snow."

"Is that why you're so late? Because you were searching for her?"

"Late?"

"For the ball." He frowned and drew back her cloak. "You never intended to come here for the ball, did you?"

Rosemary looked down at her work dress that was stained from the last of her baking. "I don't know how things are done in London, but here one waits for an invitation before attending a *soirée.*"

"I sent you an invitation."

"I never received it."

His eyes grew wide. "I thought you had because you smiled so warmly when I spoke of you being in my arms again on St. Thomas's Day." His hand splayed across her cheek kept her from looking away. "Or could it be that what I saw was anticipation of something other than dancing that I saw in your lovely eyes?"

"You intended for me to attend tonight?"

"How could you think otherwise? Haven't I shown you how I enjoy being with you, Rosemary?"

"Charlotte said—I shouldn't repeat my cousin's words when she is not here to explain her misconceptions."

" 'Twas not a misconception." He glanced at the door. "I suspect as well that she has her information on the best of sources."

"I shouldn't say."

"Then I shall. Terence speaks interminably of Miss Griffydd. I'm sure he speaks as incessantly to her of the dangers you might be in to entangle your life with mine."

"But why would he do that? He's your friend!"

"Even friendship pales beside love. Mayhap he thought he could more easily win a place in Miss Griffydd's heart if he tried to protect the cousin of the woman he's falling in love with." He sighed as he rose to sit beside her. Putting his arm around her, he drew her head down to his shoulder. "He is so eager to impress your cousin that he was sure to regale her with the list of all my shortcomings. He is determined to keep you from making the mistake of believing anything I said or did was sincere."

"Was it?"

He brushed her lips with a swift kiss. When her breath caught, he cupped her chin so she could see the delight in his eyes. "How can you ask that, sweet Rosemary, when I have suffered through the longest three days of my life while I waited for you to return to Snoclyffe Park tonight?"

"And then I did not come here."

"I vow I have worn a path from the Great Hall to the front staircase in hopes of seeing you enter the house."

"In search of Cutie Pie."

"Why do you think she might be here?"

She drew a mitten from the pocket of her apron. "Do you recognize Jenna's mitten?"

"I think it is time to get some answers." He stood. "Wait here." He walked out, closing the door behind him.

Rosemary had time only to untie her cloak and fold it over the back of the settee before the door opened again. The three children came in, followed by a blushing Charlotte and an obviously chagrined Mr. Connors. Andrew brought up the end of the parade and motioned for everyone to sit.

The children rushed to sit next to Rosemary. They elbowed each other in their attempt to sit beside her. She solved the problem by lifting Donald onto her lap. Mr. Connors waited for Charlotte to sit, then chose a chair close by.

Andrew folded his arms in front of him. "It seems there have been some plots going on in this house and in Miss Griffydd's house in the village that neither Rosemary nor

I was aware of. As these plots seem to be aimed directly at us, I think it would be in the best interests of the holiday season for you to share the truth with us." His gaze focused on his friend. "Terence, I do believe I asked you to deliver an invitation to this evening's ball to Rosemary at the same time you took one to Miss Griffydd."

Mr. Connors gulped. "You did." He glanced at Charlotte who grew even redder. "We decided it might be in Miss Burton's best interests not to attend."

"Terence—"

He set himself on his feet. "No, you listen, Andrew. I admire Miss Burton and her unselfish dedication to Miss Griffydd too much to allow you to add her to your list of *à suivie* flirtations. She deserves more than court promises that have gained you the favor of other women."

"I agree." When Andrew chuckled, his friend and Charlotte regarded him with openmouthed astonishment. "You judge me, my friend, by the man who was in London, the man who savored his bachelor's fare, the man who had not learned the joy brought by vexing children." He winked at the children, setting them giggling. Then his gaze rose to hold Rosemary's. "Nor the delight of discovering that love is not something to run from, but something to run *to,* in hopes that it will be returned." Crossing the room, he picked up her hand and pressed his lips to it. "Dare I believe that you might dare to love me, too, Rosemary?"

"Yes, I love you, too." The words she had kept hidden even from herself sang from her heart like the sweetest Christmas carol.

As the children cheered and Charlotte reached for a kerchief to blot her tears of happiness, he lifted Donald off her lap and brought her to her feet. He kept his arm around her while he looked back at the children.

"There is one other scheme that needs to be explained." He picked up Jenna's mitten from the table. "You left this *carte de visites* at Miss Griffydd's house. On purpose?"

They looked at one another, then Jenna stood. "Yes, Uncle Andrew."

"And you took Cutie Pie?"

"We kit-napped her, Uncle Andrew," Donald announced with pride.

Andrew chuckled and squeezed Rosemary's shoulders. "Yes, you did. Why?"

"So Miss Burton would come here tonight," Jenna said.

Simon chimed in, "She told us when we called yesterday that she was not coming. She looked so sad that we did not want her to be alone tonight. We knew if Cutie Pie was missing and Jenna's mitten was found, she would come here."

"Ingenious."

"They certainly inherited the love of artifice from you, my friend," Terence said with a laugh.

"Where is the kitten now?" Andrew asked.

"In the nursery," Jenna replied.

"Go and retrieve Cutie Pie so that we are all assured the kitten is fine." As they rushed out, Andrew said, "Let us return to the ballroom. I think I would like to dance, if you would stand up with me, Rosemary."

"Me? In this?" She lifted the sides of her stained apron.

He untied it and lifted it off over her head. "Ta-da! You look lovely."

"This is a work dress, not a ball gown," she protested, but walked with him toward the Great Hall where beautiful music matched the lilt of her heart.

"No one will look lovelier than you, sweetheart." He smiled as he bent toward her. "And who knows? A new standard of fashion may be set by the newest Lady Snoclyffe."

"Newest . . ." She stared at him.

"Will you marry me, Rosemary?" he asked as they paused in the door of the ballroom.

Before she could answer, a shout came from the stairs leading to the upper floors. A familiar blur of black and orange and cream rushed past them and into the ballroom, with three children in pursuit. Jenna shouted to her brothers, who shouted back at her as they tried to catch the kitten that vanished among the dancers.

Andrew grasped Rosemary's shoulders and turned her back to face him. "It will not be a quiet existence such as you've known with your cousin."

"I have had enough quiet to last me a lifetime."

"Nor will it be filled with grand excitement of Seasons in London."

"No. The children will be happier here in the country."

"And I have had enough of that insanity to last *me* a lifetime. I would rather enjoy the madness of sweet passion that sweeps over me when I sweep you into my arms." He took both of her hands between his, kissing first one, then the other. "You know I love you, and you know the children love you. Say you will marry me, Rosemary."

All sound—the music, the children's excited shouts, the voices of the guests—vanished as she gazed up into his eyes. At long last, she could decipher one of the emotions burning there. It was love.

"Yes," she whispered, "I will marry you."

He tugged her into his arms, his lips on hers. As she melted to him, savoring the thrilling promise in his kiss, she suspected he would be as eager as she was to have the wedding as soon as the banns could be read.

A small hand tugged on her dress, and Rosemary drew back to see Donald's dismay.

"Miss Burton—"

"Rosemary," she corrected with a smile at Andrew.

Donald frowned. "Get the kitten down."

"Down? From where?"

He pointed up.

"The kissing-bough?" Andrew asked.

As if on cue, Cutie Pie peeked out of the greenery.

Rosemary laughed, for she was sure the kitten was wearing a superior smile. "Mayhap we should rename it the *kitten* bough."

Andrew's grin was as rakish as in all the tales repeated about him. He pulled her back to him and curved his hand around her nape. "I know you are very fond of that kitten, sweetheart, but I think I much prefer *kissing*-bough."

She had no argument for that, and welcomed his eager lips, as she agreed with a kiss that was the perfect gift for this season of love.

# *The Christmas Kitten*

Judith A. Lansdowne

# One

Lady Ellena peered down into the gathering dusk at the spot beneath the leafless elm and blinked her sky-blue eyes in wonder. He was there again! Oh, that he should be so bold as to appear before her a second day in a row, and just at dusk, when he was least likely to be noticed by anyone else. The villain! The beast! To stare up at her so impertinently, his head cocked just so, his stance and manner so very haughty, so contemptuous of the authority that forbade him entrance into her domain. And yet, there was this—particular thing—about him that engaged her attention. She could not lift her elegant little chin and turn from the window in contempt, leaving him to wonder where she had gone, though she ought. She truly ought. It was most wicked of her to encourage his impudence by remaining at the window, by staring down into the ever-increasing darkness in order to savor every tilt of his handsome head, every movement of his muscular and most seductive body. Gracious, that she should even allow herself to think of such things! She ought to blush with shame to the very tips of her ears. Her Cammy would certainly accuse her of most unladylike behavior for encouraging the impertinent rogue, but she could not help herself. No, she could not keep from staring at him any more today than she had been able to stop herself staring at him yesterday. The simple fact was that he was down there, displaying himself in the most reprehensible manner before her very eyes and, protest though she must, Lady Ellena was loving every bit of it.

*What is it he does now?* she wondered as she watched him. *He must think himself a veritable King the way he swaggers and stalks about. Truly, he is most outrageous. Oh, my dear,* she thought then, *he is climbing the elm! He is climbing right straight up the elm with not a thought in the world for who besides myself might see him!*

The fact that the highest and narrowest of the elm's branches was even then rubbing and screeking against her window as the north wind blew did give Lady Ellena pause. But despite the rogue's obvious athleticism, she could not bring herself to imagine that he might actually attempt to gain purchase upon that particular branch. And even if he did, most certainly, he would not be so brazen as to make his way to the sill of her very own window! Even the most fearless of ruffians would blanche at the thought of such a thing as that. That particular branch was far too narrow, far too likely to break beneath one's weight, though her rustic swain—for thus she had come to suspect he was—did not appear to weigh overly much. Not at all. He was slim, in fact, dark as the midnight sky, and seductively muscular.

She was watching him. He knew it to be true, and the thought of her interested gaze fastened upon him did much to bolster his determination. If yesterday he had not looked up as he had passed by the house on his way to the stables, Rowdy would never have noticed the lovely Lady Ellena poised in perfect complacency behind her diamond of window glass. Lady Ellena—the lady of his dreams. Often he had heard how intriguing, how beautiful, and how very privileged she was, though he had never before seen her and had even tended to doubt so much as her existence. But he *had* glanced upward last evening, and the very sight of Lady Ellena had stopped him in his tracks and set his poor mind to reeling. His splendid green eyes had fastened upon her, then, as they did now, and though he knew that the consequences would be dire should Rollings or one of his stable boys discover him as he paraded himself before that most remarkable creature above, Rowdy could not help himself. No, he could not. He could not have helped himself yesterday, and he could not help himself today.

He scrambled to the lowest branch of the elm, and then leaped for and caught the one above it. The winter wind was chill as it whipped out of the north with no sun to warm it. It set Rowdy to shivering, but he declined to take notice of such a paltry thing as that. *She* remained in the window. *She* condescended to watch his every move. And so, he allowed himself to take note of nothing else but *her.*

*I have lost m'mind,* he thought, scrambling up to the next branch and wobbling unsteadily for a moment a good ten feet above the ground. *Lost m'mind, an' more, even. Ain't got a bit of sensicals left, that's for certain.* But he gazed upward once again, steadied himself against the tree trunk, and began to climb even higher. *I will climb all the way to the branch that scratches against her window pane,* he thought confidently. *That I will. An' then I shall see what color those lovey orbs of hers be. I will just not look down from this moment on. That'll be the answer. If I don't be looking down, I willn't get at all nervous an' I will be up there upon that branch in three shakes of a lamb's tail.*

Daniel, Lord Cottsworth, raised the collar of his greatcoat higher against the steadily increasing wind and lengthened his stride. He ought to have dismounted at the Dunsburys' front door, but he had never trusted Dunsbury's grooms overly much and preferred to see with his own eyes that Sabre was taken into the stable, unsaddled, and provided with a warm blanket and a measure of oats and water. "Leave him saddled and shivering in the paddock, else," he muttered through chilled lips. "Laziest men I have ever seen, Dunsbury's stablehands. Fire the lot of them if I were him."

*But then, Dunsbury is not a gentleman much concerned with things of the stable,* Cottsworth reminded himself. *No. A regular virtuoso he is when it comes to investments, but talk to him about the finer points of this particular hack or that and the gentleman stares at you with those wide blue eyes glazing over as if you are speaking Summarian. Still, that is neither here nor there,* Cottsworth thought. *In little less than a fortnight, Dunsbury's eccentricities will make not the least difference. In a mere ten days, Camelia and I will be married and living at Cottsworth Manor, and no one will expect me to visit here more often than once or twice a year at the most.*

That thought appealed to Cottsworth exceedingly. He had, after all, played the role of the perfect suitor for an entire spring, summer and autumn. It was time to bring the thing to an end. Though why Camelia had chosen to be married during the Christmas Season he could not conceive. Well, yes, yes, he could, because if one were forced to have a house party for one's family over the Christmas Season regardless, why not combine that party with a wedding party? Two for the price of one. Practical really. Logical. The wind tugged at Cottsworth's high beaver hat, and he reached up to grab it in the very nick of time. And then he came to a halt. "What the deuce is that?" he murmured to himself. "Oddest thing I have ever heard. Sounds like giant hens scratching." One gloved hand holding to the brim of his beaver, he stared upward, for that, apparently, was the origin of the sound he heard—though why giant hens should be scratching about in the elm tree beneath which he was just then passing—

"By Jupiter!" exclaimed Cottsworth. And before he could say another word or decide what on earth to do, the peculiar bit of blackness that was frantically scramble-crashing down through the barren branches of the tree *kathunked* against the top of Cottsworth's hat, knocked the beaver free from Cottsworth's grasp and sent the tall hat whipping off on the wind across the park.

With a *mooph!* and a *mrrf!* the shadowy yet solid form bounced against Cottsworth's shoulder, went sliding and

clinging and sliding and clinging and sliding from one
cape to another down the entire length of the back of
Cottsworth's greatcoat, tumbled to the ground, leaped to
its feet, and bolted off in the direction of the stables like
a small black ball propelled by an enormous charge of
gunpowder.

"By Jupiter!" Cottsworth exclaimed again, staring after
it. "Never in all my days! By Jupiter!"


Miss Camelia Dunsbury was the only daughter of the
third son of the fifth Earl of Riggensby and the niece of
Colonel Anthony Dunsbury of the Royal Guard. A gentle-
woman of impeccable lineage, with a porcelain-like com-
plexion, sweetly pink cheeks, lips so alluring as to be
dangerous, and curls the color of honey, she had spent
the previous spring in making her debut into Society and
had been hailed as an Incomparable—which, indeed, she
was. Any number of gentlemen had attempted to win her
heart. A veritable army of beaux had lingered in her London parlor, trailed after her from entertainment to entertainment, implored her for but a moment of her attention.
But Miss Camelia Dunsbury had been promised from her
cradle to Daniel Orren Templeton, and despite the un-
questionably intoxicating popularity she had enjoyed at
her come-out, she had never once thought to protest that
particular arrangement made years ago between her papa
and the dearly departed Daniel David Templeton, Viscount Cottsworth's papa. She had not thought to protest
it to this very day.

"I cannot think what is keeping Daniel," Miss Dunsbury
said primly as she lifted a delicate teacup to her lips. "He
sent word that he would arrive today, did he not, Mama?
And his least word is always to be depended upon. Still, it
grows very late."

"I expect it is not an easy journey in winter, my dear,
from Cottsworth Manor to Dunsbury Dells," offered Miss

Dunsbury's Aunt Julia, the countess of Riggensby. "I have heard that there is snow in the north."

"Lord Cottsworth will be slowed by the conditions of the roads, then," nodded Camelia's mama, thoughtfully. "I have assigned him a place at table this evening, and a fire has been laid and lit in the chamber designated for his use. But perhaps I ought not to have done either. I do wish you had mentioned the snow earlier, Julia. I do hope that Daniel has not been forced to take shelter in one of those north country inns. They are quite the most annoying places, if you ask me. Still, if the snow is very bad, he will do just that. Daniel is not the sort to put himself in the way of danger, and snow is always most dangerous. Do not concern yourself over Daniel, however, my dear. He will arrive safe and sound. You may depend upon it. Though, perhaps, he will not arrive this evening as planned."

"Oh, I am not concerned for Daniel, Mama," Miss Dunsbury replied. "My fear is for the arrangements that you and Papa have made. The seating for dinner must be redone, you know, if Daniel does not appear, and one of the whist tables this evening will be short a person. And Papa's toast, which he has been practicing all day long, must be postponed. You know how anxious that will make Papa. He is not at all accustomed to toasting."

"You are such a good girl," sighed Lady Riggensby, helping herself to a piece of gingerbread. "So very considerate of your mama and papa. I do wish that Anne understood the effort one puts into such things as dinner and whist tables, and how dreadful it is to be disappointed in them."

"Oh, Mama," Lady Anne protested, rolling her fine brown eyes in exasperation. "I am certain that we all know how exceedingly considerate of *everyone* Camelia is." Lady Anne's gaze then fell with considerable vexation upon Miss Camelia Dunsbury. It was, after all, the curse of Lady Anne's life to be forever maligned by comparison to her cousin.

"Well, I cannot help but think of such things, Anne," responded Camelia politely. "It is only proper to be considerate of others, especially one's parents."

All three of the married ladies present in the winter parlor responded in a buzzing affirmative to this statement, quite taken, as they always were, with the most proper attitude of Miss Dunsbury, with whom not a one of them had ever found fault.

"Only think what a treasure she is," whispered Colonel Dunsbury's lady to Lady Riggensby.

"Indeed. Lord Cottsworth is the luckiest of all men," Lady Riggensby nodded. "To gain such a wife! I only wish that my Anne would cease all her nonsense and attempt to attain some of Camelia's sensible and laudable attitudes. That I do."

"Yes, and I wish the same for my Jane. She is so very inconsiderate at times. Her head is stuffed with nothing but fashions, entertainments, those frightful novels that she is forever withdrawing from the library, and gentlemen!"

Miss Jane Dunsbury could not help but overhear her mama's comments, and she was forced to smother a most exasperated sigh. "Truly," she whispered to Lady Anne, who occupied the space beside her upon the flowered settee, "if I have Cousin Camelia lifted up before me as an example of perfection one more time, I shall pull my hair out by the roots!"

"Oh, no, Jane," Lady Anne whispered. "You would do a great deal better to pull Camelia's hair out by the roots." Whereupon, the two cousins both giggled as quietly as they could behind their hands, so as not to draw censorious gazes from their mamas.

"I wonder how our charming Lord Cottsworth would feel about Camelia, then," murmured Jane. "Would he still wish to marry her if she were bald, do you think?"

"Oh, indeed," nodded Lady Anne. "Lord Cottsworth would marry Camelia were she bald, batty, and limped into the bargain. He is quite as much a paragon as she, and would never think to protest the understanding to which his papa and Uncle George came all those years ago. In fact, I do not think that he would oppose the arrangement even if Camelia had grown up to be a hunchbacked gnome. He cares only for his papa's honor and his own. With Lord Cottsworth this union is a matter of keeping faith. It is not as though he has developed a grand passion for Camelia."

Miss Jane Dunsbury gave a tiny shake of her head. "He is as much a cold fish as Camelia, then, is he?"

"Indeed, Jane. Have you never met Lord Cottsworth?"

"I have, but I cannot say that I *know* him. We have spoken perhaps ten words to each other since we were introduced in London this past spring. Still, he is most handsome, Anne. I tell you that I would certainly think to love such a gentleman were he to present himself to me as an eager beau."

"An eager beau? Oh, my dearest Jane, Lord Cottsworth can never be an eager beau. Eager denotes an anxiousness, an excitation—yes, I will say it—a *passion* of sorts. And Lord Cottsworth is never passionate—about anything."

"Never? Not about anything? I mean, it is understandable that he should not be passionate about Cousin Camelia, but certainly there is some—"

"Nothing. I vow, the gentleman's heart is carved from wood."

At that very moment Lord Cottsworth scowled at the Dunsburys' butler in the vestibule, and unwrapped the bright red wool muffler from around his neck. "The most impossible thing I have ever seen," mumbled Cottsworth, handing the muffler and his gloves to Perkins and allowing that worthy to assist him out of his greatcoat. "Wretched thing came bouncing down between those branches—did not cause any damage, did it, Perkins? No, no, not at the front, at the back. Slid all the way down my back, claws catching at m'coat every bit of the way."

Perkins held the greatcoat up before him and studied it with particular interest. "There are, perhaps, a few pulls in the material, my lord."

"Yes, indeed," nodded Cottsworth, gazing at his greatcoat over the butler's shoulder. "Well, Simmons will be here within the hour. Show it to him, will you, Perkins? I expect my valet may be depended upon to put things right. Where the deuce did it come from, do you think? Blasted cat! Pardon my language, Perkins. I did not mean to say blasted. But still, to fall out of a tree directly on top of a person! Of all things! And I shall never find my hat again, I expect. Purely useless exercise to send anyone out to search for it. Deucedly strong wind. Most likely blown half-way to London by now. A cat! I thought Miss Dunsbury to have only one cat, Perkins—Lady Ellena, it is called."

"Indeed, my lord. Keeps to Miss Dunsbury's chambers. Never roams about the household, and has never been outside in all its days. The gentlemen are in the billiards room, my lord, and the ladies in the winter parlor."

"I expect it must be the billiards room, Perkins. I cannot possibly appear before the ladies in all my dirt. Let me know at once when my coach arrives, will you not? And do go and whisper in Mrs. Dunsbury's ear that I am here at last. The dear lady will be concerned over her seating arrangements for tonight's dinner, no doubt."

Rowdy was so humiliated that he dared not show his face to anyone. He lay on his back in the stable loft in a pile of straw, stared up at the planking of the pointed roof, and thoroughly berated himself. What a perfect fool he had been to think that such a meager branch as that could hold his weight. And yet it *had* held—it had held long enough for him to see that the Lady Ellena's exquisite, almond-shaped eyes were as blue as summer skies—but then the stupid thing had snapped and sent him, scratching and scrambling, down through the skeletal elm to land upon a gent. Well, Rowdy was not precisely certain that the man had been a gent. He had never actually seen a gentleman before, not even Mr. Dunsbury—he had always run and hidden when he heard that Mr. Dunsbury might be coming—but he did imagine that an actual gent would look a good deal like the creature upon which he had landed, just before he had landed upon the ground.

*That Lady Ellena'll be thinking me naught but a nodcock now,* Rowdy thought dejectedly. *She'll not have nothing more to do with me, ever again. Does she look out that window an' see me coming, she'll turn away as quick as quick can. Indeed! Laughing, she be, most like. Making sport of me to anyone will listen to her. Calling me a dolt an' a dunce. An' just when I was wanting to make a good impression!*

Well, but there was nothing for it. He would simply give up all thought of the elegant Lady Ellena perched behind her diamond glass, and from this moment on apply himself wholeheartedly to his trade. Of course, he did think that he might continue to look about him for another love—a less imposing and more readily available love. One closer in rank to himself. Yes, exactly.

*There be any number of others,* he thought. *Ginger be forever inviting of me to come inside the greenhouse an' share her dinner. An' that wild little Gypsy does still be wanting to scamper about with me in the home woods. An' Abigail, she be quite pretty, an' not at all opposed to the spending of a afternoon with me while her man be working in the gardens. Aye, there be any number of others. An' they bean't dreams, neither. Ought not to be dreaming of Lady Ellena. Ought not be so much as thinkin' of that one. More trouble than she be worth, I 'spect.*

"Mrrr phflgstist brrrr murffle," he purred to himself, wiggling his right forepaw aimlessly in the air. "Mfrrrphle mrrgle mrrrphssst!"

*I ain't be goin' to attempt to gain that beautiful lady's attention ever again. No, I do not be. No matter how much m'heart aches to gaze upon that perticuler flash mort. Do she be in that window ever day from now till the end of next summer, I willn't even look up,* he told himself sternly. *But she did be exquisite. Aye, and had the prettiest eyes I ever seed.*

# Two

Lady Ellena could not think what to do. She shoved at the window with a sense of hopelessness. In summer, one of the servants might have been the least bit neglectful, the window latch might have been left ajar, and the casement might very well have moved outward. But this was winter. The latch was never left unlocked in winter. She stepped down from the sill into the very center of the window seat and looked about her, her blue eyes large with worry. It was quite unthinkable that she should concern herself over the welfare of such a ruffian, but she could not help herself. He might well have done himself a considerable injury—and all for the opportunity, mad though it was, of coming to pay her a call.

*Of course, he is a perfect nodcock,* she thought, *leaping gracefully from the window seat and stalking restlessly about the bedchamber. To climb out onto such a small branch—the very thought of it makes my heart lurch even now—oh, such a dolt! And yet, he did come, for an instant, so very near to me that had the casement been open, I might have touched him. Of course, I would not have touched him. Never. But still, I might have done.*

*And I have never seen such a fine, handsome face,* she mused. *It was a bit battered, to be sure, but that makes it all the more appealing. After all, are not dueling scars most fashionable? Indeed they are. And now I know why! Oh, but was he not gloriously grand for that moment before he fell? His thick black fur, his magnificent black tail. Everything about him demanded my at-*

*tention in that moment—most especially his eyes. I have never seen such very beguiling green eyes in all of my life. No, nor eyes so filled with pride and mischief either,* she reminded herself. *And yet, how they spoke to me, those eyes. Spoke of the most magical and wondrous things—before they departed, along with the rest of him.*

"*Mrrrgle-phfst,*" she muttered, leaping up onto the fine canopied bed and tiptoeing gracefully across the coverlet to leap down at the other side. "*Brrrrr mft mrrrow mphsgur!*"

It was most imperative to learn if the fellow had survived his fall without great injury, but how she was to go about it she was not at all sure, for Lady Ellena had never, from the very day of her birth, set foot outside the house. She had been born on the settle in the kitchen, had been carried up to this very elegant little set of chambers, and had remained here ever since. With dainty steps, Lady Ellena hurried across the carpeting into the adjoining dressing room and glanced about her.

Surely dinner time approached. Surely her Cammy ought to be here even now, changing into one of her evening dresses. Well, she would find herself a comfortable spot and wait. Yes, that was exactly what she would do—wait for her Cammy to enter and then put the problem to her Cammy as succinctly as possible.

Lady Ellena had every confidence in Miss Camelia Dunsbury. And why should she not? Whenever she suffered the least discomfort, her Cammy rushed to remedy the situation. Why once, when she was very young, she had gotten herself locked inside the armoire. One little cry and her Cammy had come dashing to her rescue. And the time that she had jumped inside the window seat to inspect its contents thoroughly and that simpleton, Priscilla, had closed the lid upon her, her Cammy had been right there opening the lid the moment Lady Ellena had begun to exclaim—in a most unladylike fashion, to be sure—against such confinement. Yes, indeed, her Cammy was to be depended upon in all things. That was why, the very moment that Miss Camelia Dunsbury stepped into her dressing room to change her gown, Lady Ellena leaped down from the top of the fruitwood chest of drawers and launched herself into a thorough explanation of all that had happened and how very important it was to learn if the fellow had done himself some injury.

"Lady Ellena, do cease and desist," Miss Dunsbury commanded after a full two minutes of *mrrrings* and *brrings* and *yeooows*. "Priscilla, I will wear the forest green velvet to dinner, as we planned. Lord Cottsworth has arrived at last. I did think, for a time, that we might be forced to proceed without him, but, thank heavens, he was not brought to a standstill by the snow in the north. Help me to slip out of this old thing, Priscilla. And I must do something with my hair. It has begun to look a good deal like a rat's nest."

*"Mrrrow-ow mrglepfhst brrr mrrr phfstgle,"* Lady Ellena began to explain again, curling herself about her Cammy's ankles as that young woman donned her robe and began to take the pins from her hair. *"Mrrrow-ow mrglepfhst brrr mrrr phfstgle!"* and she stared up at her Cammy with the most urgent light in her sky blue eyes. Her Cammy gazed down at her quite vacantly.

Throughout Miss Dunsbury's toilette, Lady Ellena spoke to her. She spoke to her calmly, then more excitedly, then rather offhandedly, and then with great urgency and feeling. She took to leaping upon Miss Dunsbury's lap, then leaping down at once and rushing to the doorway of the bedchamber, glaring back over her snow white shoulder at her Cammy with exquisite expressiveness. None of it did the least bit of good. Lady Ellena could only think that her Cammy had naught but feathers in her cockloft.

*I understand every word my Cammy says,* Lady Ellena fumed in silence. *What is wrong with her that she can never understand me, even though I speak most clearly and succinctly?*

Even so, Lady Ellena remained undaunted and determined. So determined, in fact, that when her Cammy, dressed in forest green velvet accented with ivory lace, departed the chambers, swished down the corridor and began to descend the staircase, Lady Ellena did not give over. She could not. Though she could not have said, if asked, why that impossible rogue's well-being was of the least concern to her, still, it was. Therefore she, too, departed Miss Dunsbury's chambers by dashing through the doorway, unseen, right at the maid, Priscilla's, heels—which Lady Ellena had never thought to do before—and hurried to catch her Cammy up, to come around in front of her Cammy and urge her to stop and listen to all. Unfortunately, Lady Ellena knew nothing of staircases. She was, in fact, utterly amazed to discover that one might hop down from one narrow bit of floor to another. This she did, intrigued, and upon the fourth step was beside her Cammy. And on the fifth of the steps she stepped directly in front of Camelia, who did not see her at all, and sent poor Miss Dunsbury toppling.

"By Jove!" exclaimed a masculine voice from the first floor landing, and in a moment Lord Cottsworth was dashing upward to save his intended from a nasty fall. And he would have done, too, had he noticed the gleaming white cat racing in fright around Miss Dunsbury to come in front of her again, but he did not—not until he came to the point of placing his foot upon the thing. He stopped himself upon the instant so as not to injure his intended's pet, lost his balance, and instead of rescuing Miss Dunsbury, tumbled down the staircase just ahead of her until they both came to be lying flat upon the landing, she on top, he stretched awkwardly out below her.

"Are you all right, Camelia?" Cottsworth gasped up at her, struggling for breath.

"Yes, Daniel," Miss Dunsbury managed, her cheeks aflame. She struggled to free herself from the tangle of her skirt and his lordship. She sank an elbow into the middle of his chest, bounced awkwardly upon his stomach, kicked his knee with her heel, and all in all, came near to extinguishing the poor gentleman's dignity completely before she gained her feet. "I do beg your pardon," she whispered hoarsely, her embarrassment pinking her cheeks to the most amazing and enthralling degree as she stared down at him. "I am so sorry, Daniel."

"No, no, think nothing of it, m'dear," groaned Lord Cottsworth, pushing himself up from the floor. "Accidents do happen. You must just be more careful in the future." And then he did something he had never done before. He stood and took Miss Dunsbury in his arms. He could not think why he did it. He was not the sort of gentleman who took young women into his arms and held them tightly enclosed there. And Camelia was not, for that matter, the sort of young woman who had ever desired to be held so. But then again, he had never seen Camelia so very embarrassed. Why, not only was her face aflame and her cheeks a most alluring pink, but her clear blue eyes appeared to be awash with tears. "You must not let it concern you, Camelia," he whispered into one of her pretty little ears. "Hush, m'dear. Do not cry."

Camelia could not think what to do. She had never been so very clumsy in all her years—and to bring Daniel down with her! And then to practically snuff the life out of the gentleman simply by attempting to gain her feet! She could not bear to look at him. So she did the most unCamelialike thing. It was so unlike her that her breath caught in her throat when she discovered that she had done it. She grasped Lord Cottsworth around the waist and buried her burning face in the cool folds of his neckcloth.

Shivers went through her when his arms came around her and he whispered in her ear. And when, directly afterward, he rested his chin upon the top of her head, she thought she would faint dead away. And all the while, around their ankles, Lady Ellena continued to exert the necessity of her Cammy's going out to the stable where the audacious young ruffian had fled, to check upon his well-being. *"Mrrrow-ow brrr mrrrr, murglespfsgt!"* she insisted over and over, hoping against hope that her Cammy would at last understand her, and do as she was bid.

\* \* \*

As Cottsworth tramped through Dunsbury's small wood the following morning—accompanied by the earl, the colonel, and Mr. Dunsbury, with the stable hands and the gamekeeper behind them—Cottsworth could only think how much more jolly it would be should the snow from the north begin to fall here. Always, since his youth, he had gone to seek the tree for the Yule log amidst white drifts and sizzling flakes. It did not seem quite right somehow, that the ground should be hard and cold and brown, not to mention how much more enjoyable the search would be if these gentlemen would cease to hoax him about his upcoming nuptials.

"He's a cool one, our Cottsworth," drawled the Earl of Riggensby just then. "Not a twitch or a stutter to be seen, eh?"

"Ain't up there before the parson yet," observed the colonel. "We will see how well he does once it comes to repeating the vows. Like to stutter them out in one long breath with our Camelia standing there beside him."

"No, not Daniel," protested Dunsbury with a grin. "Daniel ain't the stuttering sort. But we must remind Sir Nathan to tell him to kiss the girl, Anthony, when the ceremony has ended."

"Kiss the girl?" chuckled the colonel. "He had best, or Sir Nathan will do it for him. Will tell that groomsman of yours to poke you in the ribs to remind you, eh, Daniel? Have you kissed my niece as yet?"

"Well, of course I have kissed her," Cottsworth replied. "Kissed her in the parlor in London when she said she would have me. Expected to. Did."

"Of course you did. Have you kissed the girl since?"

"Camelia is not the type of young woman who goes about wishing to be kissed every moment of the day," Cottsworth mumbled. "No, she ain't. And I am not the type of gentleman who must be forever panting after his intended. It is not the thing."

"No, I expect not—but have you kissed her since that time when you proposed?" asked the colonel again.

"Of course I have! Any number of times!"

"What?" cried Camelia's father. "Any number of times?"

Cottsworth sank into silence. The truth was, he had not kissed Camelia since she had accepted his proposal, but for some reason, he did not wish her father and her uncles to know that. Well, Camelia was *not* the sort of young woman who cared to be kissed. He had discovered as much in that London parlor.

*And that is just fine with me,* he thought, watching his boots kicking along the path. *I am not one of these gentlemen who must have a respectable wife and a passionate one, as well. Papa wished me to marry Camelia, and I will do precisely that— passion be damned. I expect I have not a passionate bone in my body. I have never noticed any. Which merely makes it apparent to me that Camelia and I are perfectly matched.*

Gypsy scurried off the moment she heard the men coming, and Rowdy was quite determined to follow her example, but he was curious, and the wood was a fine place to be curious. There were any number of bushes and brambles from which a fellow could see without being seen. He peered about him, selected the perfect spot, and settled down behind a holly bush to watch.

*Just so,* he thought, noticing the four men in the lead and his stable hands trudging along behind with axes in their hands. *That bloke what I landed on were a gent. Just see him traipsing along aside of them others. Can't tell the difference betwixt gents an' stable hands when the lot of them be together. But what the devil be they doin' stomping through the woods?*

"Here. I expect this one will do the job," called Dunsbury. "Come up, Rollings. Bring your lads forward."

"Will it fit, George?" asked the earl. "It is near ten feet tall, I should think."

"But not so very wide," observed the colonel. "And yews always make splendid Yule logs. What do you think, Cottsworth?"

"Huh? What? Oh! I think it will do nicely. It will take all of us to carry it home once it is trimmed."

"Aye, that it will," agreed Dunsbury. "Set to, Rollings. This be our pick."

Why his stable hands cut down that particular yew and chopped all its branches off while the gentlemen stood about with their hands in their pockets, Rowdy could not guess. He had never seen Rollings and the others so much as go near a tree before. And when all of the men, gents and stable hands alike, raised the stripped trunk to their shoulders and began to sing as they carried it back toward the house, their boots tramping along the path in time to their song, Rowdy was so amazed by it that both of his ears began to twitch.

*I do got to see what they be goin' to do with it,* he thought, backing cautiously out of the holly bush. With a switch of his tail and a heart filled with anticipation of something splendidly novel to come, he bounded after them. And once he had caught them up, he marched along at the rear directly behind Lord Cottsworth, who had offered to support one of the heavier sections of the tree, but whose offer had been politely declined. "Never. You are to be my son-in-law, Cottsworth. I have vowed not to take advantage of you until you are," Dunsbury had said, laughing. His brothers had laughed with him as they had sent his lordship down the line to carry the thinnest end of the log.

Singing and laughing, the men paraded all the way back to the house, where the first footman held the outside door wide and Mr. Perkins and the other footmen stood at attention in the vestibule. It was not an easy task to get a ten-foot yew tree in through the front entrance of the Dunsbury establishment, not even with all its branches stripped off. It took a deal of concentration and maneuvering; a shouted order here; a "Look out, we be coming on to knock down the balustrade!" there; myriad exchanges of ideas and suppositions and suggestions. Broad shoulders attempted to shrink in upon themselves in order to bypass the hall table and the looking glass without shattering both. Gentlemen and stable hands both bit at their lips and balanced their portion of the load time and time again.

It was the best of all things! Rowdy could not believe what he saw. He huddled down and peeked up over the next to the top step. He blinked his deep green eyes in wonder, and blinked again. The door stood open wide, and now even the first footman had ceased to gaze about him, instead leaning in over the gents' shoulders and making suggestions of his own as to how to get the log through the vestibule and the narrow corridor beyond without smashing every object along the way to bits or gashing great scarring lines along the intricately patterned paneling.

*Ought I do it?* Rowdy wondered, watching with great consideration. *I could. I knows as I could. Just slip in past the gent's feet and up them stairs and hi-de-ho, I am in! Still, she willn't want to be seeing of me. Not after I went and maked such a fool of myself last night. And I said as I wouldn't go seeking her out no more. Still an' all, the door do be* wide *open. An' I could say to her as how I didn't* actually *fall. I could say to her as how it were all a act-like, to get her attention.*

A vision of the exquisite Lady Ellena rose up in his mind—her glorious white coat, her sturdy and seductive little legs, her haughtily elegant face, and most of all those oh, so lovely, sky-blue eyes. Rowdy shivered at the dream of her. *I be bound to do it,* he encouraged himself, his tail twitching rapidly from one side to the other as he hunkered back upon his haunches. *I be called upon to do it. I reckon as how I loves that Lady Ellena no matter what, an' I must be about the havin' of her if I can.*

"Mrglespfst," Rowdy whispered to himself. "Brrrrmrrr mrglespfst!" And, so saying, he launched himself forward, up over the top step, between Lord Cottsworth's legs, crashing into that gentleman's shin and sitting down, stunned, for a moment because of it. But then Rowdy was off and running again, veritably flying up the staircase to the first floor landing, leaving Cottsworth with but a mere glimpse of what, precisely, had knocked against his shin and sent him stumbling about, seeking something to keep him upright while the end of the Yule log bounced and jounced upon his shoulder.

"It was that damnable cat!" Cottsworth exclaimed after a full minute of attempting to regain his balance which ended with a sad thump as he sat down hard upon the vestibule floor.

"What the deuce are you doing back there, Cottsworth?" called the earl over his shoulder. "Here, Anthony, do not you fall down as well. You have set us all off balance, Cottsworth. The men up front are dancing the jig. Get up and grab hold and help us steady it again."

"It was that same black cat!" bellowed Cottsworth as he attempted to gain his feet. "Deuced thing ran between my legs just as I was taking a step. I will ring its neck do I come upon it again."

"Black cat?" asked Dunsbury. "Do not have a black cat, Cottsworth. Have a white one. Camelia's Lady Ellena. White as snow. James, did you see a black cat accost his lordship?"

"No, sir," answered the first footman, who had just helped Cottsworth to his feet and was nervously brushing at that gentleman's trousers. "No, sir, Mr. Dunsbury. I did not see any cat at all, sir."

# Three

"Not here!" cried the colonel, opening the enormous silver epergne upon the long table in the vestibule and staring down into it. "At least your cat does not favor Great Aunt Isabella's taste in epergnes, Cottsworth."

"Not in here, either," the earl called from his brother's study. "I have gone so far as to peer up the chimney, Cottsworth. Oh, wait a moment. Wait a moment. I have forgotten to check under the carpet. No, not under the carpet."

"I dare say it has gone into the kitchen," offered Dunsbury, placing an arm about Cottsworth's shoulders. "I should make for the kitchen first thing were I a cat. Just smell that bread."

"Do cats like bread?" asked Cottsworth, hoping that they would indeed discover a black cat in the kitchen so that Camelia's papa and her uncles would cease to tease him.

"No. Not particularly. But I do," grinned Dunsbury. "We shall procure a slice of bread and butter, eh? All of us. Well-deserved after bringing home the Yule log."

The four of them did precisely that, though Cottsworth's portion stuck in his throat when Riggensby suggested that they go upstairs once they had finished searching the kitchen and invite the ladies to join in the fun. "Better than a game of hare and hounds," declared Riggensby. "My Anne will enjoy it, of all things, searching about all over the house for an invisible cat."

"It is not an invisible cat," Cottsworth drawled coolly, refusing to be baited though his head was beginning to ache with their teasing. "It is a common old black cat."

"Yes, yes, we know that *you* see a black cat, Daniel," the colonel remarked, his eyes sparkling. "Apparently, it is black to you and invisible to us. But once my Jane begins to search, my boy, we will be assured of finding it. I promise you that. My Janey could find a cock in a cornfield. Has. Many times."

"I expect we shall discover the ladies in the winter day room," Dunsbury said. "All finished with your bread, gentlemen? Come along, then. Up the back stairs. From Cottsworth's description, it sounds like a menial sort of cat to me, accustomed to menial sorts of stairs. Aberration that it should appear in the entryway. Most likely aiming for the kitchen door and became distracted by our walking log. Up, up, gentlemen," Dunsbury chuckled, urging them all on before him. "And keep your eyes open. Invisible thing has attempted to kill Cottsworth twice, do not forget. Ferocious sort. Be on your guard."

Cottsworth kept his peace and pasted a frosty smile upon his face as he climbed the steps. There had been a cat, by Jove. He had seen the thing for a flickering instant. It had been the same devil that had landed upon him last evening and clawed its way down his greatcoat. He was damned if he was ever going to mention it again after this. The old reprobate might launch itself at him from off one of the chandeliers, and he would decline to so much as take note of it. *Do not take well to being teased,* he observed. *Never thought about it at all before, but apparently to take enjoyment from becoming the object of someone else's humor is not one of my virtues. Not at all.*

Rowdy, tucked neatly up beside the woodwork, stretched forward and peeked cautiously at Mrs. Dunsbury and Lady Riggensby conversing in the winter day room. They, alone, had refused to join in the hunt for Lord Cottsworth's cat, and were busily discussing plans for the neighborhood ball to be held at Dunsbury Dell in merely three days' time. *Them be* ladies, Rowdy thought in awe. Ladies. *But Lady Ellena bean't with 'em. Nope, she do not be. Well then, I best keep searching. Only I do not want them ladies to be taking no notice of me. Must dash like a thing afire, past this here open place, like a veritable flash of gunpowder, an' be gone afore they ever think to look up.*

He gathered himself, sinewy muscles tightening, into his very best crouch, hunkered there for a whisper of a moment, and then launched himself past the doorway, down the corridor, and around a corner into the Dunsburys' music room, where he gazed about him in a mixture of awe and disappointment. Lady Ellena was not in this room, either. He would certainly smell the sweet, seductive scent of her if she were here, even were she hiding from him. He had not, in fact, smelled anything at all that resembled what Lady Ellena ought to smell like in any of his wanderings through this odd place. He was beginning to doubt that he had seen the lovely Lady Ellena in a window, at all.

*Where do she be?* Rowdy wondered, standing upon his hind legs with his front paws firmly planted upon the top of a tiny bench to peer, very much intrigued, at the harpsichord. *She ain't here nowhere. What be them things?*

Rowdy scrambled up until all of him sat upon the tiny bench and studied the keys of the instrument with great curiosity. He reached out with his left paw and touched three of the keys. The sound it produced sent him leaping to the floor and scrambling behind the harp in a hurry.

*Buggers,* he thought, *be it alive? Must be. Don't like no one touching on it, neither. What be these?* He reached up a paw to pat at the harp strings. That was better. This thing weren't not alive at all, but it were fun to touch. It made his paws all tingly-like. He was just about to pat at them again, with more enthusiasm, when he heard boots clacking up the corridor in his direction. He knew the sound of boots, and he had no intention of being found in the house by anybody wearing them. Rowdy scuttled between the back of Mr. Dunsbury's bass fiddle and the wall.

"Now you think the wretched cat plays the harpsichord?" asked Mr. Dunsbury, patting his son-in-law-to-be on the back. "Never known you to be so whimsical, Daniel. In fact, never known you to be whimsical at all."

"I heard the harpsichord."

"Most likely Martha was dusting it, Daniel," offered Camelia, entering the music room beside him. "Just so. You see, there is no black cat here. No cat at all."

"Well, it heard us coming and hid itself away."

"Where?" Dunsbury asked.

"How should I know?" Cottsworth responded. "I am not a cat. Behind the draperies?"

Mr. Dunsbury crossed the room and moved the draperies aside. He looked up. He looked down. "Not behind the draperies."

Camelia, not to be thought an unwilling participant in "The Great Cat Hunt"—as her cousin Jane had enthusiastically deemed it—strolled to the harpsichord and bent to peer beneath it. Then she walked to its side and glanced beneath the raised lid.

Cottsworth paced about the room, stared down into several vases and behind the rhododendron in the corner. He went so far as to open up a violin case. He was just about to move Mr. Dunsbury's bass fiddle away from the wall when Camelia touched his sleeve and Dunsbury harrumphed. "Papa does not like anyone to touch that particular fiddle," Camelia whispered. "A string always snaps when anyone but he so much as breathes near it."

"Oh. Well. But what if the thing is hiding behind it?"

"Never!" declared Dunsbury. "No room for a cat between it and the wall. Thing must needs be no bigger than a mouse to hide there. It is bigger than a mouse, is it not, Cottsworth?"

"A good deal bigger than a mouse," Cottsworth acknowledged, allowing Camelia to turn him away and escort him back out into the corridor.

Behind the bass fiddle, Rowdy, curled up into the tiniest ball he could make of himself, gave a tiny mew of relief.

"Do I get my hands upon that reprobate, m'dear, I will— I will—well, I do not know what I will do precisely," Lord Cottsworth muttered, his extended arms filled with holly and pine branches. "But I will think of something. You may believe that."

"Do you realize that I have never seen you angry, Daniel?" Camelia murmured as she took one of the holly branches from him and arranged it carefully along the mantel of the Gold Saloon. "You are generally so even-tempered. I cannot ever remember seeing you angry."

"Yes, well, I do not generally have cats leaping down upon me from out of trees or attacking my leg while I am carrying a Yule log, m'dear."

"No, of course you do not. Still, I cannot imagine where this cat came from, because we honestly do not have a black cat, Daniel. The only cat in this house is Lady Ellena, and she is white with not so much as a black spot upon her. And we did search the entire house, did we not? Yes, we searched everywhere. It was rather enjoyable, actually. That is to say, everyone involved appeared to relish the hunt."

"You do not believe me, either," Cottsworth accused.

"Of course I do. It is merely perplexing that we should not have had a black cat, or a bit of trouble with a black cat, until you arrived last evening. Are you quite certain that you did not bring this beast with you when you came? That he did not ride in behind you on Sabre?"

"Please do not laugh at me, m'dear. I have been laughed at quite enough for one day."

Camelia turned to relieve him of another branch. Her cool blue eyes studied the glower that had arisen upon his generally agreeable face. She felt the oddest fluttering in her stomach at the sight of it. "I am not laughing at you,

Daniel. I would never think to laugh at anyone. It would be most impolite."

"Impolite. Bah!"

"Daniel!"

"Well, I cannot help myself. I am upset, Camelia. Only consider if you are right and I am wrong, for heaven's sake. In that case, I must be going mad—well, to see things that do not exist, one must be mad, eh?"

"Nerves," offered Camelia quietly.

"Nerves?"

"Indeed. Our wedding approaches, and you are becoming flustered by the thought of it. Gentlemen often do, you know. Mama said as much to me merely an hour ago."

"I see."

"Daniel, please do not glare at me so. This is to be a happy time in our lives. We are preparing for our wedding day. In three days, we are to have a ball for all of the local gentry to celebrate Christmas and our approaching nuptials. We shall open the doors between this saloon and the one adjoining and dance the night happily away with our family and friends and neighbors. Can you not think of that instead of pouting over an invisible cat?"

"I do not pout," declared Cottsworth quietly. "The cat is not invisible. And they are *your* family and friends and neighbors. My friends and neighbors remain in the north country, and my family in their graves."

"Your best friend will be here, Daniel. Sir Nathan is the only one you wished to invite, and he has assured us that he will arrive in time for the ball and remain with us until our wedding day. Are you intent upon making me angry? Because if you are, I feel I must advise you that you are succeeding quite nicely at it," hissed Camelia, hoping that her cousins, busily decorating the opposite side of the room, would not overhear her.

Cottsworth found it hard to detect if his betrothed were telling the truth about becoming angry or hoaxing him. "It must be an exceptional experience for you, then, Camelia," he replied after a long, thoughtful silence. "I have never known you to be angry before, and I have known you an interminably long time."

*What could he have meant by it?* Camelia wandered into her chambers to change her dress for dinner, but instead of ringing immediately for Priscilla she lay down upon her bed and gazed up at her intricately embroidered canopy. Upon that hanging a knight was posed upon a white charger in the act of fighting a winged dragon while a beautiful princess looked on. The canopy had been made expressly for this bed, which had once belonged to Camelia's grandmother. Camelia had always admired the canopy's craftmanship, but at the moment she did not so much as notice the fine, even stitches and the marvelous blend of colors. She did not even notice that there was a canopy.

*What could he have meant by it—I have known you an interminably long time?* "I have known you for a tediously long time is what he intended to say," she murmured softly. *Tedious. Boring. Is that how he looks upon our relationship? Upon me?* Camelia had never before given a single thought to how Daniel might actually *feel* about their approaching nuptials. She had merely assumed from the age of twelve, when her mama and papa had deigned to confide in her the arrangement that had been made, that she and Daniel Orren Templeton were one day to be man and wife. She had, from that moment onward, depended upon it. She had come out this spring knowing that Daniel would be her husband. She had not taken at all seriously any other beau. Why should she? Daniel had inherited his papa's title, lands, and fortune; he was kind and dependable; his reputation was pristine. And she—she was well-dowered, loyal, obliging, and capable, with an untarnished reputation of her own. Her practical nature had seen no reason that the two of them could not have a perfect marriage.

"Tedious," she murmured again, a solitary tear forming in the corner of her eye. "Daniel finds his association with me tedious. He finds *me* tedious."

Camelia swiped at the tear impatiently. She was not the sort of young woman who cried. She had not cried about anything since she had been in leading strings. "I am not a woman with excessive sensibilities," she told herself with a sniff. "No, I certainly am not one of *those!*"

*"Mrrrow?"* asked Lady Ellena most sympathetically, leaping onto the bed and curling up beside her Cammy, setting herself to scrubbing at one flushed cheek with her rough little tongue. *"Mrrrow mrrr brrrrmrrrow?"*

Lady Ellena had been most excited earlier. She had seen that dark, lean rogue from her window this very morning, stalking along behind the gentlemen with the odd, branchless tree as if he were an accepted part of their party. Her heart had soared at the sight of him. He had not limped. He had not paused wearily for breath. She had seen no bandages wrapped around any part of his ruggedly handsome self. He had survived his tumble, then, and seemingly without the least injury. Oh, how she had given thanks for that. Not because she was the least bit interested in the audacious rogue, of course, but merely because she possessed great compassion and had cared for what might have been his most unfortunate plight.

And when the gentlemen had turned toward the front of the house and he with them, Lady Ellena had done a most unacceptable thing. She could not think why, but she had imagined that her rustic swain was intent upon entering her house, and she had leaped from her window and dashed to the door, scratching at the bottom of it, hoping to make it open. Then she had stood upon her hind legs and groped ineffectually at the fluted glass doorknob, attempting to turn the thing as she had seen her Cammy and the maids do day after day. But she was not quite tall enough or heavy enough to do the thing. She had then run to the dressing room door and then to the sitting room door, but she discovered that they, just as effectively, had barred her way. For the first time in her one year of life, she had become aware that she was held captive. Her lovely blue eyes had grown wide with wonder.

She had given herself a little shake, then, and had determined to discuss this observation with her Cammy as soon as possible, for her Cammy loved her and could not possibly intend that she be held captive. No, certainly not. Her Cammy would speak angrily to the maids about it, and see that doors were left ajar in future.

And then Lady Ellena had remembered that one might see the front entrance from one of the windows of the sitting room, and she had scrambled up upon that particular window at once, just in time to see the rogue's bushy tail disappear into the house.

All this Lady Ellena related to her Cammy just as soon as she had finished scrubbing her Cammy's cheek. *"Murglespffft mrrrr brrrmrrrspt mrrr,"* she concluded at last. She quite expected her Cammy to sit right up and question her further—but her Cammy did not. Really, it was most aggravating. Lady Ellena knew that the ruffian had entered the house, though why he was not at this very moment attempting to gain entrance to these chambers, she could not guess. Certainly he ought to be. Why else would the rustic have wished to enter, after all, but to seek out Lady Ellena herself?

*Which does give one pause,* thought Lady Ellena, grooming one white paw with a certain degree of vanity. What a perfectly lovely paw it was—so delicate, and yet so deceptively sturdy. *Which* must *give one pause,* she thought again. *For if he is not here, right outside that very door, where has the fellow gone? And to what purpose? I have not seen him. And he did not come dashing back out upon the stoop again, for I waited and waited to see if he would do so.* *"Mrrrfrrrblef,"* she said, stepping up upon her Cammy and staring directly down into her Cammy's eyes. *"Brrrr mrrfrrrblef fluggle."*

"Oh, my dearest Lady Ellena," sighed Camelia, gazing up into those knowing, blue, almond-shaped eyes. "I did never before realize how he feels. He finds me tedious and boring. How could he say as much to me—how could he?"

And Camelia burst into sobs, amazing both herself and Lady Ellena.

*Well, he is an audacious rogue, with his swaggering and stalking and sneaking into the house,* thought Lady Ellena, *but I cannot think the ruffian so aggravating as to bring us to tears.*

# Four

The sound of the dinner bell gonging aroused Rowdy from his nap so abruptly that he banged his head against the bass fiddle and sent its strings to trembling. *What the devil were that?* he wondered, sitting up as best he could in such cramped quarters and waiting for the sound to come again. *This be the queerest place as ever I did get into,* he mused. *All of it. Queer as queer does do, and regular overflowing with ladies and gents.*

But there were none of the ladies and gents anywhere near him. He wiggled his nose the slightest bit, testing the air. His magnificent whiskers wobbled, and then his pink tongue came out a bit to taste the scents around him. *Nope, not a one,* he thought. He straightened as best he could and then backed cautiously out of his hiding place. With silent steps and a great determination to ignore all the curious things surrounding him, he made straight for the threshold and eased himself around the doorframe until he could see clearly into the corridor.

*By Jupiter!* he thought, withdrawing into the music room with alacrity. *There be more steps up at t'other side o' that flat space. Aye, there do be! Them ladies and gents be comin' down from somewheres, somehow. Got to be more steps!*

Rowdy's hope, since first he had seen the lovely Lady Ellena behind her window, had undergone more ups and downs than Rollings the first time he had stepped up onto a bucking horse's back. Now his hopes rose again and sent

a distinctive twitch to his thick black tail. He had not explored the entire place! He had covered only one portion
of it! Another portion lay above him like the stable loft,
and there were steps in place to ascend to it. His heart
thumped against his ribs in anticipation. This time, he
would find Lady Ellena. He was sure of it.

He waited most impatiently, stalking about the music
room, attending to nothing but the sounds of ladies and
gents descending the staircase. At last there came an end
to it. Cautiously, Rowdy peeked around the doorframe
again. For the longest time he waited to discover if one
more person would descend. No one came. Gathering
his courage about him, he dashed up the corridor to the
landing and discovered, right before his eyes, another set
of steps turning back upon the first and rising upward. *I
be blind as a bat,* he thought. *Didn't not so much as notice
them.* Optimistically, Rowdy began his ascent into the upper regions.


Cottsworth stared down at his turbot in utter silence.
He could not think of one thing to say to either of his
dinner partners. Lady Riggensby, of course, did not give
a rip whether he spoke to her or not, she being sufficiently
entertained by her husband, who sat above her at table.
But Cottsworth was certain that Camelia did care whether
or not he engaged her in conversation, and he felt a perfect dolt for not doing so. He poked at the dead, white
fish before him with the tines of his fork, flaking bits of it
away. Then he arranged a portion of dark green broccoli
around what remained as though laying the turbot out for
viewing before consigning it to its grave. Then he lifted a
glass of dry white wine to his lips and forced as much of
it as possible past the lump in his throat, hoping against
hope that it would help him to think of *something* to say
to Camelia. But the wine met the lump and took a wrong
turn, sending him to choking and coughing and his eyes
to watering. Two of Dunsbury's footmen rushed to pat his

back. Lady Riggensby urged him to drink more of his wine. Everyone at table, in fact, offered some suggestion—everyone except Camelia—but Cottsworth could not cease coughing, and so excused himself as best he could and left the room.

At a glare and a nod from her mama, Camelia lay her napkin beside her plate and rose to follow him into the corridor, where she waited until his coughing had stopped and he had finished attending to tears and a wildly runny nose by direct application of his handkerchief. "Are you better now?" she asked as he returned his handkerchief to his pocket.

"Yes, thank you. Much."

"Then we had best return." Camelia turned away from him and took a step back toward the dining room.

With some misgivings, Cottsworth caught her arm and turned her to face him.

"What, Daniel?"

"I—I must apologize."

"Must you?"

"Indeed. I did not intend, this afternoon, to take my frustrations out upon you, Camelia. It was most unkind of me."

"Yes," Camelia agreed, staring down at her pink silk slippers. "It *was* most unkind of you."

Cottsworth did not notice her pink slippers, but he did notice how much like silk were her honey-blonde curls, for he had nothing to study, once she had lowered her gaze, but the top of her tilted head. "Can you forgive me, Camelia?" he sighed.

"Of course I can. I do forgive you."

"You will pardon me, but it does not feel as if you do."

"No," confessed Camelia, quite overcome by her need not to gaze up into his fine gray eyes. "It does not feel to me as if I do, either. Yet, I know that I do."

"I cannot explain, m'dear, why that cursed cat should so upset me. I am not generally easy to upset. I think it is that your father and your uncles would not refrain from teasing me about it, and I felt as though—well, but that is neither here nor there. I do apologize."

"You called me tedious," whispered Camelia before she even thought to say a word. It so surprised her that she looked directly up at him, gasped, and covered her mouth with her hand.

Cottsworth's heart plummeted to the very toe of his left shoe—a totally new experience for that gentleman. Camelia's wide, blue eyes shone at him in the candlelight as sad and confused as any he had ever seen, and he could not control his heart's reaction to them. "Called you *tedious?* I never did," he replied softly. "Camelia, I would not."

"You said that you had known me an interminably long time."

"Yes, but—"

Tears mounted to Camelia's eyes and turned her dark lashes even darker.

"Camelia, do not cry!" exclaimed Cottsworth hoarsely. "I do not have so much as a clean handkerchief to hand you."

"I do n-never cry."

"No, no, you never do. I have never known you to do so. So do not do it now, Camelia. What has come over you? I have never known you to be so exceptionally sensitive. I have never known you to be sensitive at all, actually. And now, to be so very upset over such a stupid phrase as that. I did not at all mean that you were tedious. Truly, I did not. I meant that—that—" Cottsworth sought wildly for the right thing to say. Always before, no matter what the problem, the right phrase had fallen from the tip of his tongue without the least need for thought. But now—now—nothing came.

"You meant precisely that," sobbed Camelia. "I can see it in your eyes. You find me dull, and boring, and t-tedious."

"No, no, no! I find you—I did not—The thing you see in my eyes, Camelia, is panic."

"Panic?"

THE CHRISTMAS KITTEN 125

"I have never felt such as this before, but I am almost positive it is what is meant by panic. I do not know what to say to you, m'dear. I have always known what to say to everyone, and now I cannot think of a proper word. By gawd, Camelia, that reprobate of a cat has ripped up my peace and changed me into a veritable slowtop, as well!"

"Do not blame it upon the cat, Daniel. All the cat has done is to make us face the truth."

"Face the truth? What truth?"

"That I am tedious. That you have grown tired of me. That we have nothing to say to each other, nor likely ever will have. Oh, Daniel, and I thought we should make such a comfortable sort of married couple!" Camelia, most ashamedly, burst into tears.

Rowdy stalked the second floor, his heart beating rapidly, his every whisker tickling, his ears cocked for the least padding of Lady Ellena's paws upon the thick fuzzy stuff that covered the floors. She was indeed about somewhere. She was not a dream. His nose told him so. Oh, the sweet scent of her! It jumbled his mind and made his pulses pound with anticipation.

*I be upon her any minit now, by Jove,* Rowdy mused, investigating every inch of the corridor, slipping in through every door that had not been completely closed. *I be coming upon the lady soon. I be feeling it.* "Mrrrrphrrphsts!" he gasped, coming to the closed door of Camelia's bedchamber.

"Mrrr?" queried a sultry, intriguing voice from behind that particular door.

Rowdy's enormous black tail did a little jig. Such a voice as that surely belonged to Lady Ellena. It could belong to no one else. He arched his long lean body, rubbed against the oak of the door itself. "Brrrrrr," he answered her. "Mrr brr murglesphft."

"Brrrr mmmrrrr," replied Lady Ellena softly.

*She be wishin' me to come in,* he thought, his every bit of fur sizzling with pride. *Me! She do be wishin' me to come to her. I knowed she would. I seed it in her eyes right afore that dastardly branch broke last evenin'. She be in love with me!*

Lady Ellena spoke to him again, quietly and with great circumspection. She ought not to have spoken at all, but she had sensed his presence even as he had turned into the second floor corridor, and at that moment, her pulses had begun to race.

*I am such a gudgeon,* she thought as she arched her graceful body against the door that separated them. *He is nothing but an uneducated ruffian. Only look at how impossibly he behaves—strutting himself before me, staring at me, climbing the elm and now sneaking into this house. I ought to be sending him off with his tail between his legs.*

But she did not. Instead she lay down and placed her elegant little forepaws out beneath the door, tempting him mercilessly. He groaned a tiny cat-groan and ceased to rub against the door, playing instead with those exquisitely dainty paws. Touching first one and then the other of them with his own paw, patting them, caressing them.

*I be going in,* Rowdy told himself in silence. *I be going in there.* He lay down upon his back, completely forgetting he was in a forbidden place and leaving himself quite open to capture. His wide black paws pried at the bottom of the door, scratched at it. *"Mrrrfgle!"* he exclaimed.

Lady Ellena withdrew her own paws and sat up quite properly, eyeing the ruffian's attempts with considerable delight. The door actually wobbled in its frame when he pulled upon it. *Oh, what a burly beast he must be!* *"Brrrmuphf brrrmuggle,"* she whispered hoarsely, the very thought of making the acquaintance of such a strong, virile fellow sending little tremors of lust up into her throat. The thought that he might be just strong and virile enough to release her from her confinement was not lost upon her, either. Her Cammy had forgotten to instruct the maids as she had requested, and Priscilla had once again closed the doors, all three, imprisoning Lady Ellena again. *"Mrrruph brrrmuphf brrrmuggle,"* she instructed the ruffian beyond the door. *"Mrrow."*

Rowdy ceased to attack the bottom of the door, righted himself, and stared upward. *What? That thing?* he wondered. She couldn't be right. *That little tiny thing? For a door so huge as this?* Nevertheless, he stood up on his hind legs and wrapped his paws about the fluted glass knob and felt it turn.

*Well,* he thought, *I can do that. I must only catch at it from the proper angle-like, and pull it 'round.*

Having ducked back into the dining room and seized a napkin from the sideboard, Cottsworth hurried back into the corridor and dabbed gently at Camelia's tears. He was most careful of her, dabbing here and there at this tear and that. In the dim light of the corridor, her eyes sparkled up at him through lashes laced with diamonds. Her cheeks, wet and flushed, begged him to touch them again and again. Cottsworth felt a most unusual blaze rise up somewhere inside of him; then a veritable inferno roared through his entire body. The back of his neck began to perspire, along with various other parts of his anatomy that he dared not allow himself to consider. "Th-there, that's better," he murmured around the steadily enlarging lump in his throat. "We will simply remain here a few moments more and allow your cheeks to cool, and no one will ever know."

"G-good," Camelia replied. "B-because I do not wish to be thought of as some silly watering pot without a portion of self-control. B-because, I am not."

"No, of course you are not," replied Cottsworth in the most strangled whisper.

He stared down at her oddly, his fine gray eyes growing darker by the moment. And several of his dusky curls had freed themselves of the light pomade upon his hair and tumbled right across the middle of his brow. The most enormous ache welled up inside of Camelia to see it. Well, no, that was not at all the truth. The ache had actually begun this afternoon when she had discovered that Daniel thought her tedious, but it had grown since, until now she thought she would swell to twice her size with the pain of it.

Yes, and the manner in which he had dried her tears had had a great deal to do with the ache's increasing, too, and with the manner in which her heart had chosen to roar up into her ears and her pulses to pound like the drums of the red Indians from America, whom she had seen perform one very special evening this spring at Astley's. It was all so very confusing!

"Come, Camelia. We must return to dinner," Cottsworth soon murmured uneasily. "We cannot remain here in the corridor through the entire thing."

"You are correct, of course. We cannot. Shall we join the others, then?" Camelia placed her hand upon the arm he offered, and they turned together into the dining room. Cottsworth escorted her to her place and held her chair for her as she sat, helping her to move it a bit closer to table. Then he did the most surprising thing. It surprised him, and it surprised her. His hands still upon the chair-back, he leaned down and whispered into her ear. "If ever my words are the cause of your tears again, my sweet girl—I shall rip my tongue from my mouth and toss it upon whatever fire lies closest to hand. Believe me, Camelia, I find you many, many things, but tedious is not one of them."

*Now why did I say that?* Cottsworth wondered, taking his own chair and staring down at the roasted quail and onions that one of the footmen had set before him. *I have never said such a thing to Camelia in all of my life. Rip out my tongue and toss it upon whatever fire lies closest to hand? I am losing my mind.*

He stared at her, his wide green eyes unblinking for the longest time, and then he stepped farther into the room. Stepped? Swaggered, rather. He swaggered farther into the room, pride readily visible in his every movement and a triumphant satisfaction wreathing his handsome but battered face.

Lady Ellena studied him intently. With each step he took, myriad muscles rippled beneath his glossy black coat. His head cocked just so each time he stopped to study her. His enormous and most sensuous tail drifted mesmerizingly from left to right to left again, until Lady Ellena thought she could bear the sight of it no longer.

*I must have him,* she thought with the greatest sense of urgency. *He is the most magnificent beast I have ever seen—so young, so vigorous, so vital! Though he is quite unworthy of me,* she added, in an attempt to cool her rising ardour. *He is unworthy of me. I know he is. Why, he is nothing but an old, dirty, stable cat!*

That old, dirty, stable cat grinned a most knowing grin, swaggered across the carpeting and bounded, his muscles bulging, onto Lady Ellena's window seat. He gazed back over one rugged shoulder at her, then stepped up onto her windowsill and peered out into the darkness. *"Mrrrrow rrrfle,"* he growled, deep in his throat and glanced back over his shoulder at her again.

*She be the most stunnin' wench what I have ever seed,* Rowdy thought, his heart soaring with triumph. *Do some one of the ladies or gents catch me here, now, and kill me upon the spot for thinking what I be thinking, I willn't mind. No, I willn't, for I have already died and goned to heaven, and so I willn't even know if I be dead or not.*

With slow sinuous movements, Rowdy arched against the diamond panes. As black as the night behind him, darkness upon darkness, distinguishable only by the sparse glint of wavering flames upon window glass, he arched and turned and arched again. He stood upon his hind legs and stretched, his paws reaching high above the window latches, the brawny muscles of his back bulging with the effort of it. Then he turned with a studied indolence and glided like a shadow back onto the window seat.

*"Mrrrooow,"* he whispered to Lady Ellena, his tail whispering to and fro across the chintz. *"Mrrrooow."*

Lady Ellena sat openmouthed, her blue eyes glazed with passion, the elegant white fur between her exquisite shoulder blades rising upward of its own accord. *"Mrrrrrow,"* she managed shakily in answer to his most presumptuous and enticing suggestion, and in eight dainty steps and a most seductive bound she tossed all of her upbringing to the winds and lay down upon the chintz beside the reprobate.

# Five

Camelia stared at her open door in horror. It was never left open. All of the maids, and especially Priscilla, knew it was never to be left open. Her papa did not like cats in the house anymore than it appeared Lord Cottsworth did. Were Lady Ellena discovered to be prowling about where she was not wanted, Camelia's papa was like to raise a great hubbub over it and send Lady Ellena out to the green-houses, where he had long ago sent all of her brothers and sisters.

With a heart beating fast, Camelia hurried into her chambers and called immediately for Lady Ellena. She swept through the bedchamber, into the dressing room and further, into the little sitting room beyond. "Lady Ellena, do come here at once. This is not at all humorous. Oh, please come to me, dearest. I am not angry with you, whatever you have gotten into. I promise I am not." But Lady Ellena did not come.

Camelia searched beneath and behind and inside of everything in all three of the chambers, but there was not a sign of her treasured pet. With a tiny sob, she hurried back out into the corridor and stepped quickly along it, whispering Lady Ellena's name. She peered all about her, looking first one way and then the other. She checked under the small tables that lined the hallway, and into the shadowy spaces before the doors to the other chambers. She whispered Lady Ellena's name over and over.

"Whoa," cried Cottsworth in a hushed voice as he gained the landing at the top of the stairs. His two strong hands reached out to stop Camelia before she walked straight into him. "You cannot go looking one way and rushing another, my dear. You will go tumbling down these stairs again. I thought you had gone to your chambers, Camelia."

"Oh, Daniel, my darling is lost!"

"Lost? *Who* is lost?"

"Lady Ellena. Someone left the door to my chambers open just the slightest bit and she has wandered off."

"Well, but that is nothing to be upset about, Camelia. Cats do wander, do they not?"

"Not Lady Ellena. Never. Papa will not allow it. She has only been out of my chambers once since she was a tiny kitten."

"I see. And that was last evening when she tripped us upon the staircase, eh?"

Camelia nodded, gazing up at him, her eyes brimming with tears. "I know you do not understand, Daniel, but she is—Lady Ellena is like a child to me, and if Papa should discover her wandering about the house in the middle of the night—"

"Do not cry again, Camelia. I can see the tears getting ready to fall this very moment. Where do all these tears spring from so suddenly this evening?"

"I am not going to cry, Daniel. I am not the sort of woman who cries, and I never have been. Tonight in the corridor was merely—merely—an aberration."

"Good. Because even if your Lady Ellena is lost, my dear, she must be somewhere in this house, you know. And there is nothing to harm her here."

"No, but Papa—"

"Your papa is already in his chambers, Camelia. I am the last to come up. Only the servants are roaming about below. They will not betray Lady Ellena to your papa, eh?"

Camelia gave a tiny shake of her head.

"No, I did not think they would. Should one of them

come upon her they will return her to you without a word to your papa, will they not?"

Camelia nodded, swiping at just one tear that had begun to meander down her pretty cheek. The sight of her in such emotional disarray again discomposed Cottsworth to an extraordinary degree. "Oh, gawd," he moaned, and swept her into his arms where he hugged her tenderly against him. "Do not look so very sad, my dear. If you cannot feel safe until you have her with you, I shall help you to search for her, eh?"

"I—I could not ask you to—"

"You have not asked, Camelia. I have offered. Now, stiff upper lip, my little Trojan, and off we go. Have you knocked upon any doors as yet?"

"I do not wish to disturb anyone."

"No, of course you do not, but it is not so very late, my dear. The lamps are still lit all over the house, and the servants still at their duties. We will look through the rooms that stand open first. But if we do not find her in one of them, then we must begin to knock at chamber doors, or else you will not sleep at all tonight, will you?"

"No, I am certain I will not."

"Just so. Off we go, then."

Hand in hand they descended the staircase to the first floor and traversed the corridor, investigating each and every room which opened upon it. Not one glimpse of Lady Ellena did they get, but it seemed to Camelia that with each step of their search, Daniel altered. Her years-long impression of him as a cool, calm, aloof sort of gentleman—always proper, never ruffled—had been chipped away during their conversation in the corridor at dinner. And now, a previously unimagined Daniel began to rise up before her very eyes. He held to her hand tenaciously, not freeing it even when they encountered one or another of the servants going about the business of putting the house to rest.

He held it gently, firmly, all through their search of the first floor, abandoning his grip only when he found it, for some unfathomable reason, necessary to place a strong arm

about her shoulders or to tug her within the very circle of
his arms, which he did exactly three times—tugged her into
his arms. And each time he did, he gazed down at her in
the most uneasy silence with the most bewildering light in
his eyes. Twice he followed the line of her jaw with his fin-
gertip, and once, he leaned down and kissed her.

*It is not the kind of kiss Anne and Jane giggle over when they
read it in one of their endless novels,* Camelia thought as his
lips pressed hers in the middle of the well-lighted music
room. *But it is so very different from the cool, quick manner in
which he kissed me after I accepted his proposal.*

Camelia had never read about kisses herself, merely listened when her cousins Anne and Jane discussed the novels they had perused and the kisses the heroines of them
oft-times received. Camelia was positive that Daniel's kiss
could not be the same as those. Yet at this very moment,
Daniel's lips were pressing hers with a tenderness and a
warmth that made her tremble, and the very length of the
kiss was making her breathless, as well.

When at last their lips parted and they agreed that Lady
Ellena was not to be discovered upon the first floor, they
descended by way of the servants' staircase to the ground
floor and entered immediately into the kitchen, where
cook was busily banking the fires and the little scullery
girls were stowing away the last of the cleaned pots and
pans. There, upon the settle, two cats were dining in the
most splendid fashion, each with a plate of roasted fowl
set before them and a saucer of cream to the side.

Rowdy looked up at once, cream dripping from his thoroughly guilty whiskers. *Uh-oh!* he thought, his tongue licking nervously at his lips. *"Mrrrrup,"* he said, patting Lady
Ellena's paw.

Lady Ellena ceased at once to nibble daintily upon her
fowl and, following Rowdy's gaze, glanced haughtily over
her shoulder. *"Mrrrow brrrr,"* she purred upon seeing her
Cammy.

*"Mrrrrup brrrfpflgle-phst,"* hissed Rowdy, hunkering
down behind his dinner.

"It's that blasted cat," said Cottsworth. "Now tell me there is no black cat in this house, Camelia."

"Daniel, what—?" Camelia did not finish the thought, for Cottsworth had dropped her hand and was stalking angrily toward the black fellow. He reached down to seize the cat by the scruff of the neck just as Rowdy shot forward out of his crouch, between Cottsworth's legs, up over one of the kitchen chairs, skidded across the table top, and leaped for the doorway.

Cottsworth, thrown abruptly off-balance, reached out to keep from falling, pressed his hand against the hot oven bricks and gasped. "Ow! Dash it all!" he cried hoarsely but as quietly as he could, so as not rouse the household.

"Well, I never," breathed Camelia, running directly to Cottsworth and taking his hand into her own. "Polly, we must have some butter, quickly."

"Aye, miss," the cook replied, astounded to have them both in her kitchen, and at such an hour, but hurrying into the pantry as Miss Dunsbury led Lord Cottsworth to one of the chairs and pushed him down into it.

"But, Camelia, that reprobate is getting away."

"You sit right there, Daniel Orren Templeton. I am going to wet a cloth and place it on that burn and when Polly returns we are going to tend to the thing properly."

"No, but Camelia, it is merely a little burn. That blasted cat will be gone by the time—"

"I do not care. You are a deal more important than that cat. And it is not a little burn. Part of your skin, Daniel, is still upon the bricks."

*"Mrrrrr,"* observed Lady Ellena, climbing up into Lord Cottsworth's lap, placing her exquisitely dainty forepaws upon his cravat and licking with great goodwill at his chin. *"Mrrrrr."*


"I will find him," muttered Cottsworth the next morning, his attempt to tie his cravat hampered by the enormous bandage Camelia had wrapped around his hand.

"Should you like me to tie that for you, my lord?" Simmons asked quietly.

"Yes," sighed Cottsworth. "I expect so, Simmons. This is my seventh attempt, and I still cannot do the thing properly."

Simmons nodded, lifted a fresh cravat from the drawer, and set to work. "What exactly did you do to your hand, my lord, if you do not mind my asking?"

"Burned it."

"On the hearth, my lord?" asked Simmons, somewhat astonished, for Lord Cottsworth was generally not so clumsy as to do such a thing as that.

"No, upon the oven bricks in the kitchen, Simmons."

"In the kitchen, my lord? Last night, my lord?"

"Yes. Miss Dunsbury had lost her cat, you see, and—"

"You were chasing *another* cat, my lord?"

"Never mind, Simmons, just please tie the cravat."

Cottsworth felt like a small boy, having his cravat tied for him, but there was no help for it. Simmons had offered to replace the preposterously large bandage with a less ostentatious and more maneuverable one, but he could not allow Simmons to do that. Camelia had fashioned the bandage herself, and for some unfathomable reason, it seemed to him a betrayal to wear another.

*I* am *losing my mind,* Cottsworth thought, staring at himself in the mirror as Simmons fashioned a Waterfall. *But I have never before seen Camelia so—so—vulnerable. She might well burst into tears again if I do not appear at breakfast with her handiwork upon my hand.*

"There, my lord," smiled Simmons. "And you must be certain to wear your muffler, you know, when you go out this afternoon. And I have given your second-best beaver over to Perkins to keep with your greatcoat."

"When I go—ah, we are to go skating this afternoon."

"Indeed, my lord. You did wish to be reminded of it."

"So I did. Thank you, Simmons."

Cottsworth made his way carefully down the stairs, watching for cats—no telling when one or the other of them might wander beneath his feet again. Odd, he had never given one thought to cats in all of his life, and suddenly they had taken possession of a good one-third of his mind. "Impossible things," he muttered. "Expect I will need to discover a place for Lady Ellena at Cottsworth Manor, however. Expect Camelia will wish to keep her even once we are married."

He turned at the first floor landing, his hand upon the newel post and came to an abrupt halt. There, peering at him from the Dunsburys' breakfast room was a set of the greenest eyes he had ever seen. "You there," he called in a loud whisper, hoping not to attract anyone's attention. "Come here at once. No, do not go back inside. I would have a word with you, sir."

With slow, quiet steps, so as not to frighten the cat into another escape, Cottsworth virtually crept down the corridor and into the breakfast room. No one was at table. No one was anywhere at all to be seen, except Cottsworth's lithe and lanky black nemesis, strutting as audaciously as you please among the serving dishes upon the sideboard.


Rowdy was growing quite accustomed to this particular gent. Was, in fact, pleased to see the fellow. True, this gent did bellow a bit and stumble about like a one-legged swan, and go chasing through this fine house without the least direction, but as far as Rowdy knew, all gentlemen might act in a like manner. Stablehands did not, but stablehands were not to be compared with actual gentlemen. And on the positive side, now that Rowdy had had considerable time to ponder the subject, this fellow had been kind enough to step directly under the elm to break his fall; had just as much as invited him into the house; had somehow managed to distract an entire room full of searchers from looking behind the bass fiddle—well, he must have done, because Rowdy had heard him speak and then they had all departed the room and left him in peace. And only last evening, the gent had come down to see how Rowdy and Lady Ellena did in the kitchen.

*'Course I thought as how he come to chase me out of the kitchen,* thought Rowdy, pushing the cover from one of the silver servers with his paw and procuring himself a kipper, *but I were dead wrong. That I were. Did not come stompin' after me atall. Ought to have stayed an' finished m'dinner. Well, but these eats be just as good as what that lady did give me an' Lady Ellena last night. Just as good. Excellent, in fact.*

"Mrrrup brrr phst," he offered as Cottsworth advanced upon him. With a graceful arch of his back, a swishing of his tail and a subtle slink, Rowdy made his way further along the sideboard, knocked the cover from another silver serving dish, this time with his nose, placed his paws upon the cover and studied the beefsteaks piled high upon the dish. He sniffed each one of them; he cocked his head and studied them; he sniffed them again, then selected one from the middle of the pile, grasped the edge of it between his teeth and tugged it free.

Cottsworth stood spellbound. His intention had been to seize the beast, take it downstairs, and toss it out into the drive from whence it had come, but he had never seen such a thing in all his days as a cat removing the covers and helping himself to breakfast. And such a particular cat, too. A smile tickled at Cottsworth's lips. The kippers, apparently, were all of acceptable quality, but the beefsteaks at the top did not quite meet this scoundrel's standards. No, he must have one from the middle. Cottsworth remained a few feet from the sideboard and watched with rapt attention.

*Gent will like this one,* Rowdy thought proudly, tugging the beefsteak backwards through the maze of serving dishes. *This one be near perfect.* He set the beefsteak down a moment to get his bearings, spotted Cottsworth standing placidly at the end of the sideboard, picked up the beefsteak, turned about without knocking anything at all to the floor, and trotted to the gentleman, head high to keep the beef from dragging too much. Rowdy lay the prize temptingly down before Cottsworth. *"Mrrrow phrugle phst,"* he urged, giving the beefsteak a tiny shove with one paw in Cottsworth's direction. *"Mrrrow phrugle phst."* Then he trotted happily back to the dishes and procured himself another kipper.

"By Jove," murmured Cottsworth. "Is this for me, then? If you are not the most presumptuous brat I have ever seen. Inviting me to join you for breakfast as though you were the lord of the manor. Well, you will not be lord of this manor for long, my lad, because you are going back outside where you belong. Though I expect, since there is no one about to see us, you may finish that kipper and perhaps another while I have a cup of coffee. But then, you little reprobate, your social climbing days are ended, do you hear?"

*"Mrrrow,"* Rowdy replied, seated royally amongst the silver serving dishes and chewing contentedly.

*"Mrrrow,* indeed," Cottsworth muttered, placing the beefsteak upon a plate and leaving it upon the sideboard to be taken away, then pouring himself a cup of coffee and taking a seat at table. "There is only one cat allowed in this house, old man," he continued, "and it is not *you.*"

*"Burrrrr,"* Rowdy objected, noting that though Cottsworth sat at table, the excellent beefsteak did not sit before him. With careful steps, Rowdy abandoned his kipper, made his way down the sideboard once more and lifted the beefsteak from the plate. *"Murrgle,"* he managed, his mouth quite full, and he leaped from the sideboard, padded across the carpeting, leaped up upon the table and set the beefsteak directly on the cloth before Cottsworth. *"Rrrrr burrrr mrrrrow,"* he insisted.

"You cannot mean it," murmured Cottsworth, his eyes glinting with humor.

*"Mrrrrow-ow murgle-phst."*

"Yes, but I do not prefer my beefsteak covered with carpet fuzz and with little teeth marks already in it, you see."

Rowdy stomped back and forth across the table impatiently. What be wrong with the gent? It were the best beefsteak of the whole lot. Could it be that gents didn't eat beefsteaks? *"Yeow,"* he urged again, strolling directly up to Cottsworth and giving Cottsworth's arm a pat, *"Yeow mrrr."* Then Rowdy nudged at the beefsteak with his nose. *"Yeow mrrr,"* he said again. Clearly the gent were shy of acceptin' presents. That were it.

Cottsworth stared at the cat as it sat down on the cloth and studied him with the most hopeful look in its eyes. "Tarnation, but you are a one," he said. "You will have it that I eat your offering, eh?"

*"Brrrrup,"* Rowdy responded, tapping the steak a bit closer to Cottsworth with one paw.

"Oh, what the devil," chuckled Cottsworth, rising and crossing to the sideboard, where he procured for himself an empty plate, a knife, and a fork. "What the deuce can it hurt? I do not, however, intend to eat the bits with the fuzz on them or the teeth marks in them," he informed the cat as he sat back down, slapped the beefsteak onto the plate, and began to cut it. "I do hope you will not take offense because of it."

*"Rrrrr,"* Rowdy assured him, watching as Cottsworth placed the first bit of steak into his mouth and chewed. *He do like it,* Rowdy observed with a fair amount of joy. *He were just shy like.* Quite satisfied, Rowdy made his way back to the sideboard and his own kipper and began again to dine, purring contentedly.

"Well, and now you are happy, eh?" mumbled Cottsworth, thinking his cockloft must be completely empty, eating bits of a beefsteak urged upon him by a cat. "So be it. You have gained a truce for breakfast. But your time will come, my lad. As soon as this coffee cup of mine is empty, you are gone from this house. And I trust you will not give me a bad time of it, eh?"

*"Mrrrow,"* Rowdy responded, his green eyes wide with innocence, a bit of a third kipper dangling from his mouth. *"Brrrrmrrrow."*

# Six

Miss Dunsbury, her gloved hands gaining extra warmth from the fur muff into which they were inserted, skated slowly beside her fiancé upon the small lake that her papa had insisted be added to the grounds of Dunsbury Dells. All around them the members of the house party laughed and chased each other across the ice. Lady Anne and Jane had conceived that there should be a great race out to the island that sat in the middle of the ice and back again, and even their mamas and papas had decided to take part. Now, they were all attempting to gain their skating legs in preparation for the event. This was the first opportunity they had had to don their skates since last winter, and no one wished to race until they were certain that they could remain standing most of the way.

"It is to be a couples race. The winners are to be rulers for the rest of the day, and on through the ball tomorrow," Lady Anne informed Lord Easterly, who was her most favored beau, heir to Lord Hartselle, and had arrived only this very morning to spend Christmas with the Dunsburys. "And we are going to win, my dear Lord Easterly, just you wait and see."

"You think so, do you?" Easterly grinned boyishly.

"Indeed. Richard and Jane will be the ones to beat, of course, for they are brother and sister and have been skating together for years."

"You do not expect any genuine competition from your mama and papa?"

"Never. Papa and Mama?" Lady Anne giggled at the thought.

"Your uncles and aunts?"

"No, they are all much too old."

"I see. And what about Cottsworth and Miss Dunsbury?"

Lady Anne gazed at the two, who were apparently deep in conversation as they glided side by side across the ice.

"The paragons? I doubt that they will prove the least competition. Camelia skates only because it is the polite thing to do, and Lord Cottsworth, merely because she is his fiancée and he is obliged to accompany her."

"So you think," murmured Easterly.

"What do you mean?"

"Well, Cottsworth is from the north, my dear, and likely has skated all his life—earlier in the winter, and later into the spring than any of us. He will have the edge because of it."

"Pooh! He must skate with Camelia, my lord, and she will not wish to take the least chance that she might fall or her hair become disarranged, or her hat tilt in the wrong direction."

Easterly was not so certain of that. He was not very familiar with Miss Dunsbury. He laughed and took to his skates, tugging Lady Anne by the hand after him.

Camelia watched them go, but her mind was not at all upon them. Nor was it upon skating or the upcoming race. "You simply picked him up and put him out, Daniel?" she asked, gazing up at Cottsworth. "He did not scratch at you or anything?"

"Not a bit of it. Ready to go after his morning kippers. Merely wished to visit with your Lady Ellena for a time. Petted the little guy, I did. Never actually petted a cat before. Fine coat upon him, I must say."

"Daniel, you do not detest cats!"

"Eh? What? Detest cats? Whatever gave you that idea,

my dear? You do intend to bring Lady Ellena with you to Cottsworth Manor once we are wed, do you not?"

"Yes, I—"

"Just as I thought. Have I ever protested that idea to you?"

"No, but you would not, Daniel."

"Well, yes, that's so. And especially now that I come to see how attached to the puss you are. I would never think to forbid your Lady Ellena my house. Do not fear, Camelia. I shall not be like your father and insist that you confine her to your own chambers, either. You may count upon that. I shall grow accustomed to her, I am quite certain."


Rowdy stood upon the lake shore, as near the blazing fire that the Dunsbury stablehands had built for the skaters as he could possibly get without actually making himself too visible. He had hollowed a comfortable nest out of the leaves and pine needles amidst the underbrush, and if not precisely toasty warm, he was not cold, either. His admiring gaze was fixed upon Cottsworth as that gentleman glided easily along, Miss Dunsbury upon his arm.

*I reckon as I could do that,* Rowdy thought. *If the gent can do it, I reckon as I can. I only gots to figger out how. It do look like fun. I be tryin' it,* he decided after considerable deliberation. *And if it do prove as much fun as it looks, I be bringing Lady Ellena out here for to attempt the thing herself. It clearly be what the nobs do, and she'll be impressed with me for bringing her. But I expects as how I'd best be atrying of it first to be certain-sure I can do the thing.*

Not at all confident of his ability to glide over the water as he had seen innumerable ducks and now these nobs do, but certain that if the very awkward gent for whom he had developed a fondness could do it, why he could as well, Rowdy left his nest of leaves and padded around to a more deserted bit of the shoreline. Most cautiously, he placed one paw upon the ice.

*What the devil?* Rowdy wondered, thoroughly astounded.

He placed the paw upon the ice again and pulled it back again, curling it upward and studying it in amazement. *It be cold,* he observed, and licked at the paw, *but it bean't not wet like it oughta be. What the devil?*

The truth was that, think of himself what he might, Rowdy was not so very mature and wise as he might be. In fact, by the time Rowdy had been old enough to toddle off on his own last year, spring had come and the lake had already thawed, and since he had never encountered winter in his short lifetime, he had never before encountered ice, either. The very idea of it was beyond his imagination. The lake had always been a wet, slithery thing that a fellow could drink from, but today it was something entirely different.

*It be like ground,* Rowdy thought. *Jist like walking upon ground. That be why my gent be gliding along so well. He don't be doing like the ducks atall! He be jist walking.*

With a confident switch of his tail and a prideful cock of his head, Rowdy threw all caution to the winds and sauntered nonchalantly out upon the ice. And then one leg slipped one way and another leg another, and in a moment Rowdy's belly was rubbing against the frozen water.

*By Jove, my gent don't be jist walking,* Rowdy mused, attempting to gather his legs together and set them where they ought to be. *Devil if this don't be slippery stuffs like the mud what goes down into the valley when it rains. But I can be a doin' of it,* he assured himself silently. *I jist gots to be apracticin'. If I can do the mud, an' I can, then I can figger how to do this stuffs, too.*

It took him a mere three minutes of strong will and determination to accustom his paws to the ice well enough so that he could pad about on it without his paws sailing off in all directions at once. He could not achieve the gliding motion. Everything he attempted proved worthless. It occurred to him after ten long minutes of thoughtful experimentation that perhaps cats were not intended to glide about on this stuff. And his paws were cold, he noticed. Very cold. Freezing. Rowdy, who in the process of his many attempts had gotten a goodly way out upon the lake, turned around and dashed for the shore. Midway there, Cottsworth and Camelia came skating along the shoreline right in front of him. Rowdy sat back upon his haunches in an attempt to stop at once and avoid a collision, and suddenly he was sailing across the ice.

*I be doing of it,* he thought, amazed at the speed with which he glided over the frozen water, thoughts of Cottsworth and Camelia fleeing his mind completely.

"Camelia, hold on," Cottsworth said and spun both his fiancée and himself out of the way of the gliding cat. "By Jove, will you look at that! I have never seen anything like it."

"Oh, Daniel, it is your reprobate, is it not?" giggled Camelia in a most unCamelialike manner. "Look how he slides!"

Rowdy's ears filled with the wind; his fur sizzled; he had never felt such utter exhilaration in all his life. *I do be doin' it!* he rejoiced silently, too enthralled with the experience to so much as mumble a word. *I do be doin' it!* And then he hit the shore, his front paws touched the ground, and he somersaulted into the brush. Rowdy sat up and watched the world spinning about him in the most dizzying manner with a sprig of mistletoe behind one ear and a vague, happy smile upon his face.


"Ready, set, go!" called the colonel in his best parade ground voice, and they were off across the ice, skating as fast as they could toward the little island. The Earl of Riggensby and Lady Riggensby, her hand looped within the circle of his arm, took to the lead at once, but Lady Anne and Lord Easterly were a close second. The colonel and Mrs. Dunsbury came next, followed by Jane and Richard, who were saving the most of their energy for the race back. Mr. and Mrs. Dunsbury were solidly in fifth place and, just as Lady Anne had foreseen, Camelia and Daniel brought up the rear.

"Should you not like to win this race, Camelia?" Cottsworth asked with the most curious expression upon his face.

"I expect so," she replied, gazing up at him and wondering what thoughts lay behind such an expression. "But I have never won a race in all of my life."

"Never?"

"I am not made for racing, I think. Anne and Jane, one or the other of them, did always win at racing when we were young and entertained ourselves. They were never happier with me than when I lost some sort of competition to them."

"I see. And you, of course, wish to have them happy with you, especially during a Christmas house party."

"No."

"No?"

"Not so much as to lose the race on purpose, Daniel. I should like very much to win this particular race, but I do not know how to go about it."

Cottsworth grinned. "You merely skate, m'dear. Here, stop for a moment and—"

"Stop? We will be farther behind if we stop."

"No, no, it is a pause that will gain us time in the end, I promise you that. Now, begin on your left foot, Camelia, at the same time as I do so. Good, now step and glide and the right and glide. Now the left and glide. Now the right and glide." Cottsworth's grin increased as he matched his rhythm to hers. They glided by Camelia's mama and papa while Camelia was still looking down at her skates, attempting to step and glide in time with Cottsworth. She looked up, with some confidence that she had got the thing right, just as they came even with Jane and Richard, and Camelia was amazed to see that pair fall into the distance behind them.

"Do not go staring behind you, gudgeon, or you will throw us off," Cottsworth reminded her gently. "Look, the colonel and his lady have gone down. And apparently the earl and his lady have done likewise."

"Oh! There is only Anne ahead of us, with her Lord Easterly!"

"Just so," Cottsworth agreed, watching Camelia's cheeks grow red from the wind and excitement both. "But Jane and Richard will be catching us up if we do not keep at it. I can feel them closing behind us. We need not touch the island, eh? Just turn at its base and start back?"

"Yes, Daniel."

He was enthralled. In all the years that he had known Camelia, in all the years that he had known he would be her husband, he had never thought to attempt with her the thing he had just proposed so blithely—and that they were managing to do so prettily at the moment—to move forward together as one. We would do well to accomplish this same feat off the ice, Cottsworth mused, as they approached the base of the island and turned back toward the shore only seconds behind Lady Anne and Easterly, but with Jane and Richard close upon their heels.

"No, do not try to hurry any faster, m'dear," he drawled. "We are going sufficiently fast now, I assure you."

"We are? To win?"

"Indeed, for Lady Anne is taking too many steps and not allowing the ice to help her, you see. And Easterly will end by needing to pull her along, I think."

Camelia wished to reply to him, but she could not bring herself to speak. Oh, it was the most exhilarating experience! The wind roared in her ears, the ice slipped by beneath her skates, and Daniel skated beside her as though he were a part of her, his steps matching hers to perfection. Camelia's little fur hat tilted upon her head, and her honey curls slipped raggedly from some of their pins, but she did not take note. They were soaring past Lady Anne and Lord Easterly with the greatest of ease and before them lay the shore and the bonfire—and the win!

"Daniel, how are we to stop!" she shouted merrily as they neared the shore. "Are we to sail heels over head onto the ground like that silly kitten?"

"Only cease to skate when I say, Camelia," he replied, laughing. "I will stop both of us."

Cottsworth glanced back over his shoulder to discover that Easterly had indeed ended in needing to pull Lady Anne along and so had fallen a good distance behind. Richard and Jane were still up and coming, however, and surprisingly, the earl and countess were not far behind their son and daughter. "And by Jove, if your mama and papa are not closing upon Jane and Richard, as well," Cottsworth chuckled. "And Colonel and Mrs. Dunsbury are lying upon the ice laughing. Camelia, now!" he shouted, glancing back to see the shore upon them.

Camelia ceased to skate at once and found herself spun madly around, then lifted upward into Daniel's strong arms as the world twirled past the two of them. But in too short a time, their twirling came to a halt. Daniel set her skate-clad feet gently down upon the ice, his arms remained steadfastly around her and he bowed down to kiss those cold but truly smiling lips in triumph. Camelia did not at all know how to feel. "Congratulations," Cottsworth whispered, as the other skaters hissed to a stop behind them and to the side of them. "You have won the race, Camelia."

"*We* have won the race," Camelia whispered back, her heart still pumping at skating speed though her feet stood still.

"Well, I expect we shall have a dull time of it for the remainder of the day and all day tomorrow, too," sighed Jane into her brother's ear. "Think of it, to be ruled by Camelia and Daniel practically forever."

"Might not be so bad," murmured Richard, who was merely fourteen, had never been compared in anything to his Cousin Camelia, and did not at all think her a bad sort.

"Might not be so bad?" Lady Anne joined in the conversation. "Why, I expect we shall begin with the gentlemen, Richard, forced to involve themselves in a discussion of the merits of mangelwurzels and the ladies set to learning some new method of preparing lemon tarts!"

"Jolly good show, my dear!" called Mr. Dunsbury as he and Mrs. Dunsbury skated up beside their daughter. "Never thought to see the day my Camelia would win a race. Proud of you, m'dear."

"Just so, Camelia. My, but the two of you skated so wonderfully together."

"Did they not?" thundered the colonel. "Why, my lady and I were so impressed that we sat down upon the ice to watch them."

"Anthony," protested the colonel's lady. "You fell down upon the ice, sir, and pulled me down with you!"

"Indeed, but what was the reason we did not get up again? Was it not the prowess of these two lovebirds?"

"No, it was because we were laughing too hard to manage it," accused the colonel's lady with a wide smile for Camelia and Cottsworth both. "But we would have been enthralled by your prowess else, my dears, I do assure you of it."

"Well, and what will it be first?" asked the earl. "We have all had enough skating, I should think. Where to next? What must we be about? Cottsworth? Camelia?"

"I think we should return to the house and have some hot chocolate, not tea," proposed Camelia. "And Lady Ellena shall come down into the parlor to have a saucer of cream all her own."

"Oh, no," sighed her papa.

"George, you promised. Whoever wins rules the household for the rest of this day and through the ball tomorrow," hissed Mrs. Dunsbury in her husband's ear. "Camelia and Daniel have won."

"Yes, but a saucer of cream will not be the end of it."

"No, Lady Ellena shall have the run of the entire house until the ball is over. And those are merely the first of my wishes," Camelia declared.

She looked like a pixie the way she cocked her head just so. Cottsworth was quite beside himself to see her do it, standing in the circle of his arms with her hat askew, her muffler flapping, ringlets of honey-gold fluttering loose about her cherry-red cheeks, and her eyes sparkling with triumph.

"And you, Daniel?" asked Mrs. Dunsbury. "What will your first wish entail?"

"Me?" Daniel had not so much as thought about it. He gazed away from Camelia so that he might think of something besides this confusingly changeable but delicious woman in his arms, and saw a pair of green eyes peering out at him from the underbrush. "That cat," he said, pointing at a barely visible, yawning Rowdy. "I will have that cat brought to me, ladies and gentlemen. And quickly, too!"

"By Jupiter!" exclaimed Dunsbury, gazing in the direction Cottsworth pointed. "There actually is a black cat!"

# Seven

Camelia smiled still. It had been so very funny—all her aunts and uncles and cousins, Lord Easterly, and even her mama and papa, hopping and scrambling about through the undergrowth attempting to capture that cat. And Daniel had proved the most amusing of all. He had stood by the fire, with his arms folded securely around her, and doled out innumerable suggestions as coolly as you please to all them—and then he had cheered for the cat, who appeared to think it quite a wonderful game. Oh, but she had so enjoyed to be in that circle of his arms, and even more so because he had cheered for the cat. Camelia was beginning to suspect that deep inside Lord Cottsworth lay a good bit of mischief, if only one knew how to bring it forth.

*I find that I like mischief when I see it in Daniel,* she mused, gazing at herself in the long looking glass as Priscilla fastened the tapes of her deep brown, velveteen gown. *Good heavens, Daniel made me wish to be positively mischievous myself. I wonder if I could be? Perhaps I am the paragon Mama and Papa think me only because I have never thought to be anything else. I shall make an attempt,* she decided upon the instant. *I shall attempt to be funny and mischievous, just as I attempted to win the race, and see what results.*

"But how did that black rascal get into the house, then?" Priscilla asked, wishing to hear the rest of the tale. "He *is* in this house, miss. He and Lady Ellena are prowling about together everywhere. I have seen them with my own eyes."

"Yes, well, everyone came to us begging for mercy, and so Lord Cottsworth allowed as perhaps they need not catch the cat, after all, and we all started back up the path. And Lord Cottsworth called over his shoulder, 'We are going to the house, you reprobate, are you coming or not?' and in a moment that cat was tramping along at Lord Cottsworth's heels as though he made one of our party. You ought to have seen the look upon Uncle Anthony's face, Priscilla. And the look upon Mama's, as well. I thought they would both fall into whoops when they saw it."

"I never thought his lordship to be fond of cats, miss."

"No, I never did, either. I cannot think what has gotten into Lord Cottsworth to alter him so."

"The coming nuptials, miss," offered Priscilla, placing a lovely, multicolored shawl about Camelia's shoulders. "Gentlemen do seem always to grow odd the closer the time comes to wed."


"I cannot conceive what has gotten into them," Jane giggled to Lady Anne as they followed their mamas into the withdrawing room. "They are generally so deadly dull, but I have not had so much fun at dinner since I was in the nursery."

"You may think it was fun, Jane," Lady Anne protested, her tone betrayed by the sparkle in her eyes, "but *you* did not drop anything from the spoon when you passed it, and so *you* were not called upon to eat all that remained in that vile utensil."

"No, but I was the one who had to stand and recite the message that began with Lord Cottsworth and went in whispers through everyone at table," Jane grinned.

"I did like that game, Jane! Did not you? It felt so very rebellious, to be whispering in Lord Easterly's ear in front of Mama and everyone, and at table to boot."

"Yes, but how twelve people could turn 'Peas and carrots

must be vaguely related,' into 'Pecking ferrets are most sadly mated'—I should never have guessed it possible!"

"I wonder how we shall spend the remainder of the evening?" mused Lady Anne. "Dinner did bode well for a jolly time."

"Indeed. Lord Cottsworth will likely order the gentlemen into the drawing room after the first glass of port so as to begin some new game."

But he did not. Instead, a footman came and presented Camelia with a note almost as soon as the ladies had settled. "Now," it read. Camelia giggled to herself and tucked it away into her reticule. "Ladies," she announced, strolling to the center of the room, "the gentlemen have each lost a shoe, and as your ruler, I hereby command you to go and find the lot of them."

"The gentlemen, or the shoes?" chuckled Lady Riggensby from her seat upon the burgundy sofa.

"The shoes, Aunt Julia," smiled Camelia. "Though I ought to warn you of the rest of it."

"What rest of it?" asked Jane.

"Whichever gentleman owns the shoe that you find will become your partner in your performance for the evening."

"Performance for the evening?" queried Camelia's mama.

"It is my turn to wield the scepter, you see. And I have decided that everyone except Daniel and I shall perform some sort of entertainment this evening," Camelia explained.

"What sort of entertainment, my dear?" asked Jane's mama.

"That is to be decided by you and your partner. You must find a gentleman's shoe, and then take that gentleman and decide between you what talents you possess that can be put together to entertain us all."

All of this seemed quite tame, especially to Lady Anne and Jane. But then, what more could be expected of Camelia?

"If only Lord Cottsworth had continued to rule," sighed Lady Anne. "Why must he give over to Camelia?"

"Well, she did win as well," Jane pointed out. "I expect it is only fair, though it will be deadly dull."

But then the ladies set off through the house in search of gentlemen's shoes, and Lady Anne's and Jane's attitudes underwent a noticeable change. Upon finding first one shoe and then another, the ladies all attempted to identify to whom each one might belong. They began to laugh and scuffle over them, each wishing to procure the shoe of a gentleman whose talent matched her own. In the dining room, the gentlemen sat chuckling over their port and wagering which lady each of them would have, while each of them wiggled one set of toes covered only by stockings.

Lady Anne sang sweetly and wished to have Lord Easterly to play her accompaniment, but ended with her uncle, the colonel, whose only true talent was juggling apples. Mrs. Dunsbury could not remember which shoes her husband had worn, and triumphantly flourished the one she thought to be his, only to discover that it belonged to Lord Easterly—who played the pianoforte—which was particularly useless, because Mrs. Dunsbury had a tin ear and a voice like a frog, and her greatest talent was guessing at Jots and Jumbles. Jane, who recited poetry, ended with Mr. Dunsbury, who played the bass fiddle. The countess danced divinely, but got Jane's brother, Richard, whose only talent was bird calls. And the colonel's lady, Camelia's Aunt Nora, who could cut silhouettes of people with scissors and paper, was joined to the Earl of Riggensby, who had always claimed that the only entertaining talent he had ever discovered in himself was the ability to balance a stack of pie plates upon his head.

"It is going to be a long night, I fear," Cottsworth whispered in Camelia's ear as he took up residence beside her upon the silver and gold settee. "I do hope, my love, that you have asked for brandy to be delivered with our tea."

\* \* \*

*My love.* Even this spring, when he had set about courting her properly as was expected of him, Daniel had never called her "my love." Had he actually intended to say it this evening?

"And why am I pondering over such a thing?" Camelia asked herself sternly as she retied her night cap more comfortably beneath her chin, fluffed her pillows, and tugged another quilt atop herself. It was very cold, especially now that the fire upon her hearth had dwindled to mere glowing embers. "Lady Ellena," she called softly into the darkness, hoping to hear a soft purr and feel four little cat paws pounce upon the bed in response. Of course, it was a senseless hope. Ever since Daniel had invited that little black rogue into the house and Lady Ellena had been allowed to roam free, both had played least in sight.

Camelia sighed, stared up toward the canopy she could not see but knew by heart, and pondered. Had there really been knights upon white chargers willing to fight dragons for the love of a princess? She had never believed it to be so. She had never believed in romantic love at all. She had believed only that a young woman had duties to her family, society, and to the gentleman she married. She had spent all of her years learning those duties and doing her best to perform them properly. But now—now—something within her was changing, growing, bringing tears to her eyes over the stupidest things, making her giggle at the oddest moments, and causing her to long for Daniel to be more than the righteous, honorable, proper person he had always been.

"And today, he was," she whispered. "He said and did the nicest things. He was funny and mischievous and most endearing the whole evening long. I would have him love me," she said loudly and abruptly. "If there is such a thing as this romantic love, I would have Daniel to love me so. And I to love him in the same manner. But I do not know how. I have never thought to learn about such love. I only know how to be a proper, dutiful wife."

*"Mrrrrr,"* came a hushed little purr just then, and four

little cat paws pounced upon Camelia's stomach. *"Mrrrrr,"* Lady Ellena repeated, and she stalked upward until she could quite easily reach her Cammy's face. She scrubbed it thoroughly, licking at eyebrows and eyelashes, cheeks and chin, and then she stepped off onto the bed and kneaded herself a place upon the quilt at Camelia's side, considering the words she had overheard.

Cottsworth lay quietly beneath the counterpane and four extra quilts, wondering what had gotten into him. *I cannot so much as sit beside Camelia,* he thought, *without wishing to put my arms around her. Perfectly unacceptable behavior which she is right to frown upon, though I do not recall her frowning upon it. But surely she attempts merely to be agreeable by not scowling every time I do it. And to kiss her in front of the entire house party, as I did on the ice? What the devil has gotten into me? I feel so differently whenever I am near the girl than I was used to do. I cannot remember my palms ever perspiring, and most certainly my throat did never close, or my pulses pound. No, and I have never before been inclined toward such mischief as I set into motion this day. Never.*

*It is that cat,* he thought then. *It must be. Not one of these things occurred until that little reprobate came falling down out of the elm upon me. I was a perfectly cool and collected gentleman until then. And when he tripped me bringing in the Yule log, I vow I was never so peeved. And when I could not find him afterwards, and all the teasing began—Well, that set something to leaping about inside of me, and it has not ceased to wiggle and jerk and ache to this very moment. And Camelia—Camelia, of late—sets whatever that thing is to doing a veritable jig around my heart.* "What the devil?"

*"Mrrrr,"* responded an almost invisible Rowdy as he landed upon Cottsworth's stomach, stomped about upon it for a moment, then stalked fearlessly up Cottsworth's chest to scrub companionably at the gentleman's chin. *"Mrrrr brrr mrrglphst."*

"Do not do that," protested Cottsworth, shoving Rowdy

gently away. "That tickles. I did never realize that cats had tongues like sandpaper."

*"Mrrrow,"* Rowdy protested, sneaking in under the hand that shoved at him and scrubbing at Cottsworth's chin a bit more. *"Brrr mrrgurle mtzsphrst."* He ceased to scrub the chuckling viscount, then, and stepped down beside him to begin kneading at the pile of quilts. *"Mrrphluggle mrrfle mrrbrrphrst,"* Rowdy rumbled, deep in his throat. *"Mrrphluggle mrrfle mrrbrrphrst."*

"Why," Cottsworth responded, hesitantly patting that black head, "are you not settled down beside your lady love, old fellow? I returned you legitimately into this house so that you might succeed with her, did I not? That is what you were attempting to do that night in the kitchen, eh? Will she not have you, you old reprobate?"

*"Rrrrrr,"* Rowdy answered curling into a ball beside Cottsworth. *"Mrrrrr rrrrrr."*


Visions of Lady Ellena lulled Rowdy toward sleep. The seductive scent of her tickled at his nostrils. Her marvelous blue eyes opened wide and innocently before him, and her delicate pink nose demanded to have a lick placed upon it at once.

All afternoon and evening they had explored the house together. They had romped through the attics, chased each other back and forth through every open chamber upon the second floor, bounced upon beds, scrambled under chests of drawers, rolled about upon the thick fuzzy stuff, which Lady Ellena had informed him was called carpet. They had engaged in battle with the ball of red yarn that Lady Ellena's Cammy had given her, raced up and down the stairway to the first floor, shared an investigation of each and every thing lying about in the music room, sat in every chair they could find, and then padded down the backstairs to the kitchen, where cook, who had proved before to have a tender heart toward the pair of them, provided them a sumptuous dinner.

*I didn't never enjoy m'self so verimost much,* Rowdy thought dreamily. *She be not only exquisite an' allurin'. She be fun! It done broked m'heart to part with her. But she were right. I cannot be ignoring of my gent. He has done been kind to me, an' I be duty-bound to be kind to him in return. Only look at how quick he has goed off to sleep, just by knowing that I be here beside him to pertect him through the night. And maybe he will want to be my gent forever,* mused Rowdy hopefully. *Maybe.*

# Eight

Christmas Eve day dawned bright and brisk, portending success for the neighborhood ball that evening. Perkins and his footmen opened the doors between the Gold Saloon and the Silver Saloon, and everyone inspected the resultant ballroom. The ladies directed the placement of the furniture from both saloons around the verimost edges of the room. The footmen rolled up the carpets and carried them off to storage in the summer parlor. Both chandeliers were let down and the candles replaced in each.

"We have forgotten to decorate the wall sconces," the Countess of Riggensby observed, and dispatched some of the servants at once for more holly and pine boughs.

"And the chandeliers could do with a bit of ivy and mistletoe," added Mrs. Dunsbury.

Lady Anne and Jane and Richard attached red bows to some of the chairs and tables; Mr. Dunsbury and his brothers oversaw the erection of a platform in the northeastern corner of the Silver Saloon for the musicians, and the placement of the pianoforte upon it. A veritable bevy of maids decorated the platform's edges with silver paper and ribands of green and gold. And once the ivy and the mistletoe arrived, Cottsworth and Camelia took it upon themselves to decorate the lowered chandeliers.

In the dining room, Perkins oversaw the setting of the sideboards for the buffet supper. Family and guests would dine in their rooms upon trays this day, so that all would be in readiness for the evening.

Cook and her minions, who had risen at four, were deep in bread and pastries, fowl, fish, and beef, peas, carrots, and potatoes, crab cakes and caramel cremes. Dinner and supper alike had begun in the ovens and upon the spits. And in the midst of all, the Christmas pudding for tomorrow was in the making. Throughout the morning, each of the family members would enter to stir the pudding with a wooden spoon from east to west, in honor of the Three Kings.

In the family parlor, the remains of last year's Yule log had already been set out. At Dunsbury Dells the Yule log was always lit at midnight, upon the very twelfth stroke. And this year, all of the local gentry would crowd into the parlor to witness the event.

"You have been chosen to light the Yule log, you know, Daniel," Camelia informed Cottsworth as they twisted ivy and mistletoe through the sconces of one of the chandeliers. "Papa has decided that it must be you."

"Well, I have done it innumerable times at Cottsworth Manor without burning myself. I hope I shall have no trouble doing it here. I should not like to disgrace you, m'dear."

Camelia could not help noticing that she had become "m'dear" again, and was no longer "my love." He had not meant the least thing by those words last evening, then. He had called her so merely because of that odd mischievous mood that had overtaken him. "I have no fear of such a thing," she replied quietly. "You do never disgrace me, Daniel. You are always most proper."

"As are you," Cottsworth replied, distracted by Rowdy, who sat beside him, unfastening the ivy as fast as Cottsworth could fasten it. "Cease and desist, Rowdy, or I shall put you out."

"Rowdy? You call him Rowdy now?"

"One of the stable boys told me it is what they call him. He has lived in your stable for almost a year, Camelia."

"I did never know. My, but you are a splendidly hand-some rogue, Rowdy," she added, tickling Rowdy beneath his chin. "And such an intriguing face—complete with fencing scars. Here, sir, this will give you and Lady Ellena both something to do," and she rolled some silver paper into two balls and set the cats to batting them about.

"You are a paragon, Camelia," Cottsworth observed, and wondered what it was he had said as he watched the smile fade from her face.

Rowdy was not at all certain. The ball was in full swing and had been for some time. Lying beneath the silver and white striped settee, he had chosen to ignore the noise and rolled upon his back to play with the delicately curved mahogany leg nearest him, wrapping his paws about it, attacking it, batting at it enthusiastically. Lady Ellena glanced haughtily at him from the corner of her eye.

*It bean't atall a sure thing as it will work,* Rowdy thought, ignoring that disdainful glance and inserting his claws into the bottom of the settee to scoot himself in a circle upon his back. *Do it not work, likely my gent will not like me no more an' toss me out upon m'ear. Still, I have taked Lady Ellena for to be my heart's own love, an' I have promised her to help her Cammy.*

Lady Ellena fairly glowered at him as she lay primly proper a safe distance from the frollicking ruffian. Attacking the settee! Of all things! Although, it did look to be rather amusing. But this was not the time for it. Not at all.

"*Mrrowow,*" she demanded, reaching over to slap at Rowdy impatiently, demanding his attention.

In a gown of green taffeta and slippers to match, a sim-ple gold locket at her throat and a riband of green threaded through her honey-colored curls, Camelia joined Cottsworth upon the dance floor. Forming a set with Lady Anne and Jane, the Reverend Mr. Rogers and Sir Nathan

Berget, Cottsworth's groomsman, who had arrived at last to join the house party, they moved through the preset forms of a country dance. *Everything is going splendidly,* Camelia thought, pleased with the celebratory tone of the ball and most happy to have Daniel—who had danced with every matron and every single young woman in the room—at last beside her.

*And just see how everyone smiles and laughs,* she mused joyfully as she and Daniel came down the line. *I have never seen our neighbors so very jolly.*

"What the deuce is everyone laughing about?" asked Cottsworth quietly. "I dare say one of the gentlemen could not wait upon the wassail bowl and has added brandy to the punch."

"Daniel, Aunt Julia is waving at us from the settee and laughing even more vigorously. Is it my gown?" Camelia gasped abruptly, peering down at her bodice in fear.

"No, no, not your gown, my dear Miss Dunsbury," offered Sir Nathan as they passed him by. "Only look behind you. Cottsworth, glance at your heels." And Sir Nathan was off into a round of chuckles as was Jane, who stood opposite him.

"At my heels?" muttered Cottsworth and turned. "Well, by Jove!" he exclaimed. "Cease and desist at once, you little reprobate. You have everyone in this room laughing at us."

"What?" asked Camelia, and then she saw Rowdy, his tail high, his chin poised just so, his ears cocked forward, strutting down the line at Cottsworth's heels in time to the music. "How precious he is!" she exclaimed. "Only see how he dances, Daniel!"

"His dancing days are over," declared Cottsworth. As they reached the front of the line and parted, Cottsworth bent, scooped Rowdy from the floor, and thrust him at a passing footman. "Take him out of here," he ordered tersely. "No place for a cat. Trip someone."

*"Rrrrow!"* Rowdy protested and leaped from the surprised footman's grasp, landing gracefully upon the pol-

ished floor and scampering away through a virtual forest of dancers' legs.

"He has gone under the settee," mumbled Cottsworth as Camelia turned under his arm in the dance. "I expect he will not bother anyone under there."

"Of course not," Camelia replied. "He is quite out of the way, now. You must not be angry with him, Daniel. He is so very sweet, and only wished to be with you."

*"Mrrrrow,"* Lady Ellena said, rewarding the returning Rowdy with a beatific smile. He had begun the plan quite nicely, and she was pleased with him. She had divined that first night with him that, ruffian though he was, his word was to be depended upon, and she was not disappointed. All would go swimmingly if her Cammy and Lord Cottsworth cooperated as they ought.

Two sets later the strains of a waltz began and Cottsworth, the gold embroidery upon his green waistcoat shimmering in the candlelight, bowed once more before Camelia. Lady Ellena's eyes lit with anticipation. *"Brrrow mrrr,"* she instructed, nudging Rowdy in the ribs with her perfectly adorable pink nose.

Cottsworth led Camelia to the floor.

Rowdy squiggled out from beneath the settee, dashed across an open space, squooshed his way along beneath the gold striped sofa and two gilded chairs, and behind a cricket table.

Cottsworth swept Camelia into the waltz.

Rowdy bolted onto the floor, zipped through the maze of dancers and hurled himself at Cottsworth's knees just as that gentleman and Camelia spun into a turn.

Camelia gasped and missed her footing; Cottsworth clutched at her to save her and muttered a curse; together they tumbled to the floor. Rowdy sprinted up onto Cottsworth's lap, stood upon his hind legs, seized the twisted sprig of holly and mistletoe from Cottsworth's lapel, and dashed back into the midst of the dancers, who had all come to an abrupt halt, staring aghast at the fallen couple.

Once at the center of the startled dancers, Rowdy swaggered audaciously about in a circle, tossed the sprig of holly and mistletoe into the air and pounced upon it with commendable prowess. He then sat down upon his haunches, held it between his teeth, and grinned roguishly at Cottsworth and Camelia.

"Of all things! He tripped us on purpose, Camelia. I will box that little reprobate's ears!" Cottsworth growled, rising to his knees.

Camelia, sitting ignominiously upon the floor, took one look at Rowdy's cheeky grin and burst into whoops.

"You are gravely overcome, m'dear. And rightfully so," murmured Cottsworth, as he gained his feet and offered Camelia his hand. "Who can blame you?"

"N-no," laughed Camelia, refusing his offer to help her rise and laughing all the harder as she sat upon the polished floor. "I am not at all overcome. Oh, oh, Daniel, just *look* at him. He is so very funny!"

"I am looking at him, the brazen brat." Cottsworth's tone had lightened as he knelt back down beside Camelia. "Have you ever seen such cheekiness in all your life?"

"N-no, n-never." Camelia leaned her head against Daniel's shoulder, fairly trembling with laughter.

"Well, it is not all that humorous," offered Cottsworth, beginning to chuckle as his arms went around her and his heart rate increased considerably. "You are not hurt, Camelia?"

"N-no. Merely my dig-digni-dignity."

"Oh, is *that* what it's called?"

"Daniel!"

"Sorry. But you did say—and mine took a bit of a bruising, as well. Berget, do not just stand there, get my boutonniere back before the deuced reprobate eats it."

Sir Nathan grinned and made a grab for Rowdy, but the cat dodged nimbly to the right and dashed off with Cottsworth's boutonniere in the direction of the punch bowl.

"Got him!" cried Squire Mackleby, setting aside his cup of punch and pouncing upon the cat.

"No, no, he has squirted away from you, Mackleby.

Heading toward you now, Riggensby," advised the Reverend Mr. Rogers.

"I have him," the earl announced coolly, and then dove for the cat.

"Afraid not," observed Cottsworth, as Rowdy cut back across the ballroom and zoomed behind the draperies that covered one set of French doors.

Mrs. Dunsbury strolled confidently to the draperies and tugged them aside. In a flash, Rowdy was off again, dashing the length of the ballroom, out through the door and up the corridor, in the direction of the supper room.

"He is heading for the food," Cottsworth shouted. "I have seen him amongst serving dishes before. Pray God the crab cakes are not yet upon the sideboard." Taking Camelia's hand, he tugged her to her feet and literally dragged her from the ballroom, she giggling behind him and struggling to keep pace.

"After them!" shouted Squire Mackleby with an enthusiastic wave of his hand. "To hounds! To hounds! Tally ho the cat!"

"Charge!" bellowed the colonel, thoroughly enjoying the new turn the festivities had taken.

"I never," giggled Lady Anne, hurrying from the ballroom upon Lord Easterly's arm. "I expect I ought to apologize to you for such unseemly conduct."

"No," Easterly replied. "For such a lark as this? Onward, my lady! Into the fray!"

Rowdy swerved into the dining room, skidded across the hardwood floor as far as the carpeting, somersaulted, and soared off in the direction of the largest sideboard. *Most likely willn't do the trick*, he thought as he landed agilely amongst the serving dishes. *Most likely be out upon m'ear in a moment. Still, it do be devilish fun. Ah, there be m'lady just where she said, an' right on time.*

*"Mrrrow,"* Lady Ellena greeted him from just beside the doorframe with poised assurance, the light in her beautiful blue eyes sending a veritable shiver through Rowdy from the tip of his nose to the tip of his tail.

At that very moment Cottsworth and Camelia veritably flew around the doorframe from the other side. Lady Ellena launched herself directly in front of them. "Watch out!" cried Cottsworth, attempting to stop upon the instant.

"Lady Ellena!" cried Camelia, swinging in front of Cottsworth and grabbing both his shoulders to keep from stepping upon her darling. For a moment in time, they clung to one another just so, off-balance and seeking secure ground, but it did them not one bit of good. Down they went again, this time with Cottsworth flat upon the floor and Camelia on top of him.

"Both of those cats will get their comeuppance!" Cottsworth exclaimed. "No, they will not," he revised on an amazed intake of breath as he gazed up into Camelia's once cool blue eyes. They blazed with laughter, and with something else entirely. "Camelia?" he whispered hoarsely as she lay soft, pliable, and thoroughly enticing atop him with her lips provocatively parted, her cheeks a most alluring pink, and her honey-blonde curls tumbling seductively down around her face. She breathed down at him in wonder at the sudden passion roaring through her. She moved against him, and Cottsworth's entire body erupted into flames.

"My gawd, but you are glorious, Camelia," he whispered hoarsely, his arms encircling her, pulling her closer to meet her parted lips with hungry, passionate kisses. "You are a regular hoyden," he gasped between one kiss and another. "A veritable minx. A temptress beyond resisting. You will be my paragon and my paramour as well when we are married, Camelia. I vow it."

"No," Camelia whispered back, raining kisses upon him in return. "I do not think I ever wish to be a paragon again. Oh, Daniel, you do love me, do you not? Love me enough to fight a dragon for me?"

"A dragon? Two of them! Six of them! Love you, Camelia? I love you, want you, need you, you gudgeon. You are my heart's burning desire."

"Well, I'll be—" Mr. Dunsbury exclaimed as he maneuvered his way to the front of the throng rapidly gathering upon the threshold to the supper room.

"Mind your language, George," interrupted Mrs. Dunsbury, giving her husband's arm a squeeze.

"Will you look at that, Dunsbury," declared the squire, studiously ignoring the pair lying upon the floor before his very eyes. "Two cats, sitting bold as you please amongst the serving dishes. And they have knocked the cover off of that one, too."

"Hush, Neville," murmured Mrs. Mackleby. "You will betray our presence to the lovebirds."

"Lovebirds?" The squire cocked an amused eyebrow. "There are birds in the supper room, as well?"

"I told you Daniel was not so perfect as you thought," Sir Nathan whispered to Jane, moving into the supper room, her hand held tightly in his. "I have known him forever, and he is not such a paragon as everyone thinks."

"I expect not," giggled Jane, poking at Camelia's shoulder with one finger. "But I would have wagered that Cousin Camelia's perfection could never slip." Jane poked again.

"Oh!" cried Camelia, suddenly become aware of just where she and Daniel were, and what they were doing.

"Everyone, but everyone, is watching you from the threshold, Camelia," Jane informed her, smiling.

"Except Miss Dunsbury and I, who are watching you from right here, Cottsworth," Sir Nathan added. "Need some help to untangle yourselves—to attempt to stand up and look somewhat respectable?"

"I expect we had better," sighed Cottsworth. "Where's that blessed reprobate?" he added when at last he and Camelia had safely gained their feet.

"There," laughed Jane, pointing, as the rest of the guests crowded exuberantly into the room. "He is sharing our crab cakes with Lady Ellena, and using your boutonniere as a centerpiece."

"Better he should have held that mistletoe over our

heads," laughed Cottsworth, his arms going 'round Camelia. "It would have given us an excuse for our reprehensible behavior."

"Oh," Sir Nathan replied, his eyes brimming with mischief, "you require an excuse?" He strolled to the sideboard and plucked the boutonniere from the crab cakes. "You will not mind if I borrow this, eh?" he asked Rowdy. "Your fellow reprobate has need of it, my friend." Whereupon he crossed back to Cottsworth and Camelia and held it above their heads. "Must kiss the girl at least one more time, Daniel," he urged. "Cannot let this mistletoe go to waste."

*"Mrrrphgle mrrzphstf!"* Rowdy agreed heartily, glancing slyly at his idiotically smiling gent.

*"Brrrr mphzphstf!"* Lady Ellena added fervently, giving her reprobate's head a loving whack and stealing what remained of his crab cake.

# A Place
# by the Fire

Regina Scott

To my grandmother, Ruby Ellen Harris, for being
the kind of courageous, loving woman the
countess was trying to be.

# One

Miss Eleanor Pritchett, teacher of literature at the Barnsley School for Young Ladies, slid into place along the wall of the headmistress's office, tucking her light brown hair up into the black mop cap all the teachers wore. She had never liked the shapeless black bombazine uniform of the school staff, but now she was thankful for the way it hid the fact that her slender chest was heaving after her dash from the second story. As it was, Eleanor arrived just in time to hear Miss Martingale's nasal voice proclaim, "What is this creature?"

So it was true. Dottie had been caught with the kitten. Eleanor knew she should have dissuaded the farmer who brought the eggs from giving the tiny bundle of fur to the girl, but the gleam in Dottie's dark eyes had been too precious to waste. Wincing at the thought of the consequences of that act, Eleanor slipped a little farther along the back wall until she bumped into the quivering form of the school's art teacher. A quick look at Miss Lurkin's pale, narrow face confirmed Eleanor's suspicions about who had had the misfortune of finding the kitten, and the lack of foresight to keep from mentioning it to Miss Martingale.

From her new position, Eleanor could see around the two, high-backed leather chairs that stood in front of the massive, claw-foot walnut desk. Dottie stood between chairs and desk, her black mourning gown of fine silk making her look thinner and more fragile than usual. Behind the desk, Miss Martingale's considerable bulk was trembling with ill-suppressed indignation, one gloved hand holding aloft a small, squirming black kitten, who hissed with equal indignation.

"I believe you have been taught to answer when spoken to by your elders," Miss Martingale said sharply. "But I shall repeat myself just this once. What is this creature?"

Dottie raised her head to meet the outraged headmistress's gaze, and Eleanor had to stifle a shout of triumph. There was determination in those chocolate eyes, and not fear. Since returning to the school three months ago, the girl had never looked more like a daughter of a peer than at that moment. All this furor would be worth it if it brought the child out of the unresponsive cocoon she had built since her parents had been killed in a boating accident in Naples.

Miss Lurkin obviously didn't have the stomach for the tension that coiled through the room. "It's a cat," she burst out. Then, as Miss Martingale's cold blue glare turned her way, she shrank into herself. "That is," she ventured timidly, "I believe it is a cat. Is it not?"

Eleanor rolled her eyes. Nothing incensed Miss Martingale more than idiocy, except perhaps outright rebellion.

"To be sure," Miss Martingale sniffed. "It is a cat." The wrinkle of her long nose and the sneer on her thin lips made it obvious what she thought of cats. The kitten spat at her.

"To be precise," Eleanor felt compelled to put in kindly, "it's a kitten. And a rather tiny one, at that."

The icy gaze swept over her, and she dutifully lowered her own. As an employee of the Barnsley School, she owed Miss Martingale her loyalty. Having been the recipient of one of the woman's few bouts of kindness, she owed her far more. She would be forever grateful that the taciturn headmistress had agreed to take in an orphaned twelve year old whose soldier father had died without even leaving enough to pay for her schooling. She was even more grateful that an allowance from the school's patrons, the Darbys, had allowed that child to learn and ply a trade for nearly fifteen years. And all Miss Martingale and the Darbys had asked in return was complete and total submission.

Until the seven-year-old Lady Dorothea Darby had returned to the Barnsley School, Eleanor had been more than
willing to do anything Miss Martingale asked. Since then,
she had had more than one infraction. In fact, the last week
she had had to try to be on her best behavior to ward off
Miss Martingale's suspicions. Still, it certainly wasn't Dottie's
fault. Eleanor knew she saw too much of herself in the girl's
sadness at being orphaned. She had done everything in her
power to ease the child's pain, sneaking sweetmeats from
the kitchens, taking Dottie on walks about the fields near
the school on her day off, and staying with the girl when she
had nightmares. It was only for a time, Eleanor had assured
herself and any of the other teachers who noticed. It wasn't
something worthy of Miss Martingale's attention. If they all
just kept quiet, Dottie would be herself again in no time.

And the plan had been working. Dottie would never have
been able to stand before Miss Martingale's fury three
months ago. Now she stood so tall that Eleanor's heart
swelled with pride. If only she could get Miss Martingale to
see how the girl had blossomed, and not see the act as full-
scale defiance!

"Thank you for that clarification, Miss Pritchett," the
headmistress sniffed. "However, the size of the creature is
immaterial. We have a policy at this school that forbids the
keeping of pets, including cats, of any size. I am sure you
are familiar with that rule, Miss Pritchett."

Eleanor fixed a smile on her face and kept her tone pleasant. "Of course, Miss Martingale. Dottie would never seek
to break one of the school rules, would you, dear? You
weren't actually keeping the kitten, I'm sure. You were just
showing the other children, and were going to return the
kitten to Farmer Hale in a day or so."

Even though Eleanor was sure Dottie remembered the
agreement they had made, she smiled encouragement
when the girl glanced quickly back at her, biting her lip.
Beside Eleanor, Miss Lurkin bit her own lip. Miss Martingale
frowned.

Dottie turned to face the headmistress again. "No," she

sighed. "I wasn't going to give him back. I want to keep Jingles."

Eleanor nearly groaned aloud. The request was impossible. Dottie could only be disappointed, and Miss Martingale could only be made angrier. She wracked her brain for a way out of the mess.

Miss Martingale's eyes flashed fire. "Then you admit, Lady Dorothea Darby, to purposely breaking the rules of this school?"

Eleanor held her breath. The delicate black head rose a little higher. "Yes, Miss Martingale, I do so admit."

Eleanor exhaled and closed her eyes. They were done for. She had no idea how strict a punishment Miss Martingale would exact for outright disobedience, but it would be stinging. Miss Martingale had an infallible belief in the structure of life. Everything and everyone had a place, a role to play. Keeping that place was an honorable pursuit. Anything else condemned one to the fires of hell.

Eleanor opened her eyes in time to see Miss Martingale thrust the kitten at Dottie, who clutched him to her. Jingles's fur was raised, his ears were laid back, and his yellow eyes glared. The white, bell-shaped patch of fur at his throat, which had earned him his name, stood out, as did the pale oval of Dottie's determined face. Eleanor remembered suggesting that the girl name him Alexander the Great, for from the first he had made it clear he intended to explore and conquer the world. Now, like Dottie's courage, his tiger's heart could only get them in deeper trouble. Eleanor wanted nothing so much as to scoop them both up in her arms and take them out of the room before doom could fall.

"I'm sorry to have to do this," Miss Martingale sighed with martyr-like patience. "The Earl of Wenworth and the Darby family have always been very generous to this school: donating the school grounds out of the Wenworth estate, inviting the staff for an annual tea, encouraging the students in their studies." She fixed Eleanor with a baleful glance.

"Miss Pritchett has benefitted from such generosity a number of times."

Eleanor felt the color rushing to her cheeks. She did not need Miss Martingale's reminder of how much the Darbys had done for her. She would never forget the summer they had asked her to help the second son, Justinian, study. It was she who had learned—how it felt to love, and how to remember her place.

Dottie pulled the kitten closer and bowed her head. "My grandmother says the Darbys are known for their kindness. If my father was alive, he'd let me keep Jingles."

Eleanor's heart went out to the girl. She gazed at Miss Martingale imploringly. "It is a very little kitten, Miss Martingale. Perhaps, since Dottie is still in mourning . . ."

Miss Martingale slapped her hand down on the desk. Everyone else in the room jumped. Jingles started hissing again. "The rules must be obeyed, by all students, at all times. Anything less is anarchy, and I will not condone anarchy. This kitten is obviously a symptom of a much larger rebellion, a rebellion that appears to have infected you as well, Miss Pritchett. You have left me with no choice but to take the creature out and drown it."

Eleanor gasped. "Miss Martingale, no!"

"No!" Dottie cried, stumbling back out of reach. "No, I won't let you!"

Miss Martingale sniffed. "Lady Dorothea, you appear to have been spoiled terribly. We do you no service by allowing you to continue this way."

Eleanor felt a pang of guilt. If Dottie was spoiled, there was only one person to blame. She took a deep breath. Perhaps there was a small chance that they might get out of this unscathed. And it all depended on how much fifteen years of loyal, unstinting service meant to Miss Martingale. "Please don't blame Dottie, Miss Martingale. She is only being belligerent to shield someone else. The kitten doesn't belong to her. It's mine."

Miss Lurkin collapsed against the wall. Dottie turned to stare at her, wide-eyed. Jingles growled.

"I see." Miss Martingale nodded. "Yes, that does make a difference. You may go, for now, Lady Dorothea. We will speak again later. Please release that creature into Miss Pritchett's care."

Solemnly, Dottie handed over Jingles. Her dark brows were knit in concern, but Eleanor smiled encouragement at the girl's trusting gesture. Dottie dropped a less-than-respectful curtsy to Miss Martingale and slipped toward the door. Jingles twitched in annoyance in Eleanor's grip.

"As for you, Miss Pritchett," Miss Martingale intoned, "you may collect your things. You are dismissed."

Eleanor stared at her, feeling as if her stomach had dropped to the soles of her feet. The kitten sank its claws into the bombazine to protest being held so tightly, but she barely noticed. "What?" she managed in a whisper.

"You know very well how I feel about disloyalty. You have either brazenly ignored the rules of this school and the safety of its residents, or you have shamelessly cozened the girl against my expressed wishes. You had an earlier infraction involving the Darbys, one I chose to overlook against my better judgment because the late earl himself pleaded your cause. You do not have him to hide behind this time. You are dismissed. The matter is closed. Mrs. Williams will have the pay due you through today ready by the time you are packed. Good-bye."

"But—" Eleanor started. Miss Martingale turned her broad back on her. Eleanor looked toward Miss Lurkin in appeal, but the art teacher refused to meet her gaze. Jingles nipped her hand. Absently, she disengaged him and settled him more gently in her arms. She wandered to the door in a daze.

Dottie was waiting for her in the drafty corridor. She flung her arms around Eleanor's waist and hugged her tight. Jingles mewed in protest at the additional pressure. "Oh, Miss Eleanor, I'm so sorry! I heard what she said! What will you do?"

Eleanor reached around the kitten to stroke the girl's trembling black curls. She should be furious with the child's former willful display, she was sure, but somehow she couldn't be angry with the heartfelt sobs. "It's all right, Dottie," she lied. "I'll be fine. You mustn't worry."

Dottie let go of her, sniffing back tears. "But where will you go?"

"I'll find another post, I suppose," Eleanor replied with far more assurance than she felt. Her mind whirled at the thought of leaving Barnsley. She'd lived in the school since her widowed father had brought her there at six years of age. She had never been farther away than the village of Wenwood, some eight miles over the fields. She knew the city of Wells was reported to be about thirty miles in the opposite direction. Perhaps that was where she should go. There must be several girls' schools there, or someone who needed a governess or nanny. It struck her suddenly that worse than her own situation was Dottie's. The headmistress would be sure to withdraw all privileges, and none of the other teachers would dare give Dottie the attention she needed. The child was once more alone at the school. And this time there was nothing Eleanor could do about it.

"Do other schools accept kittens?" Dottie asked hopefully.

Eleanor glanced down at the black kitten who wriggled in her arms. Jingles glared up at her in high dudgeon. Smiling at his utter ferocity, she bent to let him free on the hardwood floor. He scampered away, losing his footing with every other step on the polished wood, until he fetched up against the far wall. There he sat, as if he had intended to arrive at that position all along, and began licking his paw. The king was graciously allowing his subjects a moment to converse in private before attending to his needs. They should be suitably grateful.

The antics of the eight-week-old kitten—the runt of the litter Farmer Hale had called him—had never failed to raise Eleanor's spirits. Now her smile faded into despair. How was she to find a position with no recommendation, limited funds, and a small black kitten?

As if she had followed Eleanor's thoughts, Dottie spoke

up. "You must take him to my Uncle Justinian. He'll know what to do."

Eleanor started. Face Justinian again? She wasn't sure she had the strength. She had carefully avoided the public sitting room whenever he called on Dottie. Even ten years later, she had not forgotten the shy, gentle young man she had fallen in love with. His father, the earl, had made it clear when he had sent her back to the school in shame that she had no right to tell his son good-day. She could hardly go now and ask him something as important as what to do about her future. It had been all she could do to convince the late earl to keep from having her turned out then and there for her brazen behavior. A penniless nobody, daring to love a Darby? Perish the thought! "Somehow I don't think your uncle can help me, Dottie," she replied as gently as she could.

"Uncle Justinian helps everyone," Dottie corrected her. "He might even have a post for you, himself."

"Your uncle is still a bachelor, I believe," Eleanor tried tactfully. "He'll hardly have use for a governess or a nanny."

"Take Jingles to him," Dottie insisted. "He'll know what to do."

*Perhaps he might, at that,* Eleanor thought suddenly. At the very least, the staff of Wenworth Place might be prevailed upon to keep the kitten for Dottie, leaving Eleanor with one less impediment to finding another post. She could go to the kitchen door. She wouldn't even have to see Justinian. And perhaps she could mention to Mr. Faringil, if he was still the butler, that Dottie might need a different school after her confrontation with the volatile headmistress. Perhaps she could even convince him to ask Justinian to bring the girl home. It would certainly ease her mind knowing that Dottie and the kitten were well cared for.

She bent and hugged the girl. "All right, dear. I'll take the kitten to your uncle. Don't worry. Everything will come out fine."

# Two

Justinian Darby, the recently declared ninth Earl of Wenworth, stared at the stack of papers his steward had brought him and sighed. He couldn't help glancing at the credenza next to the doors to the patio. Raindrops were reflected in the cover of a small, leather-wrapped portfolio. With the work before him, it would be days if not weeks before he could touch his writing again. He ran his hands back through his hair and bowed his head. How had his brother managed all this and still found time to gallivant all over the Continent? The answer lay before him: his brother had sadly neglected the estates, and now Justinian was left to pick up the pieces.

It was hard to be angry with a man who had died in his prime with his devoted wife beside him. He missed Adam and Helena terribly. But the truth of the matter was that Adam had had the training and personality to be a great earl, had he chosen to be. And Justinian had the disciplined mind and introspective personality to be exactly what he had planned to be, a scholar. It was duty that found him over a hundred miles from his beloved Oxford, wrestling with matters of enclosures and harvests rather than the lofty realms of literature and philosophy.

Everywhere he looked he found more problems awaiting his attention. His younger brother, Alexander, had refused to resign his commission after the war, staying on in France while their mother despaired of seeing him again.

His youngest brother, Jareth, had set himself on the path of a wastrel, and just as firmly refused to be pried from the pleasure dens of London. Neither had even returned home for Adam's funeral. He could count on them only to provide additional headaches.

His niece Dorothea seemed unsettled in the Barnsley School, although he understood from his mother that the girl had been happy there before her parents died. The seven times he had visited over the last three months, he had noted only minor improvements, all of which could be attributed to the child's fondness for her literature teacher. The headmistress had been adamant that it was inappropriate for him to personally thank Dottie's "Miss Eleanor," as the woman was only doing her job. However, even with her thoughtful efforts, Dottie still appeared wan and depressed to him. She had never spent much time with her parents, yet she seemed to be missing them more than he did.

Upstairs, his mother was nearly an invalid, and relied on him for all companionship. He had attempted to get her to hire someone, but she told him in no uncertain terms that she vastly preferred the company of family to that of strangers, however kind or well trained. Dr. Praxton, the local physician, assured him she was healthy enough to rise from the bed if she chose, yet she refused, and nothing Justinian had said or done since becoming earl had persuaded her otherwise.

From the few reports he had uncovered in the little-used library, the estate was also in dire straights. The levees on the River Wen, which flowed along the southern boundary, were crumbling. Unless he devised a plan to shore them up, his crops would be ruined and all his tenants would be flooded from their homes next spring. Of course, that might be a blessing, as these latest reports showed that the houses were in ill repair and barely habitable. His logic told him there were simply too many tasks for one man. A smaller part of him urged him to flee for the halls of Oxford and never look back.

Someone moved silently into his peripheral vision. He did not have to look up to guess it was Faringil, his butler. He stifled a sigh, trying once again to find an ounce of patience for the man. Faringil had the dignity and bearing of the butler to a great earldom. His thick hair, now a snowy white, was always pomaded in place. His posture was erect, his gaze serene. When he looked down his bent nose and set his thin lips together, the other servants scurried to do his bidding. However, Justinian had only recently noticed how utterly deferential the man could be. Faringil entered a room as if he tiptoed toward a deathbed, gliding to a spot just to one corner of his master and waiting patiently to be noticed. He paused respectfully before speaking, and waited to be granted permission to continue. Both habits only served to further Justinian's frustrations. "Yes?" Justinian dutifully asked, suppressing another sigh.

"Sorry to disturb you, my lord."

Justinian waited. The butler waited, as well. Justinian grit his teeth and took a deep breath. "What is it, Faringil?"

"There is a woman at the door," the butler replied calmly. "She claims to be from the Barnsley School."

A sense of foreboding struck Justinian, and he rose, dreading his butler's next words. "Has something happened to Dottie?"

"I do not believe so, my lord," Faringil replied with measured calm, and Justinian felt himself relax. The butler's next statement only served to make him tense again. "However, the woman appears to be ill, and isn't very coherent."

Justinian frowned. If it were merely another request for donations, he would have had Faringil refer the woman to his steward. However, as Faringil wasn't certain the woman wasn't here about Dottie, he should probably handle the matter himself. "I'll see her, then. Is she in the sitting room?"

Faringil wrinkled his nose, making him look a bit like a rabbit. "Certainly not, my lord. I would not bring an ill person into the house, not with her ladyship's delicate constitution."

"My mother is safely in her room, a story above us," Justinian replied. "Somehow I doubt any infection could pass through the floor to reach her."

"Yes, my lord, of course," Faringil sniffed, but Justinian knew the butler was placating him. Annoyed more than he should be, he allowed the man to lead him back through the corridors to the kitchen, where the woman waited.

Eleanor huddled miserably on the oak bench that stood in the many-windowed breezeway between the back coaching yard and the kitchen. For the fourth time since setting out from the Barnsley School she wondered what had possessed her to agree to take the kitten this far. True, it was only five miles across the fields from the school to the house's rear door, but she hadn't reckoned on the rain. She also hadn't reckoned on the sodden state of the fields, or the fact that she had to walk all the way with all her possessions in a carpetbag Miss Lurkin had been persuaded to part with and carrying a black kitten who only wanted to escape. He had actually slipped through her grip twice, forcing her to drop the bag and prevent him from conquering the muddy grain. As a result, she was soaked, filthy, and thoroughly tired.

Mr. Faringil had not recognized her, which she supposed was something to be grateful for. Unfortunately, the man had also been unable to comprehend what she was asking, and had gone off to seek assistance. To make matters worse, she seemed to have developed a sudden case of the sniffles.

Jingles poked his head out of her cloak, where she had put him for safekeeping, and rubbed his wet head against her chin. She sneezed six times in rapid succession. For once, she succeeded in startling the little tyrant, sending the kitten cowering back under her cloak. Unfortunately, the sneezes did her no more good, leaving her feeling bleary-eyed and exhausted.

There was a movement in her peripheral vision, and she grabbed her bosom to make sure Jingles hadn't gotten farther than her waist. She was certain kitten claws could do no damage to the flagstone floor at her feet, but she wasn't going to take any chances that Lord Wenworth might take the kitten in dislike. She felt the comforting wiggle in her lap, and patted him through her sodden cloak.

Someone cleared a throat. Looking up, she saw that Mr. Faringil had returned with a tall gentleman. Even though her eyes refused to focus, her heart told her who it was. Clutching the kitten to her, she rose and dropped an unsteady curtsy. Her only hope was that he might not recognize her any more than the butler had.

Justinian stared at the apparition before him. From the light brown hair escaping her limp straw bonnet to the hem of her serviceable brown cloak, she was dripping wet. Her half boots and the bottom quarter of the cloak were caked with mud and leaves, and dead grass flecked her slender figure to her waist. Although she kept her head bowed as she rose from her curtsy, he could hear her sniffling, and had no doubt that her eyes would be as red as the pert nose he had glimpsed.

Eleanor could not resist a quick glance up at him, blinking her eyes to focus them. She had always thought Justinian Darby handsome. Ten years had hardened the youthful face into clean lines of maturity, but the heroic aspects that had attracted her in the first place were still there. He had shared her love of literature, and she remembered thinking that he embodied so many of the traits common to the heroes of old. His hair was as tawny and thick as Samson's must have been. His brow was as wide and as thoughtful as King Arthur's had surely been. His eyes were a gray as deep and sharp as those she imagined had belonged to Merlin. His shoulders were broad, his waist narrow, and his legs long enough to resemble any god in the Greek pantheon. At the moment, all of him was clothed in the immaculate black of mourning. "Lord Wenworth," she breathed, and had the misfortune to start sneezing again, seven times in a row.

When she sniffed her way to silence once again, she

found the butler was staring at her in alarm, and Justinian was frowning. Whether it was concern or annoyance, she couldn't tell.

Justinian was certain he knew the woman before him. It did not seem possible, for the young lady he had known ten years ago would surely have married and left the school by now. In fact, he had long ago resigned himself to the fact that he would never see her again. He tried once more to get a better look at her, but she proved adept at avoiding his gaze.

"Faringil," he said, "will you introduce the young lady?"

Faringil shook himself and collected his bearing. "Of course, my lord. Justinian Darby, ninth Earl of Wenworth, may I present Miss Aledor Brigid."

Eleanor winced. No doubt that was exactly what she sounded like, with this infernal sniffing. Still, it was probably better if she did not correct him.

To her surprise, Justinian bowed deeply, and she was afraid he knew the truth. "Miss Brigid," he said in a voice that was as deep and comforting as she remembered, "an honor to make your acquaintance. If I'm not mistaken, it's Miss Eleanor, isn't it? You are my niece's literature teacher."

Eleanor nodded, swallowing around the scratch in her throat. "Yes, that's right." She told herself she should be glad he didn't recognize her, and ordered the part of her that was hurt to be silent.

Justinian also ignored that part of him that fell with disappointment that it was not his Norrie, after all. The last thing he needed right now was a romantic entanglement. "I've heard a great deal about you from my niece." He smiled politely. "What can I do for the school today?"

Inside her cloak, Jingles squirmed, reminding her of why she was there. She pulled him gingerly into the light. Faringil recoiled as if she had pulled out a bludgeon. She opened her mouth to explain, and her nose exploded again. The rapid succession of sneezes doubled her, and with a surge of panic, she realized the kitten was dropping from her grip. She snatched at him, but two large, long-fingered hands came between her and the little animal. By the time she could recover, Justinian was staring down at the black ball of matted fur that crouched in his open hands, hissing in annoyance.

"It's a kitten," she offered.

The kitten returned Justinian's stare with unblinking yellow eyes. He stopped hissing and cocked his head. Justinian had the strange sensation that his soul was being examined, and felt an absurd sense of relief when the kitten nodded approval.

Eleanor felt a similar relief. "He likes you," she noted. "I'm so glad. Dottie was hoping you might be willing to keep him for her. There is a policy against pets at the school." There, she'd made it sound like a logical turn of events rather than the tragedy it had nearly turned out to be.

The kitten rose with the obvious intention of exploring the palms of Justinian's hands, and he turned to offer the little animal to Faringil. The butler took a step back, blinking, then seemed to recall his duty. With a sigh, he accepted the kitten, holding it at arm's length so that its muddy back feet dangled. Jingles's ears went back.

Justinian frowned at his butler before turning to Eleanor. "Of course we'll keep the kitten for Dottie," he replied. "Please assure my niece that . . ." He paused with upraised brow.

"Jingles," Eleanor offered helpfully.

"Jingles will be well taken care of, and waiting for her when she comes home at the end of the month for Christmas."

Eleanor's smile froze. She'd love to be able to tell Dottie exactly that, but she wasn't very likely to be allowed inside the door of the school again. Besides, if he went to visit soon, perhaps Dottie would confess how unhappy she was, and he would be moved to take action. "Thank you," she replied. "But perhaps you could tell her yourself? I know she would love to see you."

The noble brow clouded, and Eleanor knew she had gone

too far. No Darby ever accepted suggestions from anyone outside their exalted social circle. She had thought she'd learned that lesson on her first visit to Wenworth Place.

Justinian grit his teeth to keep from offering a sharp rejoinder. How dare the woman imply that he was neglecting his niece! She clearly had no idea of the work he was forced to do. It wasn't as if he had time to visit even once a week. The kitten hissing in Faringil's grip suddenly seemed like one more burden.

"Christmas will be here soon enough, Miss Brigid," he replied coldly. "Now, if you're quite finished, I must see to other matters."

His tone left no question in Eleanor's mind that those matters were far more important than a small black kitten and a wet, impertinent schoolteacher. She hurriedly dropped another curtsy as he turned away. *Be thankful he took the kitten,* she told herself firmly. *You have no right to expect more. Remember your place.*

Justinian paused, catching sight of a bedraggled carpet-bag sitting in a puddle of water near the door. Had the woman walked all this way with the kitten in the bag? "Faringil?"

"My lord?" This time the butler's step forward was quick enough, even though he had to juggle the kitten in his grip.

"Have the carriage brought around to return Miss Brigid to the school."

"That won't be necessary," Eleanor put in before the butler could promise to comply. As two pairs of inquisitive eyes turned in her direction, she struggled to think of some logical reason why she wouldn't be returning. "I'm not going back to the school," she hedged. "I'm . . . I'm returning home . . . to York . . . on holiday. Yes, for Christmas." She felt the guilt of the lie as much as she felt the tickle in her nose, but she couldn't bear to have Justinian know she had been disgracefully dismissed.

He glanced out the multipane windows, noting how the

day was rapidly darkening. "It is late. You'll never make Wenwood before nightfall. Faringil?"

"My lord?" The answer was not quite so swift. The butler had made the mistake of pulling the kitten closer and was now engaged in a battle over the possession of the top button of his waistcoat. The kitten's claws were firmly imbedded in the patterned satin on either side of the gleaming metal button, and his tiny teeth nipped at the Darby crest. What the king wanted, he generally got.

Justinian frowned at the display, although he was terribly tempted to laugh. "Have a room made up for Miss Brigid."

"My lord, I wouldn't dream of imposing," Eleanor began. She hadn't stopped to think about where she'd sleep that night, but nothing short of a winter snowstorm would have compelled her to stay at Wenworth Place alone with him. Even if he didn't remember her, her memories were still potent.

"Nor would I dream of turning a lady out into a winter's night," Justinian countered. Sensing her reluctance, he forced himself to continue more gently. "Have no fear for your reputation. My mother lives here, as well. Besides, I will not be able to entertain you. I have pressing matters I must attend to, as I mentioned. If I do not see you again, have a pleasant journey tomorrow."

"Thank you," Eleanor managed, deciding to be relieved by the kind gesture. If she didn't have to see him again, perhaps it might be all right to stay the night. It wasn't as if she had anywhere else to go.

Justinian bowed and turned from her curtsy. However, grateful Miss Brigid might be, the fact of the matter was that she had handed him another problem, at least for the night. And he felt another premonition that she would be far more difficult to deal with than an aristocratic young kitten named Jingles.

# Three

Morning would prove Justinian correct. He hadn't even started on the blasted pile of papers when Faringil slipped into the room to stand rigidly behind him. It seemed that Miss Brigid was more ill than anyone had suspected, and Faringil was clearly concerned that she had brought some dire disease upon them that would decimate the entire area. Justinian had dispatched a footman for Dr. Praxton, who had arrived in due course.

Justinian considered going up to see the woman himself, but thought she somehow wouldn't appreciate a visit by the lord of the manor if she wasn't feeling well. It was a rather cowardly excuse, but he kept thinking that if he could just get through a third of the papers that morning, he might be able to sneak away that afternoon and write. Jareth had sent him one of the recently published novels from London, which read like so much drivel that he itched to try his hand at something finer. Not that he'd ever go so far as to admit to anyone but his scapegrace youngest brother that he was writing a novel in the manner of Walter Scott. A Darby didn't parade anything so common as artistic abilities in public. No, he crafted his stories in the library's quiet, assuring himself that the work had literary merit. Hoping to finish soon enough to write, he plunged into the report on the state of the levees.

Unfortunately, after only three pages, the hairs on the back of his neck rose, warning him that he was not alone.

"Yes?" Justinian clipped, hoping the tone of his voice would let Faringil know that the interruption was unwanted.

"Pardon me, my lord."

"What is it?" Justinian demanded.

"Dr. Praxton would like to speak with you."

"Then send him in," Justinian replied. He lowered his eyes, scanning the page to find where he left off. Faringil did not move. "Well?" Justinian snapped.

"He's with Miss Brigid, my lord. He would like you to come there."

Justinian rolled his eyes, but sighed and rose to follow the man from the room.

He was not a little chagrined to find that Faringil had placed the kindly schoolteacher in the servants' quarters at the top of the house. Dr. Praxton stood waiting for him before the door. The doctor was a small, slender man with an unruly shock of thick gray hair he never seemed to trouble to comb. His eyes were close-set, and nearly black. Justinian had heard that some of the local women thought him shifty-eyed, considering him to resemble a rat. He had always found the man professional in his dealings and intelligent in his conversation. Now Dr. Praxton nodded in greeting.

"Sorry to disturb you, my lord," he said in explanation, reaching for the door handle. "I thought you would want to see this."

Justinian felt another premonition of dread. He shook his head. He had to get over these feelings that everything was going to turn out badly. Miss Brigid hardly seemed the type to have brought a gallon of port with her in her carpetbag, although her lying inebriated certainly would have been enough for the servants to suspect she was deathly ill, and for Dr. Praxton to want his attention.

"What is the difficulty?" he asked, hoping to be prepared for whatever lay beyond the door.

"Hold your nose, please," the man replied, "and I'll show you."

Justinian frowned at him. "Hold my nose?"

Faringil obligingly shook out a lace-trimmed handkerchief and handed it to Justinian. "Your nose, my lord."

Still frowning, Justinian accepted the white lawn square and held it against his nostrils. Doing the same, Dr. Praxton opened the narrow door, and they all peered in.

Justinian could have sworn the very air in the room swam with the noxious odor that reached him even through the handkerchief. *Ammonia,* the scholarly part of his brain asserted. *Cat piddle,* the more practical part of him corrected. What had possessed Faringil to shut the poor woman up with the kitten? It had been over twenty hours since he had seen Miss Eleanor. If she had been ill and too weak to rise, she could hardly have cared for a cat. Now, thanks to Faringil's sensitivity, or lack thereof, the woman must be nearly dead.

Eleanor lay on the narrow bed in the small room, eyes closed against a pounding headache. The last thing she remembered was feeding Jingles the remains of the dinner she had had little interest in eating, changing hurriedly into her pink flannel nightgown in the chilly room, and burrowing beneath the counterpane with the kitten beside her. Just before falling asleep she had thought of Justinian again, remembering his appreciative smiles years ago when she had answered a question he could not. Their minds had seemed so attuned, then. That was obviously no longer the case. She started to regret that she had agreed to stay, then promptly scolded herself for her lack of humility. She was considerably warmer and more comfortable than if she'd had to sleep in a barn, and the little room was no smaller than the one she'd lived in all her life at Barnsley. She had fallen asleep telling herself to remember her place.

Waking up, however, had proven far more difficult. Instead of getting better, she felt much worse. Her eyes were nearly swollen shut, and her tongue was thick in her dry mouth. Twice now she had felt as if someone was watching her, but both times she had found herself alone when she had managed to raise her head. Now she felt the same sensation, and tried once more to look. Her body seemed willing enough, but her chest felt as if there were an anvil on it. Glancing down, she met Jingles's gaze. The kitten yawned, showing sharp white teeth, and stretched, kneading the counterpane over her chest with its tiny claws. He minced toward her, and she began to sneeze. After the eighth time, she managed to bring herself under control. The kitten was nowhere to be found, but her chest still felt constricted.

"You see the problem, Lord Wenworth," someone said in the distance. "It's small wonder the woman is ill."

Lord Wenworth? Her heart plummeted at the very thought of Justinian seeing her like this. She had some pride, after all. She turned on her side and drew the bedcovers over her head, hoping they would all go away and leave her alone.

Justinian fought down his frustration. Did none of the estate staff have a brain? Must he do everything? However much he had adored school, he had always wondered why his father had sent him away so often. Now he knew—with such a staff, the poor man could hardly have slept, let alone spent time with a child! "Faringil," he snapped, not waiting for the man to answer, "fetch a footman and have him carry Miss Brigid to the family wing."

Faringil turned as white as his hair. "But, my lord, the disease! The countess!"

"I wager there isn't a thing wrong with the woman that a clean room and good food won't fix," Dr. Praxton put in.

Faringil seemed to relax on such reassurances. "Very good, then. If you will be so kind as to wait for an hour or so while the maids make up the room and get a fire lit. And I will have to reassure the rest of the staff that the woman isn't infectious."

Justinian glared at him, and Faringil quailed. "If none of the many footmen I've seen wandering about this place is brave enough to rescue an ill woman, I will carry Miss Brigid to the family wing myself."

"My lord, no!" Faringil gasped.

"Mr. Faringil, yes," Justinian assured him. "And unless you'd like to see me fetch coal and fluff bed linens as well, you will have a footman and chambermaid meet me in the room. I expect it to be ready by the time I arrive, which will be in precisely five minutes, if I am not mistaken. Do I make myself clear?"

"Yes, my lord. Completely clear." Faringil hurried down the corridor to comply.

"Thank you, my lord." Dr. Praxton nodded, watching the butler. "I couldn't seem to get through to him. I know the Darby household has always been large on protocol, but if you really wouldn't mind—"

"Let's get this over with," Justinian replied. He took a deep breath of the fresh air in the corridor and plunged into the room. Keeping away from the puddles and piles that edged the wall of the little room, he made his way to Eleanor's bed and bent near her. She was huddled under the covers, with only the top of her disheveled hair showing. Gingerly, he pulled back the bedclothes. Her face was red and blotchy; her breath came in sharp, wheezing gasps. Alarmed, he bent closer.

Eleanor felt someone pull away the counterpane and forced open her eyes. Justinian's face swam into focus before her. "Oh, no," she moaned. Her voice came out more like the croak of a frog. She struggled to rise again, anything to escape his concerned gaze, and Justinian slid an arm under her shoulders and another under her thighs.

"Good morning, Miss Brigid," he said in what he hoped was a calm, reasonable voice. "You seem to have gotten worse because of our hospitality. I'm trying to rectify that. Dr. Praxton is here. He's a physician."

She should have been alarmed to find that they all thought her so ill that she needed a physician, but Justinian's voice was as warm and as comforting as rose hip tea with honey, or hot chocolate on a cold morning. "I know Dr. Praxton," she replied. He's visited the school." The words sounded a little clearer now that she was partially upright. His reassuring smile told her he had understood her.

"Excellent. I'm just going to move you to another room where you'll be more comfortable. You won't mind if I pick you up?"

Mind? Her head spun at the very thought, and she was certain it wasn't from her mysterious illness. She felt his muscles tense under her, and then she was rising. A moment more and she was up against his chest. Her face flushed with heat, but somehow she didn't think she had a fever. How many nights had she dreamed of what it would be like to be held in his arms? Between them lay nothing but the sleeve of his coat and the worn flannel of her nightgown. If she hadn't already been too ill to walk, she would have gone weak at the knees.

Justinian wondered that he didn't flush, too, under her steady regard. There were two bright spots of pink on her high cheekbones, and the color was rapidly spreading down her long, elegant neck below the collar of her nightgown. This was the first time he'd really gotten a good look at her, and even with her face swollen, he felt again that he should know her. Trying to remember when he had met her before, he kept a reassuring smile on his face as he maneuvered his way out of the room. When they reached the narrow stairs, however, and he had to hitch her closer to start down, her chest brushed his and he was suddenly uncomfortably aware of how tightly he held her. Only one woman had ever made him feel so self-conscious. He stumbled, and caught himself immediately.

"Narrow stairway," he mumbled in excuse. Could it be? He shot a quick glace at her face again. Ten years and the illness could not completely erase the girl he had known. As red-rimmed as her eyes were, he would know that blue anywhere, so deep it was nearly violet. He still dreamed of those eyes, and the smile that had lit them when he had the courage to flirt with her. But if it was really Norrie Pritchett he held, why was she pretending to be someone else? The possibilities troubled him. He was quite glad when they reached the main corridor on the second floor and a maid guided him to a room not far from his mother's.

The fire was just starting to glow in the grate as he lay Eleanor on the clean flannel sheets. She trembled as he pulled away, feeling suddenly chilled. A maid hurried forward to tuck her under the bedcovers. Justinian withdrew out of her sight. Disappointment shot through her. "Thank you," she called.

Dr. Praxton clapped Justinian on the shoulder. "And I thank you, too, my lord. I'll let you know my diagnosis before I go."

Dismissed, Justinian nodded and wandered from the room. He should confront her, demand an explanation, he supposed. He'd certainly wanted one ten years ago.

"She can't have just returned to the school," Justinian remembered protesting. "We had an understanding."

His father had put a hand on his shoulder. "My dear boy, one cannot form an understanding with someone like Miss Pritchett. She most likely won't remember you beyond tomorrow."

Justinian had shrugged off the touch. "I don't believe you." Even in his memory the words sounded like those of a petulant four year old denied his favorite candy. "She has more character than that."

"Justinian," his father had sighed, "you have been among your books too long. A young lady bills and coos with every charming young man who comes along. I daresay she ran off when she realized you were taking her far too seriously. You've worn your heart on your sleeve. Even your mother has remarked on it. The poor girl was likely frightened out of her wits by your obsessive devotions."

He had recoiled, stung. He had never had the courage to do more than press her hand fervently and recite the most passionate of love poems. Surely this would not have been enough to scare his brave Norrie. Yet there had been times when her blue-violet eyes were troubled when she looked at him, and his words had fired her cheek in a blush. "If what you say is true," he had mused aloud, "then I have done her a disservice. I should at least apologize."

"You will only embarrass the girl further," his father had assured him. "You are young, Justinian. Your heart will mend. Return to your work at the university. That is far more important than this momentary infatuation with Miss Pritchett."

Remembering now, he closed his eyes and shook his head. He'd been young, all right, far too young to realize what a mistake he was making. He had graduated, then gone on to additional studies, then teaching and research. One month had piled onto the next, and before he knew it, ten years had passed. Looking back, he knew them for the empty years they had been.

But had anything changed? Would she be any more receptive to his suit now? Ill as she was, now was obviously not the time to ask. He should return to his papers, he thought, but somehow the idea was depressing. Even his precious novel didn't suit him at the moment. Instead, he found himself at his mother's door.

The countess looked up as he entered. Small and fine-boned, she made him feel like a gawking giant of late. She lay down the book she had been reading and smiled at him, patting the satin covers beside her. "Justinian, how delightful. Have a seat and tell me how you go on."

He bent and kissed her cheek, but found himself too restless to sit. "Good morning, Mother. I'm doing well. How are you?"

She frowned at him. "My liver is peevish, and I have indigestion. You never ask about those things. It isn't like you to discuss banalities. What's wrong?"

He smiled at her. "You read me too well." Even though she did, he could hardly confide his suspicions about their guest. It would only trouble his mother. He resorted instead to something that might be of more interest to her. "Dottie has adopted a kitten, which the school has sent home to us. Unfortunately, the messenger who brought it appears to have come down ill."

"Poor man," his mother murmured. "Nothing serious, I hope."

"I hope so as well. But it isn't a gentleman. It's one of the teachers." He could not bring himself to name her.

"Not Dottie's Miss Eleanor?" his mother asked hopefully. "I have so wanted to meet her after your description of Dottie's stories."

Justinian sat at last beside his mother. "Yes," he admitted reluctantly, "the very same. But meeting her will be out of the question until we know that she is well. All I need is for you to come down ill, too."

His mother cocked her head. "You're taking on too much again, Justinian. No one has asked you to single-handedly save England, you know."

He rose. "No, just an estate that covers a considerable portion, as well as the livelihood of everyone who dwells on it. And now a small black kitten, too."

"A kitten is hardly a chore, my love." His mother smiled, watching him. "All a kitten needs to be happy is a place by the fire. And perhaps a nice ball of string. Ask my Mary for one, if you'd like. And bring her to meet me when you can."

He didn't have to ask to know she wasn't referring to her abigail. Perhaps that might be a solution, after all. His mother studied people as he studied literature. If she confirmed that the woman really was Norrie Pritchett, then he might have the courage to question their guest. If not, it was one less thing he would have to trouble himself about.

He offered her a smile. "Very well, Mother. When the redoubtable Miss Eleanor is better, you will get a chance to meet her." *And,* he added silently, *the sooner the better for all concerned.*

# Four

Justinian waited until the following morning to inquire after his guest. The day was the longest of his life. Dr. Praxton had assured him that Miss Eleanor had inflamed mucous membranes that were making her breathing difficult; however, he felt it was neither croup nor pleurisy. He prescribed cold compresses on the face and chest, and laudanum to help her sleep. Mary, his mother's abigail, had been pressed into service. Faringil had reported before retiring that Miss Eleanor appeared to be sleeping easier. And Justinian made sure that the kitten had been properly cared for, and it was now sleeping in a basket in the corner of their guest's room.

He knew if he were a better host he would take a greater part in all these matters, but he couldn't bring himself to interfere again unless absolutely necessary. He told himself it was because of the papers piling higher every day on the great mahogany desk, but he suspected there was another reason. Holding Miss Eleanor in his arms, even sick as she was, had made him painfully aware that he was celibate. He hadn't had much time for women at Oxford. And then, he had never entirely gotten over Norrie.

Now that he was the title holder, he supposed it was his duty to marry and continue the line. He would have to choose a woman of impeccable breeding and understanding, such as Dottie's mother had been. She would have to know how to manage a great house, how to deal with a

strong-willed dowager like his mother, and how to host
parties for everyone, from the tenants, to the family, to
members of parliament. She would also need to know how
to raise children, Dottie and their own. She would surely
be one of England's finest. Nothing less would do for a
Darby. However, no matter how hard he tried, whenever
he thought of the woman he'd marry, she looked exactly
like Norrie Pritchett.

She had come from the school to help him study when
he had been sent home mid-term his second year at Oxford with a bad case of pleurisy. Fearful of losing his position as one of the top scholars, he had been only too
glad for someone to quiz him on various subjects. Unfortunately, the first woman who had been sent from the
Barnsley School had found his course of study incompre-
hensible. The second was so awed to be in the Great House
that she barely spoke above a whisper and jumped every
time he questioned her.

"For all the donations we supply that school," his father
had mumbled, "the least they could do is send someone
with brains and backbone."

"You haven't given them sufficient motivation in this
case, my dear," his mother had countered. "You must give
them incentive to send their best, not just those who would
improve their social standing. Give all the older students
a test, with the most difficult questions Justinian can contrive. Whoever scores the highest shall spend each summer
day at Wenworth Place."

"Capital idea!" his father had proclaimed. Justinian had
dashed off one hundred or so fairly challenging questions
covering literature, history, science, and the arts, and his
father had presided over the test himself.

The winner, an apprentice teacher named Norrie, had
arrived on the doorstep of Wenworth Place two days later.
Her gaze at the ivy-hung walls of the Great House was no
less awed than her predecessor—but she soon proved herself an able scholar. In fact, he found himself impressed

that she had learned so much with no more training beyond the Barnsley School for Young Ladies.

"And what do you think young ladies learn?" she had replied when he voiced his thought aloud. "We may not be privileged to attend Eton or Harrow, but we are perfectly capable of learning any subject a boy can learn. Besides, what else have I to do but read and learn? Sometimes I think it is a blessing that the nights are so long and I have nothing better to do than read."

"It is a blessing," he remembered agreeing with envy, for then the only thing in life that seemed to matter was his studies. "You aren't expected to entertain hunting guests or dash off to London to attend someone's debut."

"We all have our crosses to bear, Mr. Darby," she had replied with a twinkle in her expressive eyes. "I expect yours was to have been born wealthy. Only think how lucky you were to have been born the second son. If you had been born the eldest you'd have to spend all your time having fun."

He had laughed with her, then, though the words haunted him now. The duty pressed upon him was anything but enjoyable. By midday, he knew he had to learn the truth about the woman upstairs or go mad. Mary answered his cautious tap. He entered to find the schoolteacher sitting up against the elaborately carved headboard, quilt drawn up to her chest, teasing the kitten with a piece of red ribbon.

"Good morning, my lord," Eleanor replied to his greeting. She hunched a little lower in the bed and bowed her head, hoping that just enough of the illness remained so that he still wouldn't recognize her. If only she could have avoided another meeting. He had, after all, repeatedly claimed to be needed on urgent matters. An ill schoolteacher hardly ranked high enough to distract a Darby. Another day might give her the strength to walk to Wenwood, where she hoped to find someone who might be going on to Wells. If only he would leave her alone until then!

Now that the illness nearly had passed, her voice was gentle and rather melodious, he noted, deeper than he remem-

bered Norrie's being. He peered closer. Even with her head
bowed, he could see that the swelling and redness were
gone from around her eyes, and nose as well. In fact, her
skin glowed with health restored. He seated himself on the
chair Mary had recently vacated beside the bed and cocked
his head, trying to get her to meet his gaze. Jingles must
have caught Justinian's movement, for he leapt to his feet
and stalked across the coverlet to investigate. Eleanor
quickly dangled the ribbon in front of him to keep him
from jumping onto the earl's lap. She cast a look of appeal
at the silver-haired abigail, but little round Mary had busied
herself at the wash basin and refused to notice her.

"You look much better this morning," Justinian remarked, hoping to get her to raise her eyes. He realized
as soon as he said it that it was rather tactless. His mother
would have rapped his knuckles for such a statement, and
Helena would have stared at him through the lens of her
quizzing glass until he had dropped his gaze.

Eleanor only nodded, sinking lower until the covers were
under her armpits and her head nearly rested on her chest.
"Yes, whatever was bothering me seems to have disappeared
in the night, just as Dr. Praxton predicted. I'm very relieved
it wasn't infectious after all, as Mr. Faringil suspected. I
would never forgive myself if I made you all ill."

The illness he felt, Justinian thought, had nothing to do
with her sickness and everything to do with the lady herself. "It does indeed seem to be a passing thing," he replied with assurance. "I take it none of the students at the
school were ill."

At the mention of the school, she started. If she was
forced to endure his company, at the very least she could
mention Dottie's predicament. She would have to go carefully this time, remembering her place and how the Darbys
considered things. She pulled Jingles to her and began petting him to hide the trembling of her hands. "You have
been very kind, my lord. I wonder, could you spare another
moment?"

"Certainly," Justinian replied, far more pleasantly than

he felt. He could not understand why she continually refused to face him. If she was Norrie, surely she knew him
well enough to meet his gaze. The unwarranted sensitivity
was nearly as annoying as Faringil's deference. But perhaps
she was about to explain. "Is something troubling you?"
he prompted hopefully.

Eleanor smoothed her hands over Jingles's fur. The kitten deigned to suffer her touch. Justinian was regarding
her fixedly, she could see out of the corner of her eye, so
that she wasn't certain how to start. She forced herself to
remember the tableau in the headmistress's office. "I am
nearly recovered, as you noted," she replied. "But I am very
concerned about Dottie—that is, your niece, Lady Dorothea."

"I'll visit her soon," Justinian promised, wanting only
to get on to more urgent matters. "I am well aware that I
am neglecting her."

"Neglecting her?" Eleanor blinked in confusion. "Certainly you are not neglecting her! Dottie receives more
visits from you in a month than many of the girls receive
in a year! You are obviously the most loving of uncles."

Justinian felt as if he were going to blush, and shifted in
his seat in embarrassment. "Thank you," he murmured,
unsure of what else to say in the face of her unexpected
praise.

"Your behavior does not concern me in the least,"
Eleanor assured him. "It's Dottie's. The loss of her mother
and father is too fresh for her to have returned to school.
She cannot concentrate on her studies. She needs reassurances. I'm sure that's why she became obsessed with Jingles."

Justinian glanced down at the kitten, who stretched out
and relaxed in pleasure under Eleanor's petting. If Norrie
paid him such attentions, he'd probably react in exactly
the same manner. The thought unnerved him, and he hurriedly rose.

"Is she unhappy, then?" he asked, pacing the room and
willing his mind to focus on the newest problem that had

been handed him and not on the way Eleanor's long-fingered hands slid across the shiny black fur.

"Dreadfully so," Eleanor confided, watching him. She was a little surprised by how strongly he reacted to her words. When his father had sent her away and he had never pursued her or sent a word of encouragement, she had convinced herself that he was not a person of strong feelings after all. Either he had changed, or she had been wrong. Both possibilities sent a chill through her. She shook herself and plunged on. "I think she would be much happier here with her family for a time. I don't wish to be impertinent, but would you consider bringing her home sooner than Christmas?"

It was a reasonable suggestion. Any other time he would have applauded her good sense. However, at the moment, Jingles had rolled onto his back, and Eleanor was tickling his stomach in ways that made Justinian flush. "No impertinence," he all but panted, backing toward the door. "But it can't be done. No one to care for her."

Eleanor looked up in wonder that the usually eloquent Justinian Darby was all but stammering. His tawny hair curled about his damp forehead, and he was swallowing almost convulsively as he attempted to meet her gaze. All thoughts of modesty fled. Eleanor scrambled from the bed, thrusting Jingles at a startled Mary.

"My lord, are you ill?" Her own concerns forgotten, she hurried to his side and raised a hand to his forehead. She could not have brought a disease upon him! She would never forgive herself!

Justinian backed away from her in horror, bumping up against the solid panel of the door. The flannel nightgown draped her body effectively, but his memory conjured up the feel of her curves against his chest.

"I'm fine," he yelped, ducking to avoid her touch.

She blinked, surprised, and hesitated. His voice seemed unusually husky to her, and his face was certainly reddening. The symptoms were very like her own illness. Could Dr. Praxton have been wrong about the nature of the disease? Determined, she plastered her hand to his sweaty brow.

Justinian groaned at the cool touch. Her nearness, her sweet concern, and his body's reaction convinced him whom he faced. "Norrie, please!" he gasped. "I assure you, I'm fine. Return to the bed."

Eleanor stared at him. She could feel the blood draining from her face, and suddenly the room seemed to dim. Justinian's alarmed face receded rapidly as her knees buckled. He caught her easily and swung her up into his arms. For the second time in two days, she found herself pressed against his chest.

"It is you, isn't it?" he murmured.

Knowing it impossible not to meet his gaze, Eleanor nodded. She wavered between misery and embarrassment. "Yes, I used to be known as Norrie Pritchett. The headmistress thought my full name, Eleanor, was more fitting for a teacher. I promise you, I won't faint. Would you please set me down?"

"Need I remind you that you have been ill?" he replied, relishing the feel of her so close. He remembered how noble he'd felt at twenty to refrain from doing more than pressing her hand fervently. What an idiot he'd been. Life was entirely too short to forego such pleasure. He pulled her closer and tried to smile reassuringly when her eyes widened in obvious alarm. They both knew that in another minute, he would kiss her.

"Put that down," Mary commanded, and Justinian started. Then he realized she addressed Jingles, who had picked up a piece of fuzz off the counterpane and was attempting to swallow it, nearly crossing his eyes in the process. Eleanor was blushing in his arms. All he needed was servant's gossip to frighten her away again before they could get reacquainted. Reluctantly, he crossed the room and set her on the bed.

Eleanor lost no time scrambling beneath the covers and snatching Jingles to her, burying her burning face in his soft fur. The telltale tickle began in her nose even before

Mary bustled forward to tuck the bedclothes more tightly about her. The look she cast Eleanor out of the corner of her eye made Eleanor redden even more. *They will all think I have forgotten my place,* she thought with shame.

A thousand questions crowded Justinian's tongue, but none found its way forward. It seemed insipid to ask her whether she was all right when he could see she was greatly distressed by his recognition. He didn't have the heart to press her with more important questions. "We must speak," he started, and saw her turn from red to white. "About Dottie and about other matters. But I'll come back when you're recovered."

As he strode toward the door, Eleanor thought that he would have a very long wait. She had never recovered from his regard the first time. What made him think this time would be any different?

# Five

Eleanor Pritchett was running away again. She didn't seem to have any other option. She was entirely recovered from her mysterious illness. The only time even a remnant of it returned was when she held Jingles too close to her face. Then she was sure to sneeze several times in quick succession, and she could feel her eyes tearing. It seemed that the illness was directly related to the little kitten, although that explanation did not account for Justinian's strange symptoms the day before. He had hardly been holding Jingles at the time. Still, she could be reasonably assured that, as she was leaving the kitten behind, the disease would trouble her no more.

She had to leave. Justinian had indicated that he wanted to talk, but she could think of nothing they could say to each other that she had not told herself a dozen times over. She knew her place. His father had taught it to her, and Miss Martingale had made sure she never forgot the lesson. If she had been an unthinkable mate for a second son, she would never be suitable for the earl. She could never have his love; she would not have his pity. Ten years ago she had slipped away and hidden herself at the Barnsley School. She had been a girl of seventeen, then. Now she was a woman of twenty-seven, and the prospect of running away held even less solace, especially when this time, she had nowhere to run.

As she dressed in her black bombazine and traveling

cloak, now cleaned and pressed, Jingles sat by the fire,
licking his fur and eyeing her between flecks of his little
pink tongue. For all his nonchalance, she had a feeling
he might miss her. Certainly no one else in the household
had made much effort to care for him. She had hoped
Mr. Faringil would attempt to settle Jingles into his new
home. Unfortunately, the butler seemed only too happy
to leave the care and feeding to her. She had managed to
convince Mary to bring water and kitchen scraps for the
kitten, and to let him in and out and watch him when he
needed to relieve himself, but it was clear to Eleanor that
the abigail did so under duress. If only Dottie would come
home sooner! Then Eleanor would not have any qualms
about leaving Wenworth Place behind.

Before the Tompion clock on the mantel struck eight,
she set out. Determined to find someone to take charge
of the kitten, she let him scamper about her feet as she
started down the corridor. Doors like her own dotted the
satin-hung walls on either side in both directions. When
she had visited the estate all those years ago, she had never
had occasion to rise above the ground floor, so she scarcely
knew her way. Farther to her right, she thought she saw a
wider archway that must be the main stairway. Clucking to
Jingles, she started in that direction.

Partway there, she saw a door open and Mary back into
the corridor, a tray of empty serving dishes in her arms.
Eleanor paused to keep from bumping into the abigail.
Before she could cry out, Jingles stalked around Mary's
legs and into the room beyond. The king was intent on
inspecting his holdings. Mary was equally intent—on bal-
ancing the tray; she obviously did not see the kitten. Before
Eleanor could speak, the abigail trotted off in the opposite
direction, oblivious to her presence.

Eleanor bit her lip. Someone had been in the room, or
Mary wouldn't be cleaning afterwards. But was it the breakfast room or a bedchamber, and if the latter, whose? She
hardly wanted to meet up with Justinian in his nightshirt.
Just the thought made her blush. But if the room was

empty, ought she to leave Jingles alone? They might not find him for days in this huge house!

From inside the room came a thud and a startled mew. No human voice responded. Encouraged, Eleanor opened the door and peered inside.

The room was a bedchamber, considerably larger than the one in which she had stayed. In the center stood a walnut box bed with yellow and gold hangings. A fire blazed in the grate of the walnut-framed fireplace, and the gold velvet drapes were closed against the dawn of a winter day. Nowhere under the long curved legs of the dark dressing table, armoire, or washstand could Eleanor spy a small black kitten.

"Jingles," Eleanor hissed, unable to see beyond the hangings of the bed to determine if anyone was still in it. For all she knew, Mary had merely been cleaning away a breakfast long eaten. She tiptoed a little farther into the room. "Jingles? Here, kitty, kitty."

"He's here," a voice called. Eleanor swallowed, not sure whether to be relieved that the voice was not Justinian's or concerned that the room was indeed inhabited. She peered around the hangings to see a tiny elderly woman nearly lost amongst a mountain of white-lace-covered pillows piled up against the headboard. Her skin was as pure as fine bone china, crinkling around the sharp blue eyes and soft pink mouth. In fact, her eyes and mouth were the only spots of color from, the white lawn cap trimmed with lace and dripping ribbon to the white coverlet that was pulled up to her chest—the only color, that was, except the very black kitten who was trying to cross the white counterpane. Every time he minced across the uneven surface, the woman gently seized his hind foot and drew him back. Outraged, he dug his claws into the fine material and pulled it back with him. Eleanor couldn't help but smile.

"You must be Miss Eleanor," the woman murmured. "I am Eulalie Darby, Countess Wenworth."

Eleanor's heart skipped a beat, but she managed a curtsy. "Your ladyship. An honor to meet you."

The countess quirked a white brow. "An honor, is it? That is yet to be seen." She nodded to where Jingles was once more attempting to reach the foot of the bed. "Is this my granddaughter's kitten?"

"Yes, your ladyship," Eleanor nodded, reaching to catch the kitten. "I'm sorry Jingles disturbed you. I was just looking for someone to take custody of him."

Deprived of his freedom, Jingles squirmed in her grip. Lady Wenworth held out her frail arms. "You needn't take him away. I'm sure I can find something to entertain him."

Eleanor wasn't sure that was the best choice. If the kitten somehow was transmitting the illness, it would hardly do to infect someone as frail as the countess. She hesitated, and a vaguely familiar light came to the countess's eyes.

"I am not accustomed to having to repeat myself," Lady Wenworth murmured, the steel evident behind her gentle tone. "Give me the kitten."

Swallowing, Eleanor complied. Jingles stared up at the countess before deigning to rest in her arms.

"Very good," Lady Wenworth nodded. "Now, sit down, Miss Eleanor. I should like to get to know you better."

Surely the woman could see she was dressed for travel. Eleanor hesitated again, but as the blue eyes narrowed she hurriedly sank onto the hard-backed chair beside the bed. She certainly didn't want to give the woman apoplexy. On the other hand, it was apparent that Justinian hadn't mentioned her connection with a certain Norrie Pritchett, whom the last earl had accused of fortune hunting, and Eleanor didn't want to refresh her ladyship's memory. An invalid even then, the woman had only met her a few times. Still, it seemed the better part of wisdom to escape as soon as she could. She tried to remember Miss Partridge's classes on etiquette at the school. Beyond forms of address and curtsys, she didn't think topics of conversations suitable for dowager countesses had been covered. She vaguely remembered that fashion, weather, and health were considered safe gambits. Unfortunately, she knew nothing about the latest fashions, and it seemed rather impertinent to discuss matters of health with an invalid. "Lovely weather for December," she said with a pleasant smile.

The countess regarded her sternly, although her blue-veined hands were gentle on Jingle's fur. "Stop that at once. I was positive from Justinian's description that you would make better conversation than that."

"Sorry," Eleanor murmured, abashed. "What is it you would like me to converse about?"

Eulalie waved a hand airily at everything and nothing. "Whatever you like. So long as it is original and witty."

Eleanor felt as if her mind had suddenly frozen. She had never been called upon to discuss anything with anyone other than the staff and children. Certainly, no one had ever demanded that she be witty. She gazed at the countess, whose look was turning surly again, and suddenly she recognized a resemblance. "I see where Dottie gets her determination," Eleanor replied. "She's just as likely to put me in a difficult position when she makes up her mind to have something."

The countess laughed, a surprisingly hearty sound for one so frail. "And what do you do when she does?"

Eleanor returned her smile. "I have a choice of scolding her or hugging her. So far, the latter has worked rather well."

"Very well then, I submit." The countess threw open her arms, sending a startled Jingles dashing to the end of the bed, where he eyed them both unforgivingly. Eleanor stared at her a moment in disbelief, but there was no mistaking her gesture or the curious moisture behind those blue eyes. If the countess had been one of Eleanor's charges, she would have said the woman was lonely. Her heart went out to Lady Wenworth, and she hugged her tiny body close.

After a moment, the countess released her, eyes over-bright. Eleanor felt tears in her own eyes, as well.

"How lovely." Lady Wenworth sighed. "We must have more of those while you're here."

Eleanor glanced down at her traveling cloak. "I'm terribly sorry, your ladyship, but I shan't be here long. I was just on my way, actually."

Eulalie frowned. Something about the intensity of those knitted brows reminded Eleanor of the lady's son, as well. "That will never do. We have hardly had time to get acquainted. No, you must stay, at least through Christmas."

The thought was so alarming that Eleanor had to press her lips together to keep from vehemently protesting. The countess was not what she had expected, but that didn't mean she would ever be welcome here. She could not let a moment's pleasantness cause her to forget her place. Collecting herself, she straightened. "I'm sorry, your ladyship, but I simply can't."

"Pish tosh," Eulalie replied. "You can't, or you won't? If that school is the problem, I shall simply write and tell them your presence is needed here at the estate."

Eleanor managed a polite smile. She had been in that position once before. It had not ended well. "But it *isn't* needed. We both know that, Lady Wenworth. There is no possible reason for me to stay on. I would only feel as if I were taking advantage of your hospitality."

The countess's eyes narrowed again. "I'm not offering you hospitality, girl. I'm ordering you to stay and visit. That should assuage your sensibilities. Didn't your mother teach you to defer to your betters?"

Eleanor felt herself grow cold. She could hear the echo of Lord Wenworth's words: *Do not strive to mimic your betters, girl. Your place is at our feet, never at our sides.*

"I know what is expected of me, Lady Wenworth," she murmured, clenching her fingers inside her gloves. "But sadly, I have a tendency to speak my mind. You would not find me a pleasant companion for long, I fear. I might tell you that you are quite impossible."

Eulalie grinned at her. "Only my husband ever had the courage to say such to me, more's the pity." She reached out and squeezed Eleanor's hand. Eleanor raised her head, surprised by the kindness of the touch. "Please stay, dear. Justinian doesn't have time for me, and Mary hasn't the

courage to stand up to me. Even when Dottie is home . . ."
She trailed off and clapped her hands. "That's it! Of course.
Dottie must come home for Christmas. Justinian mentioned you recommended she come home sooner. You can
tell the school you stayed on to get things ready for her."

Much as she knew she must leave, she felt the pull of
the countess's offer. How sweet it would be to make a home
for Dottie, a place where the girl could find happiness
again. Still, she could not risk seeing Justinian. "I'm sorry,
your ladyship, but I don't see that that's necessary."

The countess waved her hand airily as she had done
before. "Children need routines, schedules. At the very
least, no one has lived in the nursery on a regular basis
for years. Someone has to see that it is fit for my granddaughter. And it shouldn't be too taxing, so you would
have time to visit me. What do you say, my dear?"

She had to say no. She couldn't be in the same house
as Justinian for the three weeks remaining before Christmas and hope to avoid him. They would meet, repeatedly.
As a sort of governess and companion, she would be in an
impossible position, she could see—neither peer nor servant. She should leave before her heart could be bruised
any further. She should walk out of the house and never
see Jingles, Dottie, Lady Wenworth, or Justinian Darby ever
again. What did she owe any of them?

"Lady Wenworth," she heard herself say, "I would be
delighted to stay. Consider me your Christmas helper."

# Six

From the frown on his mother's face as he sat at her bedside, Justinian knew he was not reacting as she had expected to the news that Miss Eleanor would be gracing them with her presence through the Christmas season. "You asked her to stay!" he all but yelped.

His mother eyed him with such intensity that he wondered whether his remark had been taken as annoyance or joy. The truth of the matter was, he wasn't sure which had prompted it himself.

"Really, Justinian," she sniffed. "You simply must stop acting the part of martyr. Miss Eleanor will hardly get in your way. She will spend most of her time getting things ready for Dottie, and the rest of the time here with me. You won't have to lift a finger. On the contrary, you might even find her helpful. I would imagine that as a teacher she writes with a fine hand, and she must know something about summing. I daresay she can't be as bright as that girl we had up from the school that summer for you, but she might be able to help you with your estate work."

Justinian had a sudden vision of Norrie seated at the mahogany desk, the winter sun making a halo of her light brown hair, dust motes glittering around her. He swallowed. "No, thank you, Mother. I prefer to work alone."

His mother shook her head. "And will you dig your own grave, as well? It isn't a sin to need assistance, Justinian.

You weren't so prickly when you were younger. I think you actually enjoyed having that young lady as a tutor."

Was she reminding him of what Norrie had meant to him? She needn't have tried so hard. He had never been able to forget. He peered closer at the guileless blue eyes, the dimple that was still evident in the wrinkles beside her mouth. His mother had ever been the master manipulator. What was her game this time? She obviously did not recognize the woman, or she would be teasing him about it now. Or were these reminders her way of showing that she *had* recognized Norrie? "Perhaps you should tell me exactly what you and Miss Eleanor discussed. If some agreement has been made, I should understand it better."

She waved an elegant hand. "Oh, fah, we have nothing so formal as an agreement. She is pleasant company. Haven't you been harping at me to find a companion? I liked her, and persuaded her to stay." She frowned again, gaze sharpening. "And it took some persuading. Have you taken her in dislike, Justinian? Did you say something to make that poor girl feel unwelcome?"

Despite himself, he flinched. Was he so obvious in his attentions once again that she should feel the need to flee? Why could he not be more civil in her presence? "All the teachers at the school know they can count on the Darbys for assistance," he hedged. "I'm sure Miss Eleanor is no exception."

"Yes, well." His mother sniffed, obviously dissatisfied. "She seemed in a tearing hurry to leave. It was all I could do to convince her to stay until Christmas. Has she family, do you know? Have I intruded on pressing business of some sort?"

Now Justinian frowned. "She has no family, of that I'm certain." He remembered her comment the first day about leaving for a holiday in York. What bamming! Norrie Pritchett was an orphan. There was no family. His frown deepened as he wondered why she had felt compelled to lie. Worse, why would she want to keep him from mentioning her presence to the school? He had no time to puzzle further, for he caught his mother leaning forward, for all the world like a hound who'd caught the scent, and forced a pleasant smile. "Most likely you merely put her in a difficult position with the school," he offered. "I'll send word you've appropriated her. I'm sure they won't mind."

His mother tossed her head. "Of course they won't mind. We are Darbys."

"Of course." He chuckled, rising to go and bending to kiss her cheek.

"You should also know that I asked her to dine with me every meal she's here," the countess said. She eyed him for a moment, then smiled brightly. "You may join us if you'd like."

The last thing he wanted was to spend a cozy meal with his mother and the woman of his dreams. "Thank you, but no, Mother. I have matters that I must see to."

She sighed, lowering her gaze and plucking at the bedcovers. "Oh, very well. Leave an old woman to her own devices. Small wonder I'm reduced to picking up strays when my own sons can't find time for me."

Justinian felt a stab of guilt. "Mother, you know I'm not trying to avoid you. Besides, there isn't room here for three." He blew her another kiss, but she refused to look up. Annoyed, he shook his head and turned to go. As he opened the bedchamber door, he found himself nose to topknot with Norrie.

She dropped a deep curtsy, treating him to the view of the crown of her golden-brown head. As she rose, he saw that she was completely recovered from her malady, noting the line of her cheek and the way her lashes wreathed her eyes in gold as she demurely lowered her gaze. He wanted nothing so much as to tip her chin up with his finger and press his lips to hers. Instead, he returned her curtsy with a nod.

"Miss Eleanor. My mother tells me you will be staying with us a while longer."

Was that regret or pleasure she heard in his voice? Eleanor glanced up quickly, and he was smiling politely. It seemed to her the smile was forced, and her answering smile must have been all but gentle. "Just until things are set to rights for Dottie's return, my lord. I have other things I must see to."

"Oh?" the countess prompted from her bed. "Justinian and I were just discussing that, dear. What other things are troubling you? Perhaps we could help?"

Just thinking of her empty future made Eleanor pale, but she wasn't sure she wanted to know how the Darbys would react to the plight of a servant. Besides, the countess couldn't do anything about it, and she could not ask Justinian. "It's nothing so very pressing, your ladyship," she replied, lowering her eyes once more and hurrying past him to the countess's bedside. "It can easily wait until after Christmas."

"There, you see." His mother nodded, patting the coverlet beside her for Eleanor to sit. "Everything has been arranged quite nicely. There is nothing about this that should disturb you, Justinian. You may go."

*Nothing to disturb me, indeed,* he thought as he offered his mother and Eleanor a bow and quit the room at last. *Only a house guest in the one woman I've ever loved but who seems afraid of my presence, the impending return of my niece with potentially no one to care for her after Christmas, and a small, black kitten named Jingles. By Christmas I predict I shall be quite disturbed, indeed!*

Justinian was not the only one disturbed by the turn of events. Eleanor soon regretted her impulsive decision to remain. While Justinian did not press her as she had feared, she still could not seem to avoid him, no matter that the great house was huge. He came to wish his mother good morning and inquire after her health while they breakfasted each morning. Mr. Faringil brought him up with annoying frequency to answer a question or inspect her work in the nursery and schoolroom, to the point that she jumped whenever she saw a movement out of the corner of her eye. He was a shadow on the terrace outside the library while she took Jingles out to play in the gardens behind the manor. She found him listening to her read Shakespeare to the countess in the evenings. And she saw him when the countess sent her on some errand to the ground floor, each time she passed the open door to the library.

The door was not often open, but when it was she found she could not keep her gaze from straying to the figure behind the desk. Sometimes his brow would be knit, and he'd be studying the papers before him with such intensity that she wondered if he were not grappling with the fate of the Empire. Other times he would be leaning back and staring at the ceiling as if invoking heaven's assistance. The times that wrung her heart, however, were when his leonine head was cradled in his hands and his broad shoulders were slumped over the desk, as if the burden he bore were simply too great.

And she could see that he did bear a burden. However much she had once teased him about the difficulties of being born to the manor, she could now see that that gift came with a heavy price. Nothing happened on the estate without Justinian's consultation and advice. The steward brought a steady stream of issues and concerns from the tenants; Mr. Faringil seemed unable to manage the household without appealing to Justinian for each decision; and even the cook requested his preferences for dinner as if she were cooking for the Prince Regent and not an elderly woman, an overtired earl, and an impoverished ex-schoolteacher. He seemed to have no time to himself, and little appreciation for his efforts. She only wished she could find some way to help.

Unfortunately, with visiting the countess, keeping the kitten out of trouble, and finishing her work in the nursery, her days were also busy. After inspecting the nursery and schoolroom, she had worked with the countess to identify furniture and linen that could be used to refurbish and brighten the little-used rooms. Using paper, pen, and ink that Mr. Faringil provided her from his lordship's library, she drafted a schedule for Dottie that included time to study, to play, and to exercise in the gardens or on horseback. She had to make the schedule twice, as the first time Jingles had jumped onto it in mid-scribble and proudly smeared the ink into small, paw-shaped patches.

Although she delighted in spending her evenings reading books from the Darbys' excellent library, each afternoon while the countess napped she borrowed the several-days-old *Times* from Mr. Faringil and scanned the ads for positions. She had seen any number for governesses and nannies. There had even been two for teachers at girls' schools in London. Somehow, she found a reason not to respond to most of them. The one time she did sit down to compose a letter, Jingles had jumped into her lap and reached up for the paper, and she had put the quill and ink away for fear of another mishap. She knew she could not keep hiding away from her future, or her past, but for now, only the present was even tenable.

As for Justinian, he was finding the present to be completely untenable. It seemed to him that he was constantly on the verge of breaking into two people. One, an impertinent fellow, wanted to drag Norrie Pritchett off to a secluded corner of the manor, kiss her nearly senseless, and demand to know why she had reappeared in his life if she wasn't willing to acknowledge his existence. The more scholarly fellow, who had been forced to be an earl, raised an eyebrow at such brutish behavior, reminding the impetuous fellow that he had frightened her away in the first place with far more gentle actions than that. The scholar cautioned prudence; all good things came to those who waited. Justinian wanted to follow the latter advice, but he found his good intentions ruined every time he happened upon Eleanor. Luckily, the habitual coolness with which she greeted him convinced him that he should not speak; however, it did not seem to keep him from remembering. Now there were new memories overlaid on the old: the loving attention she devoted to setting up Dottie's apartments and schedule, the sparkle in her beautiful eyes when she showed them the newly refurbished schoolroom, the sound of her laughter at some quip of his mother's, the soft hush of long skirts passing his door and the absurd longing to hear them pause. She distracted him from his routine, she distracted him from his work, she distracted him from his writing. He did not have an answer for how to stop her bittersweet distractions, and wasn't entirely sure he really wanted one. His very ambivalence only served to trouble him further.

He was trying once again to determine the appropriate course of action one night about a fortnight before Christmas when he found his supper, which he had been wont to take alone in the library at the desk, very much disturbed. It started innocently enough. He was just spooning up a mouthful of chicken broth when there was a distinct thump overhead. He frowned at the frescoed ceiling, but soon returned to his reading. The second noise occurred as he was starting his ragout of beef; that sound was definitely more of a thud. His salmon tart was taken to the tune of repetitive drumming that made him wonder whether he had been invaded by the Scottish army. The feet running back and forth during his lamb brisket made him sure of it. Before the blueberry trifle Mrs. Childs had promised him arrived, he was taking the stairs two at a time to find out what was going on.

His mother didn't even look contrite when he appeared in her doorway. Both Mary and Norrie dropped a curtsy, and it was not lost on him that both had red faces and appeared winded. Indeed, Norrie's slender chest was heaving, and she was biting her full lower lip as if she was afraid she was going to burst out laughing at any second. The laughter sought escape through her twinkling eyes, instead.

"Good evening, Justinian," his mother heralded. "So good of you to join us. We were about to ring for dessert. Will you have some?"

He took a deep breath. "No, thank you, Mother. Is everything all right up here?"

The countess raised a finely etched white eyebrow. "All right? Certainly. We are all fine, aren't we, Eleanor?"

Eleanor thought she would explode if she didn't let the laughter out. Until this evening, she had been successful in keeping the lordly little cat from exploring the countess's bedchamber. For some odd reason, the countess had demanded that he remain through dinner, and Eleanor had hardly eaten a bite before he had begun stalking about. His reactions to different pieces of furniture and belongings at the floor level had been funny enough, but when he jumped up on the dressing table and scowled at himself in the mirror, the countess had whooped with delight. Both Mary and Eleanor had repeatedly tried to distract him, but the calling, pulling, and petting had been to no avail. His highness Jingles was determined to play in the face powder and other interesting items. She had just spent the last few minutes in a wild chase about the room as the kitten bounded off furniture and scampered around the harried abigail's legs. As Justinian's gaze swept her direction, she sucked in a breath. Consequently, her voice came out entirely too high and tight. "Perfectly fine."

"You hear that?" the countess smiled serenely. "We're purrr-fectly fine."

Eleanor choked and bowed her head, clutching her heaving sides.

Alarmed, Justinian took a step toward her. "Miss Eleanor, has your illness returned?"

Eleanor waved him away. "No, no, really. I'm quite all right. Please don't let us disturb you."

The countess cocked her head. "You know, Eleanor dear, I think Justinian may be right. You look quite done in. You should go to bed immediately. Justinian, would you be so kind as to escort her?"

Eleanor froze, and Justinian frowned at his mother, who sighed gustily as if suddenly quite weary herself.

"I'm sure Miss Eleanor would rather have Mary," he replied so quellingly that Eleanor felt herself pale.

"Out of the question," his mother snapped, drawing her

shawl more tightly around her shoulders. "She can't be spared. Good night, Eleanor dearest. I'm sure you'll feel better in the morning. Don't forget to take the kitten with you."

Eleanor had no choice but to hug the countess goodnight, as she had been wont to do. "Yes, your ladyship, thank you." As she pulled away, she swore she saw the countess wink. Discomposed, she could only peer under the dressing table, where she had last seen the kitten. "Jingles? Here, kitty, kitty."

"Allow me," Justinian clipped, reaching up the bed hangings beside his mother and untangling the kitten's claws from its precarious hold. Jingles blinked at him and had the audacity to yawn. Eleanor hurried forward to accept the little animal.

"Thank you, my lord," she murmured, burying her face in the kitten's fur to hide her embarrassment. Unfortunately, that only set her nose to itching, and they hadn't even reached the door before she was sneezing again.

"Give him to me," Justinian commanded as they started down the corridor. Face reddening, she complied.

"I'm very sorry we disturbed your work," she told him, eyes following the scroll pattern in the Oriental carpet underfoot. "The countess does so enjoy Jingles's antics. I had no idea our hilarity was carrying beyond the room."

"It is of no significance," Justinian assured her and was surprised to find that he meant it. "My mother needs something to take her mind off her problems."

"Is she so very ill, then?" Eleanor couldn't help asking. For as long as she had been at the Barnsley School, the countess had been bedridden. It struck her now that she had never been told why. She supposed it was not a subject for a lowly schoolteacher.

Justinian answered her readily enough. "Dr. Praxton tells me there is nothing wrong with her outside the normal changes that come with age. My father married late. My mother was nearly forty-five when I was born. She will be seventy-five this year."

"Shhh," Eleanor cautioned. "I don't think she likes that fact to be well-known. Besides, if she isn't unwell, why does she remain in bed?"

Justinian sighed. "I wish I knew. But she seems happier now than any time I can remember." He glanced at her, and decided to speak his mind. "You seem to have that effect on people."

Eleanor blushed again, and wished she had Jingles to hide it. She glanced quickly at the kitten, who lay cuddled against Justinian's broad chest. Jingles's yellow eyes were closed, and his cheek nuzzled against the black waistcoat, not far from Justinian's heart. She could imagine no finer place to rest. She swallowed and averted her gaze.

"Norrie." He stopped in the corridor, and she had no choice but to stop beside him. "Norrie, we must talk. We cannot be expected to live in this house for the next fortnight as if we are nearly strangers."

"But we are nearly strangers, my lord." She was as insistent as she was quiet-spoken, and she knew he was listening. "It's been nearly ten years. I have heard that you went on to be a great scholar, just as you had planned. And now you are being the earl, which I know you had not planned, nor even wished. Our lives were different, then. The paths have only diverged even farther. You are no longer Justinian Darby, and I am no longer Norrie Pritchett. You are Lord Wenworth. And I am Miss Eleanor, the schoolteacher. That is how things are. It took me some time to truly understand this. Now, if you will please hand me Jingles, I will say good night."

She was so calm and sure of herself that any nebulous ideas of professing undying devotion blew away like mist in the wind. Solemnly he handed her the kitten, who snuggled just as contentedly against her breast as he had against Justinian's chest moments before. "Very well, Miss Eleanor, if that is how you feel. I guess we have nothing to discuss, after all."

Norrie couldn't understand why her eyes blurred as he walked away. It must have been the illness returning, after all.

# Seven

Eleanor assured herself that it should have been easy to act nobly so close to the Christmas season, but she found it progressively difficult. She should have been relieved that Justinian did not mention their past relationship again, but was not a little disappointed to find that he gave her a wide berth. She should feel pleased that by reminding him unselfishly of his greater duty—which was to marry someone far more important in the world than one insignificant schoolteacher—she had put a wall between them. That was what she had meant to do, and she had succeeded. Now she just had to finish her business and leave.

There was still over a sennight before Christmas on the day the snow began to fall. She had taken Jingles out to play in the gardens that edged the back of the house, and was surprised to find how cold it had grown. They had only gone a little ways along the house from the kitchen when the first flakes descended, large and heavy. Jingles didn't notice them at first. When he did, he proceeded to pounce upon them as interlopers in his kingdom, lifting his paws in approval to find nothing but a thoroughly vanquished puddle. As Eleanor's own cloak was beginning to dampen, she soon scooped him up and hurried up the steps to the terrace to find the nearest entrance to the manor.

She knew the first door she came upon would lead into the library; she had seen Justinian standing outside it often enough. She almost continued on, but a quick look through the open curtain on the double doors showed the chair behind the great desk as empty as the room beyond. She thankfully slipped inside, setting Jingles down long enough to shrug out of her damp cloak and wrap the wetness away from the papers and books. She glanced about the lamp-lit room again, reassuring herself that Justinian was indeed not in residence, although a warm fire glowed in the grate and papers were spread upon the desk. Unfortunately, in the brief moment she had surveyed the room, she had lost sight of Jingles.

She tiptoed farther into the room, peering under the legs of the various chairs and book tables, but could not find the kitten. A dull thud behind her sent a chill through her. Whipping about, she found not Justinian but something far worse.

"Jingles, get down!" she cried, rushing back to the desk where the kitten was capering about on the open papers. Jingles ignored her, pushing the stack of crackling parchment ruthlessly to the floor as if annoyed it dared share the desk with him. Eleanor grabbed him up and held him firmly against her. "That is quite enough, my paper despot." She glanced down at the parchment, and her heart sank. What was once nicely written prose was now muddy blobs of watery ink dotted with the unmistakable footprints of a kitten. Remembering how much Justinian's work had always meant to him, she shuddered to think how he would react when he knew it was ruined.

"We must find a way to fix this," she told Jingles, bending closer. The page that had been smeared, she saw, was nearly the last page of a rather long piece. Perhaps if she took it and some of the earlier pages, she might be able to recopy it on the parchment in her room and then replace it before Justinian knew it had gone missing. It was certainly worth a try. If he discovered it before she finished, she would simply explain the circumstances. She wouldn't have to give him another task to undertake.

That night in her room, however, she was surprised to

find not some weighty estate matter or a legal writ before her, but the finale of what was surely a novel. The descriptions conjured pictures in her mind, she found herself liking the character who was obviously the hero, and she was so caught up in the scene of the hero confronting the villain that when she found she had not picked up the final pages, she nearly cried in disappointment. It was some of the most well-written prose she had ever read, and it had surely been written by Justinian Darby.

She sat back in her chair at the writing table in her room and pulled Jingles away from the precious pages. Justinian Darby, a novelist. She envied him, and she pitied him. As a renowned scholar, he would never have been respected for publishing anything so frivolous as an adventure story, which this obviously was. As the Earl of Wenworth, it was unthinkable. She doubted whether anyone but herself had ever read so much as a page. That was the greatest pity, for it was as good as any she had seen. How difficult it must be for him to find time to write it, and to hide it away.

Over the next two nights it was a labor of love to decipher and copy the smeared sections. As she did so, her respect for the piece only grew. Surely there was some way he could publish it. He deserved the literary acclaim it would certainly receive. Lord Byron and Walter Scott published their works under their own names. Yet, they did not bear the proud name of Darby. Perhaps he could publish it anonymously, as the woman was doing who had written *Sense and Sensibility*.

She pondered the matter so thoroughly that the countess caught her wool-gathering the next day. Eleanor jumped as Lady Wenworth rapped her knuckles sharply with her quizzing glass.

"And what is more important than my most entertaining story of the bruise on my toe?" she demanded, eyes narrowing.

Eleanor shook her head with a smile. "Oh, certainly nothing *I* might think of."

The countess grinned. "That's my girl. Seriously, my

dear, is something troubling you? You have seemed rather pensive of late. You aren't thinking of leaving us, are you?"

Eleanor managed to keep a pleasant smile in place. "I promised to stay until Christmas, did I not? But I regret, my lady, that my plans have not changed. Once Dottie is home and settled, I must move on."

"That school cannot need you as much as I do," the countess sniffed, pursing her lips into something very much resembling a pout. "This is most vexing. I've done everything I can think of, and still you and Justinian do not seem to have come to an agreement."

Eleanor swallowed. The woman could not mean what she thought. "An agreement?"

The countess was watching her, and there was no mistaking the shrewdness in those blue eyes. "Yes, an agreement. My son may sometimes be obtuse, but I'm sure he noticed that you bear a striking resemblance to Norrie Pritchett. I must admit, however, I find Eleanor much more elegant."

"You know?" Eleanor whispered.

"Whatever other ailments I may have, I'm not blind, my dear."

"But you couldn't have met me above four times!" Eleanor protested.

"I believe it was five, and you are very memorable, dear. A mother usually remembers her son's first love, if she is lucky enough to be privy to it."

"He didn't love me." Eleanor shook her head, and she wondered suddenly whom she was trying to convince.

"Oh, but I disagree. Justinian quite wore his heart on his sleeve, the poor lamb. Why else did you think my husband felt he must send you away?"

Eleanor hung her head "He thought I had designs on the Darby fortune. I assure you, your ladyship, I didn't then, and I don't now."

"Ah." The countess let the word hang in the air for a moment, then sighed. "Then you don't love my son."

Eleanor couldn't lie about that. She kept her head

down. "Your husband was very convincing. It isn't appropriate for someone like me to love a Darby."

"What exactly did he say to make you think that?"

She didn't stop to wonder why the countess would ask. "He said a great many things. The one I remember most often is 'the best you can hope for from my son is to bear his bastard.' I didn't stay to hear any more."

"I should think not." The countess's blue-veined hand reached out and lay on top of her clenched fingers. "My husband was very opinionated, my dear, and I'm ashamed to say that I condoned it. Goodness, I most likely encouraged it. I'm very opinionated myself, in case you hadn't noticed."

Eleanor sniffed back tears and managed a smile. "I had rather gotten that impression."

The countess's smile was gentle. "And you are not opinionated enough, if you let yourself believe all that was told you. We Darbys are famed for our arrogance, as well as our generosity. Thank God Justinian seems to have inherited only the generosity of spirit. I've seen the way he looks at you, my dear. You could still have him."

Eleanor surged to her feet. "If you are suggesting as your husband did that my best hope is becoming Justinian's *par amour,* the answer is no. Do not suggest that again, or Darby or no Darby, I shall pack my things and leave this house immediately."

"Oh, honestly," Lady Wenworth sighed, "you young people are entirely too volatile. I had to wait until I was at least sixty before throwing such ultimatums at my elders. I am suggesting nothing of the sort. You would make my son an excellent wife."

Eleanor's legs suddenly refused to bear her weight, and she sank back onto the chair. "His wife? Me?"

"Oh, you are so delightful. You shock so easily. I vow it's simply too much fun. Yes, dear, his wife. I could plant the idea in his mind, if you'd like."

"Yes, no! I mean you certainly are capable of doing so, but I wish you would not."

The countess raised her eyebrows. "Whyever not? You have as much as admitted you love my son. You have all the qualities I would wish for in a daughter-in-law—you are devoted and caring, and you aren't afraid to speak your own mind. If I read my son correctly, it would take very little to sway him."

"No," Eleanor repeated, scarcely knowing what to think. "I cannot let him make such a mistake. He has his family name to consider, your family name."

"Pish tosh. I was a Burns long before I was a Darby. The old line could do with some new blood."

Eleanor shook her head. "No. Please do not tease me on this. If you care anything for me, you will let things stand the way they are."

The countess's eyes narrowed. "You should know by now that the only person I care for is myself. I do as I please around here."

Eleanor rose again, shaking out her skirts and trying to hide the fact that her hands were trembling. "Then you do it without me. Persist in this line, and I will leave tomorrow morning."

The countess glared up at her and Eleanor glared back. They stood locked, gaze to gaze, lips compressed, jaws firm.

With a determined thud, Jingles overturned the countess's face powder. The countess lowered her gaze with a shrug. "Ungrateful kitten," she sniffed. "He has yet to learn the appropriate manners for a Great House."

Eleanor went to scoop Jingles out of the pink dust, which coated his fur from tail to nose, leaving kitten tracks across the surface of the rosewood dresser. "Some are not born to the manor, my lady," she replied, dusting him off. "Jingles's pink nose twitched, and he sneezed. "Some of us are content with only a place by the fire."

"Yes, well, even those can learn to be of service."

Eleanor bit her lip to keep from responding. *From potential countess to serving girl in a few moments,* she thought with a shake of her head.

"He needs your help, you know," the countess continued doggedly.

Eleanor held the kitten up and turned him about. "Yes," she tsked, "he is a bit dirty. I suppose I'll have to wash him off."

"Not the infernal cat—my son!"

She turned to find the countess sitting straight up in the bed, color high.

"I thought we just agreed," she replied to the countess, "that there was nothing appropriate I could do for Lord Wenworth."

"You have chosen to see yourself as beneath him. That makes you so in my eyes. Yet you might still be of use to me. He won't listen to me. He is working himself to an early grave. What am I to do then, eh?"

Eleanor's mind flashed to his bowed head and felt a chill. "Nonsense," she replied firmly. "Your son is a brilliant scholar. He'll find a way out of whatever is wrong."

"A brilliant scholar he may be, but who's to know? Do any of them care how brilliant he is?" She waved her hand as she had been wont to do, but there was anger in the movement. "His brothers, his steward, those dolts in Wenwood, the people on the estate? They hound him and hound him, and never listen to his reasonable answers. A scholar, you say? He is a scholar because I wanted a scholar. Adam was always my husband's son, and Alex and Jareth belong to no one, but Justinian, Justinian was all mine. I wanted a great philosopher, a poet, a genius. I'm afraid the old adage is true. One should be careful what one wishes for. Justinian is all those things, and as a result, he is a miserable earl."

"He is a wonderful earl!" Eleanor protested. "He takes his duty seriously, which is more than I can say for the last few Earls of Wenwood."

The countess raised an eyebrow, and Eleanor felt herself blushing, realizing she had just criticized the lady's husband and elder son.

"You see, you *do* have some opinions," the countess remarked. "Much as I admire your willingness to stand up for the boy, the truth of the matter is, if he is not a miserable earl, he is miserable *because* he is the earl. You could help him there, I think."

"How?" Eleanor asked suspiciously, though in truth a part of her would have liked nothing more than to sincerely help Justinian.

"Christmas is nearly here. Distract him long enough to let him enjoy it."

Eleanor gazed at her, a plan beginning to form. Could she truly give Justinian a happy Christmas? Could the schoolteacher find a gift worthy of giving a Darby? "I can try. But I'll need your help, as well."

The countess gazed back just as suspiciously. "What must I do?"

"You can start by giving me the addresses of your other sons."

She frowned. "Why?"

"Never you mind. You wanted me to trust you enough to have you arrange my marriage to your son. You can learn to trust me for a simple Christmas. Besides, the addresses are the easy part. If I can contrive to have a Christmas Eve celebration in honor of Dottie's return, you must agree to dress and come down for dinner."

Lady Wenworth collapsed back upon her pillows. "I haven't dressed for dinner in over twenty years."

Eleanor smiled. "Then it's high time you started, don't you think?" As if in agreement, Jingles sneezed.

# Eight

Justinian found himself unaccountably depressed as Christmas drew near. He had yet to arrive at a workable solution on the levees, his mother seemed unusually agitated, and he had not had time to touch his novel outside of a short evening some days ago. All those things would have been enough to depress any gentleman, but he suspected that in reality the main problem was that Norrie had cut him off so abruptly. His attempts to renew their acquaintance had only served to push her farther away. She seemed to be sensitive to his least remark, so confronting her would hardly prove a remedy. It seemed perhaps his father had been right all along. Somehow, that thought was the most depressing of all.

Trying to ease his mind, he threw himself into his estate work, remaining closeted with the beleaguered steward from early in the morning until long after the sun had set. He was therefore surprised to find, when he left the library late one afternoon, that Faringil and three strapping footmen were busily draping evergreen boughs along the railing of the great stair. Glancing about, he found a similar swag festooning the doorways to the morning room, the withdrawing room, and the dining room. "Are we having some sort of celebration?" He frowned.

Faringil motioned the footmen to keep working and stepped down to his side, dusting off his hands on the apron he wore tied about his waist. "I believe we may be doing so, my lord," he replied.

Justinian waited, but no more answer was forthcoming. He wagered a guess. "Christmas?"

"Just so, my lord," Faringil agreed.

"How many days away now?" Justinian asked, almost afraid to hear the answer.

"Three days, my lord?" Faringil tried hopefully.

Justinian rolled his eyes. "Good God, man, it's perfectly all right to have an opinion on something that is a matter of fact. Is it or is it not three days to Christmas?"

The footmen paused in their work, throwing not so covert glances over their shoulders at the butler, who was reddening. "If his lordship thinks there are three days," he replied solemnly, "there are three days."

"And if his lordship thinks it's a balmy summer's day?" Justinian countered, exasperated.

"Then," Eleanor replied, exiting the parlor with an armload of holly, "his lordship will be noted as having taken leave of his senses, and life will continue."

The footmen's eyes widened in amazement. Faringil choked on whatever he was going to say, covering it with a discreet cough behind his hand. Justinian found himself grinning.

He swept her a bow. "Ah, the sweet voice of reason at last. I take it this is all your idea."

Eleanor felt herself blushing. "Actually, your mother got me started. We thought we might decorate the house for Dottie. You will be going to get her the day after tomorrow, won't you?"

Justinian nodded. "I will indeed. And by the looks of it, this will be a festive homecoming for her."

"I hope so," Eleanor smiled. "We've gathered greenery for all the rooms, and Mary and the other maids are making boughs for the mantels and doorways. Now, if I can just keep Jingles from helping with the decoration, all should be well."

"How is your little charge?" he asked, noting the way

the greenery brought out the color in her cheeks. *Black is entirely wrong for her,* he thought. *I should ask the school to change its teachers' uniforms to something less somber, pink perhaps.* He blinked the absurd thought away.

"He is well," Eleanor replied. She straightened, then continued resolutely. "That is, he is as well as I have been able to make him. I do hope, with Dottie coming home and me leaving right after Christmas, that someone will be given charge of him?"

"That's right, you are leaving." Somehow that thought was the most important of anything she'd said. The new year seemed to stretch on drearily.

Eleanor bowed her head. "That was my plan," she replied, knowing that at least four pairs of ears were keenly listening to her response. "I have been given no reason to change it."

He stared, and she hoped perhaps he had understood. Before she could glance up to be certain, she spied a black tail disappearing into the dining room. "Oh, dear!"

"What?" Justinian snapped, clearly pulled out of another thought.

She dropped a quick curtsy. "Forgive me, my lord, but I must see to the kitten." She hurried around the stair toward the dining room.

"Infernal animal," Justinian muttered. Had he understood her correctly? Was she actually encouraging him to offer? He watched her disappear into the darkened room. Around him, the footmen quickly busied themselves with their work, moving farther up the stairs with each turn of the boughs. Nonchalantly, Justinian crossed the entry and wandered down the corridor to the entrance to the dining room.

As his mother took her dinners, in her room and he had been taking his in the library, the room hadn't been used since his brother died. He was surprised to find the long oval table polished, with a silver epergne of greenery in the center. More boughs draped the satin-hung walls, and ivy wreathed the back of the sideboard. The silver chandelier glittered brightly in the light from the corridor and he thought each of the one hundred some candles was new.

The room appeared to be empty. "Miss Eleanor?" he ventured, his voice echoing to the ceiling high above. "Norrie?"

There was a muted thud and a muffled cry. They sounded from very near the floor. Frowning, he bent and peered under the table. "Are you all right?"

"Fine, fine," came the response from somewhere down the table. "I'll be out directly."

He strolled along the row of lyre-backed chairs, head cocked to scan under the table "You're sure?"

"Yes, completely. If you'd just be so kind as to go away."

Justinian paused, raising an eyebrow. "Go away? Why?"

As if in answer, Jingles strutted out from under the table. He stalked past Justinian and paused impressively in the doorway, eyeing him with apparent disfavor. Then he turned his back on Justinian and began washing himself.

Justinian turned his gaze to the table in time to see Norrie backing out from under it on all fours. He was ashamed to admit it was a rather fetching picture, but when she turned and saw him, he suddenly wished he had found some other way to occupy his time. Her lips were compressed, and her eyes snapped fire.

"I distinctly told you to go away," she clipped out, stalking past him every bit as stiffly as the kitten had done.

"Ah, but you see, this is my house," Justinian replied, hurrying to catch up with her.

"And that should be your kitten," Eleanor countered, averting her gaze, hoping her embarrassment could be hidden beneath her anger. "I fail to see why I must continually take care of him."

"Simply because you're so very good at taking care of people," Justinian answered truthfully. He touched her shoulder, stopping her, then managed to secure her hands in his own. "I must thank you for being so kind to my mother. She has been rather gruff of late. She tells me she shall miss you greatly."

"I'll miss her, too." Eleanor sighed. "But I must move on. You understand, don't you?"

Suddenly, he didn't understand at all. Still, he tried to remain congenial. "I don't understand, actually, but as you have pointed out we do seem to be different people these days. However, I have not forgotten my manners. I was trying to thank you, for doing this for my mother, and for Dottie." He glanced about the room again, and his gaze lit on the bough that had been hung over the dining room door. The shape and make of the materials were unmistakable. A grin spread across his handsome face. "And I must compliment Mary on her work, as well. That is the finest kissing bough I have ever seen."

Eleanor glanced up, horrified. The mistletoe and apples stood out in the dim light. She glanced wildly out the door, but the footmen and Mr. Faringil must be nearly at the top of the stair, for they were nowhere in sight. She was quite alone, with Justinian.

He could see she was frightened, but he could not seem to stop himself. If he was branded as being in love, perhaps it was time he started acting like it. "It would be a shame to waste such a lovely kissing bough," he murmured, bending his head to hers.

His kiss was like nothing she had dreamed. No poem he had ever read to her, no story she had imagined, captured the sweet fire of it. The love she had felt for him all those years welled up inside her, adding to the warmth of his embrace, making her press herself against him, returning his kiss with all her heart. She willed the moment never to end, prayed that he would feel what she felt at that moment, for if he did, surely he would never let her go again.

But he did let her go, drawing a shaky breath and gazing down at her with a warmth in his eyes that took what little breath she had remaining away. Norrie could only stare at him. His lips looked as warmed and swollen as hers felt.

"Norrie," he started, voice husky. "Forgive me. I should never have . . ."

Her heart nearly broke at his words. She held up a hand and sealed his mouth, feeling the sweet pressure of his lips against her fingers. "No, please, don't. I don't want to hear apologies. I've always wished I knew what it was like to kiss you. Thank you for granting that wish. You needn't worry I'll read too much into it. I know my place."

"Your place!" The force of his words pushed her hand away. "After a kiss like that, your only place is with me."

Eleanor paled, stepping away from him. How could he, after what they had shared? Was her love so cheap, after all, that all she was worthy of was to be his mistress? She bent and scooped up Jingles, thrusting the kitten into Justinian's arms. "My place," she said clearly, "is belowstairs, with the other servants. At least they have some dignity. I pray you'll leave me a little of it, and not mention that subject again."

Head high, she stalked from the room. Shaken and confused, Justinian could only peer after her, noting that before she even reached the door to the kitchen Norrie Pritchett was running as if her life depended on it.

# Nine

Justinian Darby prided himself on being a scholar, but he had been the first to admit he knew very little about women. After his encounter with Norrie two days ago, he was prepared to admit he knew nothing. He had puzzled and puzzled over her reaction, but he could not understand it. The only conclusion he could come to was that she had mistaken his comments for an offer of a *carte blanche*, but that made little sense. He would hardly offer someone like Norrie the opportunity to be his mistress. In the first place, she was entirely too much of a lady to even think of doing anything so reprehensible, and in the second place, surely she knew he would never dishonor her. Still, he had felt it only proper to honor her request and leave her alone, at least until he understood his own mind.

Now, after two days of pondering, he was no closer to understanding her, but he knew what he wanted. If there was any good thing that might come from his being made the earl, it was that he was now the one to make the decisions. And he had decided that the best thing he could possibly do with his life was to marry Norrie. Now, all he had to do was convince her of that fact.

He was feeling rather optimistic when he arrived at the Barnsley School just before lunch to retrieve Dottie for the Christmas holiday. Unfortunately, that was the last time he was to feel optimistic for quite some time. Miss Martingale, the headmistress, was her usual obsequious self, fawning over him from the moment he arrived. Her attitude set his teeth on edge, just as much as Faringil's did. Given all the matters on his mind, he supposed it wasn't surprising when he cut short her excessively long welcoming speech with a curt, "May I see my niece now?"

Miss Martingale blinked, snapping her mouth shut. She nodded to one of the other staff who had been assembled to receive him, and he offered the mousy little woman a grateful nod. As she scuttled from the room, he was thankful that Norrie had somehow managed not to be infected by the sheer subservient attitude that seemed to dominate the place. Perhaps she was right in having him remove Dottie permanently.

Thinking of Norrie made him remember that he should at least thank Miss Martingale for letting them appropriate her. "Miss Pritchett seems quite recovered from her illness," he offered as they waited in what was becoming a rather chilly silence.

The large headmistress affixed him with a cold stare. "Indeed. I wish her well."

"I'm not sure when we will be returning her to you," Justinian continued. "My mother seems to have taken a fancy to her." *Not to mention the fancy I seem to have taken,* he added silently. He wondered how the woman would take it if he succeeded in getting Norrie to marry him. The scandal would be one of the few ever to enliven the Darby reputation, but he was certain his family name would survive.

Miss Martingale frowned, and he was sure any child seeing such a face would run screaming for the door. "Am I to understand, my lord, that you have taken that woman in?"

Something in her tone told him this conversation was going to unnerve him. "I must object to you referring to Miss Pritchett as 'that woman,' " he replied. "But yes, she is staying with us. My mother asked that she remain until Christmas. I thought you had been informed. My apologies for detaining her from her duties. You must have been frantic."

"As she was released from her duties in early December, I had no reason to care as to her whereabouts," Miss Martingale sniffed. "I must say, I'm very sorry to see that she finally managed to ingratiate herself into your family, my lord. Your father warned me about her years ago, but I thought that he and I together had curbed her tendency to think beyond her station. Unfortunately, only recently I realized she was using Lady Dorothea to get to the Darbys. Of course, I summarily sacked the wretched woman."

Justinian stared at her. "Are you trying to tell me that Norrie Pritchett is a social climber, a fortune hunter?"

"I regret to say that I believe so, my lord. I tried to teach her otherwise, but I seem to have failed. I hope you know, Lord Wenworth, that I expect all my teachers, and my students as well, to know their places in life."

Justinian flinched as she echoed the words Norrie had used only days before. "I can only say that you must be mistaken, Miss Martingale," he replied. The coolness of his tone was not lost on the headmistress, who paled.

"Of course, my lord. You would know better than I."

It was all Justinian could do not to close his eyes in frustration at the familiar refrain.

His spirits nearly recovered on the ride home with Dottie, who fairly bounced in her seat beside him in the sleigh. The snow that had started a week ago had continued off and on, so the fields lay under a blanket as white as the countess's counterpane, with the Mendip Hills in the distance piled as high as her pillows.

"And Jingles is really waiting for me?" she asked him for what was surely the fourth time since leaving the school.

Justinian smiled. "Yes, he is really waiting for you. Your Miss Eleanor has been taking very good care of him." He paused, eyeing his niece. "Miss Eleanor is very good at taking care of people, isn't she, Dottie?"

Dottie bit her lip, lowering her eyes, and Justinian's fears increased. "Miss Martingale and Miss Lurkin say I was unkind to Miss Eleanor," she murmured. "It isn't right to make friends with people not of one's class. It gives the wrong impression and encourages coaching."

Justinian frowned. "I think the word you're looking for is encroachment, Dottie. And Miss Martingale and Miss Lurkin are no doubt teaching you what they believe is right. However, you must form your own opinions on that matter."

Dottie glanced up, a small light of hope in her eyes. "Then it's all right if I just love Miss Eleanor anyway, even if she isn't a Darby?"

Justinian's smile returned, hearing his own hopes echoed in her words. "Yes, sweeting, it's perfectly all right to love Miss Eleanor."

"Oh, that's famous!" Dottie exclaimed, her enthusiasm restored as quickly as it has been lost.

Justinian wished he could recover his good spirits so easily. After the conversation with the headmistress and his niece, it was apparent to him where Norrie got her notions about her place in the world. However, he could not subscribe to Miss Martingale's belief, or his father's if the tale were true, that Norrie was a fortune hunter. Everyone kept telling him that his emotions were obvious, yet she had not encouraged him in the least. In fact, she had gone out of her way to discourage him. Of course, if his initial conclusions were right, and she thought he was offering his love but not his position, she might only be holding out for a better offer.

His conviction was put to the test that very afternoon, however, for Faringil was waiting for him when he returned with Dottie. The homecoming was everything Eleanor had worked to make it. Dottie exclaimed over the decorations and ran through the renovated schoolroom, touching this, holding that, and smiling at everyone. When he took her to see her grandmother, she threw her arms about Lady Wenworth, and his mother's eyes shone with tears of joy. Eleanor, however, was nowhere to be found. The idea that she would "keep her place" and not witness the joy she had worked to bring about infuriated him. Before he could seek her out, Faringil was standing silently behind him. When Justinian frowned at him, he merely bowed and beckoned. His frown deepening, Justinian followed him into the corridor.

"Begging your pardon, my lord," the butler intoned in a whisper, glancing up and down the corridor.

"Yes?" Justinian asked, refusing to lower his own voice.

"I don't like to interrupt Lady Dorothea's homecoming, but I have been given some rather disturbing news." He glanced up and down the corridor again, and Justinian had to hold himself back to keep from throttling the man.

"Well, then, out with it," he commanded.

Faringil drew a sheet of paper from inside his black satin waistcoat and carefully unfolded it. "Betsy found this in the trash, my lord. She originally kept it to use the back side of the paper for writing a letter to her mother, but Mrs. Childs saw it and recognized the handwriting. Or should I say, the attempt at the handwriting." He handed it to Justinian. "Someone appears to be trying to forge your name, my lord."

Justinian stared at the parchment. The page was filled with nothing but his name—"Justinian Darby, Earl of Wenworth,"—over and over again. The first few times bore little resemblance to the elegant script he had learned at Oxford, but gradually, something resembling his hand appeared. "Where did you find this?" he demanded.

"I regret to say, my lord, that it was under the writing table in Miss Eleanor's room."

Justinian felt a chill run through him. He thrust the paper back at Faringil. "There must be some logical explanation."

Faringil bowed his head. "Of course, my lord. Just as you say."

"Stop that this minute," Justinian thundered. Faringil jumped and took a step back, eyes widening. "I refuse to have a man in my employ who cannot or will not think for himself. I am not infallible, for God's sake! I am asking for your opinion, man. Have you lived so long under the

Darby roof that you don't know how to have a thought of your own?"

Faringil paled. "I would never presume, my lord—that is—I have the deepest respect, that is . . ."

"In other words," Justinian sighed, "the answer is yes. Small wonder I feel as if I'm the only one making decisions around here." He eyed his man, who seemed to have been reduced to a quivering pile of Christmas pudding. "Stand up, Mr. Faringil. I appreciate you bringing this to my attention. I will give the matter considerable thought, you can be sure. For now, say no more about it."

The butler bowed, relief written in his every movement. "Of course, my lord. Thank you, my lord." He hurried away from Justinian with steps easily twice as fast as his usual measured tread.

Justinian shook his head. He glanced down at the sheet of paper, which Faringil had refused to take, and saw that it was clenched in his hand. Relaxing his grip, he eased the sheet back to its full size. His name stared back at him. And something else. Along the bottom of the paper lay the smudged track of a kitten.

# Ten

Eleanor waited in the door of the dining room, clasping her hands to keep them from trembling. She didn't need to look up to be reminded of the kissing bough over her head, or of the scene that had taken place only days before. The kiss must not distract her, not tonight. She glanced again about the room, from where the candles blazed in the glittering silver chandelier to the crystal bowl of frothy eggnog on the sideboard. The great table was draped in damask, with six places set near the head, the gilt-edged bone china and gold cutlery glimmering against the expanse of white. A strand of ivy was entwined around the base of each crystal goblet, and in the center of the table lay an immense wreath of evergreens, holly, ivy, and dried red roses. Everything was ready for Christmas Eve dinner.

Dottie scampered down the stairs, resplendent in a red velvet dress with a satin bow hanging down her back. Lady Wenworth had decreed that the child could put off mourning, at least through the Christmas season. Dottie stopped before Eleanor and threw her arms around her.

"Happy Christmas, Miss Eleanor," she proclaimed, pulling her down to plant a kiss on her cheek.

Eleanor hugged her and straightened. "Happy Christmas to you, too, Dottie. Thank you for keeping your Uncle Justinian busy this afternoon. Your grandmother and I were also quite busy. Is everything ready in the withdrawing room?"

Dottie nodded, eyes sparkling. "Just as Grandmother and I talked about. Oh, Uncle Justinian won't know what to make of it."

"I certainly hope you're right," Eleanor replied, keeping her smile in place when she wanted to bite her lip in concern. What she was going to do tonight was the most daring thing she had ever done. If it succeeded, she would at last feel that she had done the Darbys a service. If it didn't . . . despite herself, she shivered.

Dottie apparently didn't notice, skipping to her place near the head of the table. "Where is everyone?" she pouted. "I don't want to wait."

"Now you sound like a Darby," Justinian said in the doorway. Eleanor took a hasty step back, and his welcoming smile seemed to dim. He bowed to her, and she curtsied, fingering the deep green velvet of the dress the countess had found for her. It had belonged to the countess's mother. Accordingly, the waist was far too low and the skirt far too wide for current fashion. The light of appreciation in Justinian's eyes as she rose from her curtsy made it the most beautiful dress in the world.

Justinian had spent the better part of the afternoon getting his niece settled. After visiting her grandmother, she had been surprising reluctant to let loose of him, confirming in his mind Norrie's assertion that Dottie sorely missed her parents. Twice, when her attentions were distracted by a new toy or dress, he had attempted to locate Faringil to take charge of her, only to be unable to find the man anywhere. Seeing the dining room now in all its glory told him how his butler had passed the afternoon. The only remaining puzzles were why six places had been set for himself, Dottie, and Eleanor, and why Eleanor had been writing his name. Once again, however, it was not the right time to ask.

"When my mother suggested I dress for dinner, I had no idea I'd be having such lovely company," he said, his nod taking in Dottie, as well. Dottie beamed at him and waved toward the head of the table.

"Take your seat, Uncle Justinian," she chirruped. "We're all famished."

He obligingly moved to do so, chuckling, but Eleanor remained at her spot. When he reached the head of the table and saw that she had not followed him, he frowned. Would the woman persist in keeping her place even on Christmas Eve? "You *will* be joining us for dinner, won't you, Miss Eleanor?"

The question could well have been a command. Eleanor curtsied again. "Of course, my lord. As you wish."

Justinian gazed at the ceiling. "Lord, give me patience."

"You can't say grace yet, Uncle Justinian," Dottie piped up. "Grandmother isn't here."

He lowered his gaze to hers. "The countess doesn't come down for dinner, Dottie," he said with a gentleness that touched Eleanor's heart. "You know that. Even though you've come home, you mustn't think everything is going to change."

"Christmas, my lord," Eleanor heard herself say, "is a time of miracles. That's what I've always been taught."

He glanced down at her, pride in her warring with what he knew to be reality. "You've been taught a number of things that appear to be in error, Miss Eleanor. But we can discuss that later."

Eleanor paled.

"Christmas, Justinian," said the countess from the foot of the stairs, "is no time for one of your scholarly lectures."

"Hurry, Grandmother!" Dottie urged. "You'll miss all the fun."

Justinian straightened, eyes widening in disbelief.

"Patience is a virtue, child," the countess replied, leaning heavily on a gold-tipped ebony cane and Mary's arm. "One you will probably not learn until you're past my age, if you're like most of the Darbys. Good evening, Eleanor. That dress is just as lovely on you as I thought it would be." She offered her cheek for Eleanor, who kissed it gratefully, the wrinkled skin soft beneath her lips. The countess winked at her as she labored past, lace-dusted lavender silk gown rustling with each step.

Justinian hurried from the head of the table to take Mary's place beside his mother. "Mother, are you sure you can do this?"

The countess thumped the tip of the cane very near the toe of his evening shoe. "Don't ask ridiculous questions. If I was completely sure of everything before I did it, I wouldn't do anything at all." She nodded to Mary, who quietly withdrew. Justinian escorted the countess to her place at his right. From the door at the back of the room, Mr. Faringil and the footman silently materialized. Faringil himself held out the chair for the countess to sit.

Justinian turned to see Eleanor standing still in the doorway. He frowned at her, but her face was turned toward the great stair, smiling in welcome. His frown deepened at the sound of footsteps on the stair.

"And then I told Wellington he could jolly well do without me for just one Christmas," Alexander Darby proclaimed, striding to the door in full dress regimentals. "Good evening, Miss Eleanor." He offered her a sharp bow as Justinian stared.

"You've been in the military far too long, Alex," Jareth Darby quipped, bumping his elder brother aside with the elbow of an immaculate black evening coat. "One does not bow when one catches a lovely lady under the mistletoe."

Eleanor blushed as he politely pecked her cheek. The light in those gray eyes, so like his brother's, told her he would prefer to do far more, but was being a gentleman for his family's sake. "Happy Christmas, Miss Eleanor," he murmured, then turned to the room. "Happy Christmas, all."

"Happy Christmas, Uncle Jareth, Uncle Alex!" Dottie exclaimed. "Come sit by me!"

"As there is only one seat beside you, infant, that is architecturally impossible," Jareth replied, strolling up the room. "And since Alex is far more comfortable with the infantry, I shall leave the honor to him." He took the chair beside his mother's, bending to kiss her cheek as well.

"Bravo, old girl. You're in fine looks. Makes me wish I wasn't related."

The countess rapped his knuckles where they rested on the back on her chair. "Jack-n-apes! You promised to behave tonight."

He pulled back his hands, grinning. "And so I shall. A Darby always keeps a promise. Isn't that so, Justinian?"

"Certainly," Justinian managed, although he had not fully recovered from seeing them all in the same room. What could have possibly induced his brothers to appear on Christmas Eve? His gaze seemed drawn down the table to where a lovely young woman stood under the mistletoe.

Eleanor watched his amazement with amusement and no little trepidation. The countess had confided that her sons had not been together for Christmas in over fifteen years. Eleanor was a little afraid how they might react to seeing each other again. She hadn't thought they would agree to come in the first place. Yet everything seemed to be going well.

Alex made his way stiffly up the table, stepping to Dottie's side. "Captain Dorothea, requesting permission to sit."

"Permission granted," Dottie replied with a solemn bow of her head. The giggle that escaped as he did so spoiled the effect.

"In polite society," the countess said to no one in particular, "the host generally escorts a guest in to dinner."

Justinian shook himself. Their guest deserved far more than his escort for what she had done this night. He came down the table toward her, watching her smile waver on her face, her hands clasping and unclasping. The only desire in his heart was to make her feel welcome in this house she had made into a home once again.

Eleanor watched Justinian as if from afar. All three of the brothers had inherited the thick golden Darby hair, the tall slender build, the planed features. While Jareth was a little rounder and far more dapper in his stylish cutaway coat and trousers, and Alex a little leaner and far more commanding in his uniform, they were in her eyes shadows compared to Justinian. He moved with the power and assurance of his position, his family, his own accomplishments. The light in his eyes made the black evening clothes seem all the more elegant. He bowed and offered her his arm.

"Uncle Justinian," Dottie sang out, giggling. "Remember what Uncle Jareth said about ladies under mistletoe."

Eleanor gasped, then shook her head at him, begging him with her eyes not to kiss her again, not in front of the countess and Dottie, Alexander and Jareth, Mr. Faringil and the footman. Justinian looked up as if he had just noticed the bough swinging overhead.

"I remember, Dottie." Following his brother's lead, he bent and placed a chaste kiss on Eleanor's cheek, which she knew was turning as red as the velvet of Dottie's dress. "Happy Christmas, Miss Eleanor," he murmured.

Words seemed stuck in her throat, but she managed a watery smile as she accepted his arm and let him lead her to her place next to Alex.

It was as merry a meal as Eleanor had prayed it would be. The countess was in rare form, teasing all of them until even Justinian was laughing and blushing. Dottie's enthusiasm was infectious. Jareth kept his quips kind, and Alex made an obvious effort to refrain from military cant. The food Eleanor and Mrs. Childs had decided upon was delicious, and Mr. Faringil went so far as to whisper, "Well done, Miss Eleanor," when the dessert, a steaming Christmas pudding, was served.

The countess rose as the last dish was cleared away and Justinian and his brothers rose with her. "Do not tarry long over your port, dears," she commanded them, moving slowly down the table with Dottie beside her. "We have need of you in the withdrawing room."

As Eleanor rose to follow them, Justinian moved around the table to catch her arm. "Thank you," he murmured, conscious of his brothers' gaze on him. "What you did tonight makes me believe you are right about Christmas. It is indeed a time of miracles."

Eleanor swallowed, blushing under the warmth of his regard. "We are not finished yet, my lord," she replied, pulling gently away. "Please join us as soon as you can."

"Every moment will seem an eternity," Justinian promised, sending a flood of fresh color to her cheek.

He knew he should refuse the port Faringil hovered to pour for them and follow Eleanor from the room. But the dinner had caught him completely by surprise, and he needed time to collect himself. Accordingly, he sat back in his seat and let his man fill the goblets.

Jareth picked up his glass, rolling the stem between long fingers. "She's a treasure, that one. I assume I should wish you happy, brother."

"One should not assume, Mr. Darby," Alexander countered, taking a quick shot of his port. "Miss Eleanor is undoubtedly charming, and she certainly won this battle, but has she got what it takes to win the war?"

"By war, I take it you mean the famed Darby consequence?" Justinian replied, voice laced with sarcasm. "I find it difficult to remember that we are so very high above her when in her presence."

"Women have a way of clouding one's logic," Alex nodded. "Dangerous thing that, very dangerous."

"For once we are in agreement," Jareth put in. "However, as I leave the logic to you two, I say marry the chit. Either that, or set her up in a nice flat in London."

Justinian glared at him. "That is unthinkable. Surely after meeting her you would advise marriage."

Jareth grinned. "For anyone but me, of course."

"Do not listen to him, Justinian." Alex scowled. "You cannot ask the cooking pot whether the lamb should go free. You are the earl now, and certain conventions must prevail, regardless of how you might feel. It's a shame, old man, but there it is. No amount of Christmas miracle will change that."

When Justinian did not answer him, he sighed and rose, motioning Jareth to do likewise. "We will leave you to think on it, brother. When it comes to that, we always did what you and Adam agreed on."

Jareth could not pass up a parting comment. "At least, in most areas." They quit the room, leaving him alone.

The room was suddenly silent, reminding him of how it had rung with joy only minutes before. Even his brothers' counsel was a precious gift, but one he would not have without Eleanor's work. In fact without Eleanor, he feared, this is what his life would return to, this wasteland of duty and silence. Whether she knew it or not, she had just swept away any doubts he might have had on her ability to play his countess. What had he thought he needed? Someone to organize parties, entertain his mother, shepherd Dottie to adulthood. He saw now that those were superficial things, unimportant in his life. What he needed, what they all needed, was someone who truly cared, just as Eleanor did.

Suddenly, it didn't matter that his father had suspected she was after the family fortune. It didn't matter that Alex thought she was still beneath them, or that Jareth thought she would make a good mistress. It didn't matter that she had been sacked from the school for disobedience. It didn't even matter that she had been writing his name over and over again for some purpose he couldn't fathom. Everything told him that she was what he needed. This time, he would not let her get away so easily.

He rose and went to join his family in the withdrawing room.

# Eleven

Eleanor laughed out loud as Alexander succeeded in capturing another handful of raisins from the steaming silver snap dragon bowl. Jareth pouted, greatly resembling the countess, while Dottie clapped her hands with glee. Bowing, her uncle surrendered the fruits to her enjoyment.

Justinian leaned against the mantel, watching them with amusement. He had never seen his family so happy. Even the jaded Jareth was chuckling as Dottie attempted to hand-feed him the now quite squashed raisins. As Justinian shouted bravo to Eleanor's final attempt to plunge her hand into the bowl of flame-tipped, brandy-soaked raisins, something nudged his foot. Glancing down, he found Jingles sitting on his feet as if surveying from a throne. He scooped the little fellow up into his arms. Jingles sniffed but, apparently deciding the view was better, settled himself against Justinian's black, watered-silk waistcoat.

"Oh, that was fun!" Dottie declared as the footmen extinguished the flames and carried away the bowl. "What shall we do next?"

"Bring in the Yule Log, of course," the countess proclaimed from her seat on the sofa. "Eleanor, my love, be so kind as to show Justinian where we put it."

Faringil stiffened, but Justinian knew he would say nothing against the countess. Alex and Jareth exchanged glances. It was hardly a Darby's place to lug a damp log from the cellar or kitchen to the withdrawing room.

Eleanor was paling, as if she, too, realized the impropriety. He silently blessed his mother for interfering and giving him time alone with his Norrie. He swept her a bow in offer of his services, and she had no choice but to proceed him out the door.

He stopped her in the entryway, motioning her down the corridor to the library, where they were unlikely to be disturbed.

"But my lord," she protested, feebly he thought, "the log is in the breezeway."

"And there is something far more important in the library," he assured her, shutting the door behind her. She jumped at the sound and scurried toward the dwindling fire as if afraid to be near him. He took a step toward her and belatedly realized that he still held Jingles. Bending, he let the kitten free on the floor, going instead to light a lamp on the desk.

"You have already thanked me for tonight," Eleanor started, hoping to forestall anything he might say so that they might escape the library before he saw the letter lying on the desk. It was her final gift to him, and she was loathe for him to see it before tomorrow. "Let us fetch the log and return to your family."

"I would not have a family tonight but for you," Justinian countered, moving slowly closer. He didn't want to frighten her, but the need to hold her was almost overpowering. "Norrie, I cannot stand having you near but being unable to touch you."

She closed her eyes to block the view of his anguished face. "Don't. Please. I cannot be what you want."

"You don't know what I want. I've heard all the arguments about propriety and place. None of them matter. Marry me, Norrie. Let me give you the place you deserve."

Her eyes snapped open, heart leaping within her. "What . . . what did you say?"

He dropped to one knee and held out his hands to her. "Please, Miss Eleanor Pritchett, would you do me the great honor of becoming my wife?"

"Oh, Justinian!" She fell to her knees beside him and was immediately swept up in an embrace that was warmer than any place by the fire. When at last he released her, she could only lay her head against his chest, sighing. Behind them came the unmistakable rustle of paper. "Jingles!" she cried, clambering to her feet. Justinian rose just as hurriedly as she dashed to the desk. The unrepentant kitten was shoving about the papers, sending Justinian's many reports sliding off to the floor and rumpling Eleanor's precious letter nearly beyond recognition. She snatched up the startled kitten and thrust him at an equally surprised Justinian. Smoothing the letter, she found it was still readable, and heaved a sigh of relief.

"What is it?" Justinian asked, looking over her shoulder as Jingles wriggled in his grip.

Eleanor swallowed, turning to him. "Your Christmas gift. I believe it is customary for servants and tenants to give a gift to the lord of the manor on Christmas."

He frowned. "You are hardly a servant or tenant."

"Well, I must admit I wasn't completely convinced of that until a few days ago. I've run away from you once, Justinian, and I almost did so again. I was afraid I wasn't good enough for you."

"That is ridiculous," he snapped, but she held out a hand to stop him.

"Yes, it is. But you mustn't blame your father or the school. Your mother said it best, I think. She told me that I chose to see myself as beneath you, and so I was. It wasn't until I found I could help the great Darbys that I realized that it was only my own fear that kept me from admitting how much I love you."

"Norrie," he started, but she thrust the letter at him before he could deter her with sweet words of love.

"Justinian Darby, you are a great novelist. The publisher at Simons and Harding in London agrees with me."

He stared at the letter, then up at her face. It was the first time she had ever seen a Darby pale.

"You know about the novel?" he whispered.

"Jingles found it one afternoon, I'm afraid to say. I was only attempting to repair the damage to what I thought would be estate papers. I just read a few pages, my love, and it was wonderful. I knew you would never attempt to publish it as the Earl of Wenworth. But I made a few inquiries on your behalf, and it is possible to publish it anonymously. See for yourself."

He accepted the paper as if she had handed him a rabid dog, but his eyes were drawn to the words. " 'Brilliant'?" he read in astonishment. " 'Excellent literary worth'? What exactly did you send them?"

Eleanor smiled kindly. "Only the last few pages, and a letter signed Justinian Darby."

"That's why you were practicing my name."

Her face fell. "You knew?"

"Not about this," he assured her with a shake of his head. "Betsy found a piece of paper under your desk. I would guess that was your accomplice's fault." He reached up to disengage Jingles from his waistcoat, dropping the kitten back onto the desk, where he promptly pounced on the papers once again, jumping after them when they slipped to the floor near the hearth.

"Your estate work!" Eleanor cried.

Justinian slid the letter into his waistcoat and drew her close. "May he enjoy it more than I did. Thank you, Norrie, once again. Are you intent on granting every one of my dreams?"

"Yes," she replied firmly. "By asking me to marry you, you have granted me every one of mine. Can I not do the same for you?"

The light in his eyes was every bit as dangerous as the one in Jareth's when she had stood under the mistletoe. "Be careful, my love. Remember, I'm a Darby. We tend to dream of a great deal more than a place by the fire."

"My lord," Eleanor breathed, "I am your willing servant."

"No," he murmured before his lips captured hers once

again, "you are my dearest love. And before Christmas is over, I intend to prove that to you, once and for all."

And for a time, all that could be heard was the sound of a kitten purring in his place by the fire.